Lost Souls

Book One in The Redstone Chronicles

J. T. Bishop

Eudoran Press LLC

Eudoran Press LLC

6009 W. Parker Rd. # 149-913

Dallas, TX 75093

www.jtbishopauthor.com

Publisher's Note: This is a work of fiction. Names, characters, places, and incidents are a product of the author's imagination. Locales and public names are sometimes used for atmospheric purposes. Any resemblance to actual people, living or dead, or to businesses, companies, events, institutions, or locales is completely coincidental.

Author Photos by Nick Bishop and Mayza Clark Photography

Book Editing by P. Creeden and G. Enstam

Cover Design by J.T. Bishop

Lost Souls/ J.T. Bishop -- 1st ed.

Print ISBN 978-1-955370-10-3

To my Dad...
I love and miss you.

Other Books by J. T. Bishop

Chapter One

"HE'S IN THERE. I saw him. I know he's in there." Serita Avery wrung her hands. "Don't you see him?"

Mason Redstone sat on the carpeted floor and stared into the long, free-standing mirror. Other than seeing the reflection of his own face, he saw nothing, but tweaked the end of his handlebar mustache and made a mental note to get a haircut. Mrs. Avery paced behind him, every bit as distraught as when he'd first arrived. Her clothes hung on her slight frame, and her narrow face pinched more as she waited for Mason to answer.

He tried again and focused. Mirrors could be a powerful conduit for energy and in his experience as a paranormal investigator and medium, could be used by a spirit to contact the living. Mirrors had been used as a communication tool for years, and he didn't doubt Serita Avery's story; she likely had seen something come through. According to her, it was a male energy, and it had spoken to her more than once. At first, she had considered it part of her imagination, and had tried to ignore it, but lately it had become more insistent and wouldn't leave her alone.

Mason took a sip from the cup of coffee she'd given him and tried to center himself. It had been a long week. He'd just completed an investigation of a family home in which a mother and child had been affected by a malevolent spirit. Mason had made contact with the former homeowner who'd died in the house fifty years earlier from suicide, and who now tormented the current owners—especially the child, who Mason realized had her own gifts. Over the course of a week, he'd finally convinced the energy to move on and had encouraged the mother to stay in the house and support her daughter's gifts. He understood how difficult it could be to grow up hearing the strange voices and seeing the ghostly faces, knowing that everyone believed you were crazy, and keeping it all a secret so you didn't get sent to a shrink or a mental hospital.

Still feeling the effects from the difficult case, he chastised himself for taking on a new client so soon. He needed time between assignments, or his health suffered as a result. But Mrs. Avery had sounded desperate over the phone, and although his sister Mikey had attempted to push back their initial meeting, he'd agreed to meet with Mrs. Avery and investigate her mirror.

Blinking, he took a deep breath and shook out his hands. Serita Avery continued to pace behind him. "Mrs. Avery, perhaps you could wait in the other room? That might help. Your worry could be blocking anything from coming through."

She stopped, her small dark eyes darting around. "He's here. I know he is."

"Who's here? The man from the mirror?" Mason paused. "Do you see him outside of the mirror, or is it just in the mirror?"

Holding her head, she slumped. "I see him in my head. He keeps talking. Just like before he..."

Mason frowned. "Before he what?"

Dropping her hand, she stared at him blankly. Her pale skin was stark in the dusky bedroom. She'd kept the curtains closed, and he wished she'd let some sunlight in to shed the murkiness from the space. She stepped closer and picked up his cup. "I'll get you some more coffee."

Mason watched her leave. Looking around, he took in the unmade bed. Despite the covered windows, some light filtered in, and he could see her open closet. Clothes hung neatly from hangers, mostly dresses and blouses, but also pants and collared shirts. A pair of men's loafers peeked out from beneath the clothes. Settling in without Mrs. Avery's nervous energy to distract him, Mason took a deep breath, and his skin began to tingle. He tuned in and sensed a masculine presence. Was this the man his client had seen? Did the male items in the room belong to him? He went still and listened.

The presence gained strength. Mason couldn't see it but could feel it. Speaking silently in his head, he asked what the spirit wanted him to know and waited again.

The standalone mirror in the bedroom reflected only the wall behind him and his own face, so Mason closed his eyes, preferring to connect in his own way.

A chill made his skin prickle, and Mason shivered. Curious as to the spirit's intentions, he probed again and hoped for a response.

A voice sounded in his head. "Help her." It was low and raspy.

Mason clenched his eyes and responded in his mind. "How?"

"Help her. It's not too late," came the reply. "I should have listened."

"It's not too late for what?" asked Mason.

There was a pause. "Help her. You know how. She shouldn't be alone. I should have known."

"Known what? How should I help her?"

"She is lonely. Help her see what I could not. You know what to do. Trust your instincts."

Mason didn't understand. "Did she lose you? Is she grieving for you?"

"She is looking for answers. You can help. Let her know I made mistakes. I should have known better, but I was blind. She can make different choices, though. She can stop it."

"Stop what? Do you want her to do something?"

"Help her. Trust your instincts. Trust your friend."

Mason opened his eyes. He hadn't expected that. "Trust my friend? What do you mean?" he asked aloud.

"You'll know what to do," said the voice inside his head. "No secret remains hidden for long. For all of us."

Mason blinked, trying to make sense of it. It hadn't been the first time a spirit from one case had co-mingled with another, and he'd received messages before from various entities who'd used their connection with him to discuss other unrelated topics. "Are you talking about her, or me?"

He waited for a response, but the presence faded, along with the chill. He stared at the shoes in the dark closet and wondered if the man he'd just spoken with had owned them. Looking back at the mirror, he tried again to connect, but the spirit had left, and Mason no longer sensed the energy.

He stood, smoothed his shirt, and stretched his neck. His muscles were tight after a strenuous workout that morning. In an attempt to clear his head, he'd gone to the gym to lift weights and hit the treadmill before arriving at the Avery house. Exercise helped him to reset, and he'd needed it after the previous week. Expelling a deep breath, he left the bedroom.

Mrs. Avery sat at her breakfast table, looking lost in thought, his empty coffee cup beside her. Seeing him, she straightened. "I'm sorry. I never got your coffee."

He waved a hand. "That's fine. Don't worry about it."

She stood and went to the coffeepot. "I'll get it for you."

"Mrs. Avery...it's okay. I don't need any more. Thank you, though."

Putting the cup down, her face fell. "It's not Mrs. And you should call me Serita."

Mason nodded. "Okay." He paused. "Serita, can I ask you something personal?"

Her pale face lost what little color was left, and her eyes filled. "You saw him, didn't you?"

He sighed. "I saw the clothes in the closet, and the shoes. Do they belong to the man you are seeing in the mirror? Is that who's haunting you?"

A tear escaped and trickled down her cheek. "So, I'm not going crazy? It is him?"

Leaning against the kitchen counter, he crossed his arms. "Yes. It is. He's worried about you. Thinks you're lonely. He told me to help you. Said he made mistakes, which he regrets." He recalled the voice's words. "He said it doesn't have to continue. You can stop it."

Her sadness evaporated, and she stiffened. Wiping her cheek, she glared. "Is he going to keep coming around?"

Her reaction surprised him, but he understood how grief could affect the ones left behind. "In my experience, he'll stay until you get the message. It seemed important to him."

"He should have thought of that before..." Her face tightened, and she paused. "He lied to me."

"I understand. It's hard. He's not the first man to lie to a woman and won't be the last. But he knows he was wrong. I think he wants to make amends with you."

She picked up his coffee cup and dropped it into the sink with a bang, making Mason jump. "Thank you for your time. I appreciate you coming here on short notice."

Her demeanor had shifted in an instant, and Mason frowned. "He asked me to help you. I'd like to do that."

"Can you stop him from returning?" She flipped on the faucet and rinsed the cup. "I don't want to talk to him anymore. I've got nothing to say, and if he thinks he can stop me..." She shut off the faucet and turned. "...it's a waste of time."

A flare of concern rippled through Mason. "Mrs...Serita. I'm sorry to ask, but you're not thinking of hurting yourself, are you?"

Her flat face softened, and she chuckled. "Are you serious? What for? So he can thwart me in the afterlife, too? Hell, no, Mr. Redstone. It'll be a cold day in Satan's backyard before that happens."

Mason's thoughts whirled with how to respond. While he was happy to help, if the person in need didn't want it, there was little he could do. Still thinking of the connection, he wondered about the parts of the message he assumed were for him but kept that information to himself. "Is there anything else I can do for you? I wish I could tell you that he won't come around anymore, but I can't promise that. I delivered his message to you, so that may help, but if he's insistent, then you may continue to see him in your mirror."

"Figures," she said. "Just as annoying in death as he was in life." She pushed away from the counter. "I appreciate your assistance."

Something nudged at him, and he sensed her doubt and underlying anger. He followed her to the front entry. "If you need anything else, or if he should show again, you are welcome to call. Now that I've been here, I'm always available. I may be able to connect with him outside of the home."

"Lucky you. If you can, let him know he deserved what he got. He should have known better."

Mason nodded, saddened by her lingering animosity. "You can tell him your-self. Perhaps that's what he wants."

"I think what he wants and what I want are two different things. I should have realized that sooner, but I was stupid. Not anymore, though."

Mason put a hand on her elbow. "He's gone, Serita. If I could offer a small bit of advice. It's best not to hold on to old grievances. They tend to be more harmful to the holder, than the one they're directed toward."

"Not if I can help it, Mr. Redstone." Her pointed stare unnerved him, and she must have sensed his discomfort because she took a deep breath and visibly relaxed. "But I see your point, and I'll take it to heart." She opened the door. "Thank you again."

"You take care. And you have my number should you need it."

"I appreciate that. At least I now know who I'm seeing, and that it's nothing to fear."

"I find in most cases that tends to be true. It's rarely as evil as our minds make it out to be."

She hesitated, and her eyes narrowed. "I never questioned whether it was evil, Mr. Redstone. I can handle evil." Her expression softened, and she blinked and smiled. "You have a nice day."

Confused, he stepped out, and she shut the door.

Chapter Two

MIKEY REDSTONE STUDIED THE file on the monitor and typed a few notes, then saved and closed it. Pushing back in the chair, she swiveled and picked up a paper from the printer. She brought it back and placed it in a folder on the desk. After straightening a few items so Mason wouldn't complain when he returned, she stood and helped herself to some coffee from the machine on the table next to the desk.

Sighing with satisfaction, she smiled as she poured, happy that she'd finally convinced Mason to add a few items to the office that were sorely needed, one of them being the coffee maker. The spacious room in the two-story brick building that served as his workspace sported his desk, plus a couch, coffee table, and cushioned chair. The shelf-lined walls were bare other than the wooden box that sat against the back wall along with a plexiglass cube that enclosed two small stone statues. The box was familiar to her, and although she didn't like it, the statues were what gave her the willies. Sipping her coffee, she stared at their round heads and wide eyes, remembering where they had come from and why they were there. A tremble passed through her, and she thought of Detectives Daniels and Remalla, thankful they were alive and well.

Other than those items, and the new coffee machine, an open area beyond the desk was empty, except for a woven rug Mason had purchased on some overseas trip. A storage space beyond the far wall contained files and other tools necessary for Mason's business, and they were kept out of sight. Mikey smiled, though, pleased with her negotiating skills and her coffee. She'd also made Mason install a camera and intercom at the front door. Considering Mason's clients and his past experiences with those who might wish him harm, Mikey knew his safety required it and the extra security made her feel better. Now she could see and speak to anyone at the entrance and buzz them in.

Hearing the outer door open, she went around to the desk and eyed the monitor. The screen saver defaulted to the camera views up front, and she saw Mason walk through the outer office. The door to the inner office opened and Mason walked in. "Hey. How'd it go?" she asked.

Closing the door behind him, he grunted. "You were right. I should have waited." He slid his jacket off, and Mikey noted his blue, narrow-cut, collared shirt and pressed blue jeans with boots. "I told you. At least you looked nice. The blue suits you."

He ran his hands down his shirt. "You chose well. It fits perfectly."

"Well, since you agreed to the coffee machine, I figured it was the least I could do."

Mason tossed his jacket on the chair and sat on the couch. "I'm exhausted."

"That bad, huh?" Mikey leaned back against the desk. "Was she weird?"

Mason frowned. "You know I don't like that term." He rubbed his face. "But I do admit, she was a little...off."

"I told you she felt weird to me."

He frowned at her again.

"Sorry. But it's true."

"She's lost someone she loved. She's grieving. You and I both know what grief can do. Plus, from what I learned, the man she lost may not have treated her well. On top of her grief, she's angry. Pain, unaddressed, results in a myriad of unpleasant problems. She's pissed at someone who's dead. It can be frustrating, especially now when that person returns from beyond. It's a lot to assimilate."

Mikey sipped her coffee. "I suppose. I still think she's weird."

"Mikey..."

Mikey huffed. "Fine. What would you prefer? Odd? Unusual? Creepy?"

"None of those. How about lost, confused, and depressed? Any of those terms would be more accurate. I can only hope she seeks the help she requires."

"You can't be there for everyone, Mason. Sometimes, you just have to let people find their own way."

He leaned back against the couch. "I know. It's just not in my nature."

"Which is why you're exhausted." She turned and picked up the file folder. "But you'll be happy to hear that I cleared your schedule for the next couple of days." She waved the file at him. "You can look at it when you're ready."

"What about the Dunbar case?"

"I called and moved it back. They can live with a few spooky bumps in the night for a little longer."

Mason stared, and she half expected him to argue, but then he nodded and rested his head back. "All right. I like the new pink streaks, by the way."

Mikey touched her hair. She'd added pink highlights the previous day, thinking it added a little color to her brownish-red hair. "You prefer the purple or the pink?"

"You're asking the wrong guy. But if you're going to continue wearing black and keep your nose pierced, I don't think it matters."

"There's nothing wrong with the piercing, and I don't always wear black." She straightened her black t-shirt that framed her narrow waist and admired her skinny black jeans.

"Since when?"

"When I exercise."

"That doesn't count."

"Yes, it does."

He cracked open an eye at her and then closed it.

"You want some coffee?" she asked.

"No, thanks." He raised his head. "How are you? Any nightmares?"

Mikey sat on the chair across from the couch and set her coffee down. "You're hovering."

"It's just a question."

Mikey picked up a magazine from the table and flipped through it. "No, actually. Haven't had one in a while."

"Glad to hear it." He cocked an eyebrow at her. "Is that a gossip magazine? How can you read that stuff?"

"I can only handle so much of your science and medical journals. For someone who works in the paranormal, you sure read a lot about research and studies."

"The more I know, the better, regardless of the field I'm in." He shook his head. "Do you buy that crap? You know it's all lies."

"I didn't buy it. I picked it up at Remalla's. He told me to keep it." She flipped another page.

"Detective Remalla?" He paused. "You've been spending a lot of time with him."

She stopped on a page with several pictures of a famous actress who, judging by her enormous lips and too tight skin, had had yet another plastic surgery. "Don't start, Mason. We're just friends."

He pushed up on the couch. "Did you see him last night?"

Mikey chuckled. "You just can't help yourself, can you?" She closed the magazine. "Fine. Yes. We went to the movies."

"Let me guess. It had something to do with a flawed superhero who, weakened by his own moral struggles, frantically tries to find the magic power tool that will save the planet before it's destroyed by an evil villain with a scarred face."

"Close, but not really." She tossed the magazine back on the table. "*The Shining* was playing at the dollar theater. It's hard to pass up Kubrick and Nicholson."

He raised his hand. "I don't even want to know, but I'm glad you're having fun. How's he doing now that he's back at work?"

"He's adjusting. It's been hard, and he's still working through a few things. I think his captain is keeping the workload light for the moment. I encourage him to get out of the house to keep his mind off things, so we go to the movies." Mikey could almost hear her brother's unspoken question, which he finally voiced.

"You think you two might be more than friends one day?"

Mikey snorted and picked up her coffee. "Why can't two people who happen to be male and female just be friends? Why does it have to become a *relationship*?" She dragged out the word.

Mason studied her. "It doesn't have to become anything, but you two share a common thread with D'Mato, and you've both dealt with horrors better left forgotten. It makes you both strangely well-suited for each other, unless..."

Mikey gripped her mug and took a sip, uneasy at the mention of Victor D'Mato. "Go ahead. Finish your sentence."

Mason sat forward and rested his elbows on his knees. "...unless you're letting your own fears get in the way."

"Believe me, Mason. No one knows better than me how to face a fear. I've been doing it ever since I escaped Victor's clutches. I don't doubt I have a few lingering issues, but for now, Rem and I just enjoy each other's company. Can we leave it at that?"

He held her gaze. "Of course. I'll butt out, but if you ever need to talk about it..."

"I know. You're there. In fact, I can't seem to get rid of you."

"That's what big brothers are for."

"Consider your brotherly duties accomplished."

"I usually do. You're drinking that coffee you wanted, aren't you?"

"I am, for which I am grateful." She tapped on her cup and smiled. "And don't get me wrong. I appreciate your concern, but you worry too much."

He cocked a brow at her. "When it comes to you, Mikey, sometimes I wonder if I worry enough." Sighing again, he leaned back against the couch cushions. "Maybe I will take that nap."

A buzzer sounded, and Mikey swiveled toward the desk. "Who is that? You don't have any appointments today."

Mason stifled a yawn. "I'll let you deal with it. I'm going to close my eyes for a sec." He settled in and got comfortable.

Mikey stood and went to the monitor, checking to see who was at the front office door. She saw a man, tall and lanky, wearing a cowboy hat, jeans, and boots, much like Mason. Something about him was familiar, and she hit the button to the intercom. "Can I help you?" she asked.

The man spoke. "Is this the office for SCOPE?"

SCOPE was the name of Mason's business. Mikey had debated the acronym with Mason before he'd opened his agency. He'd insisted that The Study of Cryptids or Paranormal Events was the perfect choice, and she had failed to convince him otherwise. Her vote had been for The Redstone Agency, but he'd said no. She hit the button to answer. "I assume you can read. That's the name on the sign."

The man chuckled. "Is that you, Mikey?"

Mikey dropped her jaw, and Mason opened his eyes. They made eye contact, and Mason stood and came over to the desk, leaning over Mikey's shoulder and staring at the screen.

"Hello?" asked the man. "You there? Red?" The man rapped on the door.

Mason's eyes widened and his face paled.

"Who is that?" asked Mikey. "Somebody you know?"

"Son-of-a-bitch," said Mason. "That's Trick Monroe. My old partner from my Ranger days."

Mikey studied the man on the screen. "That's Trick? Didn't you two have a falling out?"

"C'mon, Red," said Trick, rapping again on the door. "I know you're in there." He grinned at the camera. "Don't tell me you're still mad."

Mason stared, his expression unreadable.

"What pissed you off?" asked Mikey. "You never did tell me why you two stopped being friends."

Mason glared, his body no longer relaxed. "He slept with Cara."

Mikey almost choked. "Your ex-wife? From Texas? He slept with her?"

"He sure did." Mason hit the button, and the buzzer sounded, and Mikey watched on the video as Trick entered the office.

Chapter Three

"SO MUCH FOR TAKING a nap," said Mason.

"What the hell is he doing here?" asked Mikey.

"I think we're about to find out." Mason went to the door and opened it. Trick was standing in the small, wallpapered, outer office, which contained only a desk and chair.

Seeing Mason, he took off his hat. "Well, hell. Look at you." He ran his fingers over the brim. "How long's it been, Red?"

Mason crossed his arms and considered his response. They'd met and been assigned together during his tenure as a Texas Ranger. There had been a time when Mason would have called Trick his best friend, and they had been as close as Detectives Daniels and Remalla. Mason had envied that bond when he'd met the detectives, recalling his old partnership with Trick, but those days were long over.

"I figured it would be a lot longer," said Mason.

Trick shook his head. "Shit. You sure know how to hold a grudge. It's been years, Red."

Mikey poked her head out, and Trick grinned. "Is that you, Mikey?" His eyes trailed over her. "You've grown up."

Mason stiffened. "What the hell do you want, Trick?"

"Trick Monroe?" asked Mikey. "I remember you."

"I like to make an impression." Trick raised his hat, looking pleased with himself.

"I recall you being a lot more handsome," said Mikey.

Trick's face fell. "You haven't changed much."

"I like to make an impression too," said Mikey.

Mason sized up his former partner. Trick looked much the same. His swagger and annoying charm remained. It was a valued skill in a Ranger, or any cop. Trick could talk down a junkie threatening suicide and waving a gun better than any lawman Mason had ever witnessed. Everything in him wanted to throw Trick out, but he couldn't do it. A tingle moved through him, and Mason opened up, letting his senses guide him. A fuzzy image appeared behind Trick, and Mason watched as Trick's grandmother came into view. Her eyes twinkled, and her silver hair sparkled. She'd died a couple of years after Trick had joined the Rangers and been partnered with Mason. Trick had invited Mason for dinner at her place a few times, and she'd been a terrific cook. Smiling, she put a hand on Trick's shoulder and her voice echoed in Mason's head.

Trick shifted on his feet and then scratched his shoulder. "You gonna talk to me, or leave me standing here like a fool?"

Mason relaxed, as the older woman faded from view. "You're lucky I like your grandmother."

Trick squinted, and Mikey shot him a confused look.

"She says 'Hi', by the way." Mason stepped back. "Come on in."

Trick gripped his hat. "God, are you talking to her? You still doing that dead people thing?" Trick walked into the inner office.

Mason closed the door. "It's my business. You know that's why I came out here. Some Ranger you are."

Trick put his hat on the coffee table. "I'm not a Ranger." He paused. "Not anymore."

"Sorry to hear it," said Mason. Despite their falling out, Trick had always been a first-rate investigator, smart as any high-ranking officer, and a solid partner. Thinking back on their days together, Mason missed being part of a team, and relying on and talking to someone who would back you up no matter what occurred.

Mikey raised her mug. "You want some coffee?"

"Love some," said Trick. "Thanks. Black is fine."

Mikey nodded and headed to the coffee machine.

Mason walked to his desk and sat. "What brings you here? And don't tell me you're just passing through."

Trick surveyed the room, his gaze briefly settling on the wooden box and plexiglass holder of the statues. "I barely saw you at your mom's funeral and you disappeared before we could talk, but I wanted to tell you it's a damn shame. She was a nice lady."

Mason interlaced his fingers and tried not to think about his mother. It would only upset him more. "Thanks." He waited as Trick stood anxiously, his face flat.

His mind wandering, Mason asked the question he should have avoided. "How's Cara?"

Trick groaned and shook his head. "You just can't let me off the hook, can you?"

Mikey finished with the coffee and brought Trick a mug. He took it and thanked her. Mikey stayed quiet, but leaned against the wall, watching.

"You don't seem to be saying much, so I figured I'd start the conversation." Mason leaned back and crossed his arms. "Did you think I wouldn't bring her up?"

"You know I haven't seen her in years," said Trick.

"How would I know that?" asked Mason.

"Don't you talk to her?"

"No. Why would I? My patience with her is about as non-existent as it is with you."

Trick sipped his coffee. "Last I heard, she married. Has two kids."

"Sorry to hear it didn't work out," said Mason.

Trick chuckled softly. "Sure you are." He gestured. "You mind if I sit?"

"Why not?" asked Mason. "You typically do what you want. Why stop now?"

Mikey pushed off the wall. "You know, I have a couple errands to run." She reached for her purse beneath the desk.

"What errands?" asked Mason.

"Oh, I don't know. I'll think of something." She tossed her purse strap over her shoulder. "You need anything while I'm out?"

Mason glared at Trick. "Maybe a shovel? I sense a lot of shit comin' my way."

Trick snorted and rolled his eyes. "While you're at it, pick up a violin. He can play it when you come back, and you can feel sorry for him."

Mason frowned, and Mikey winced and headed for the door. "I'll...uhm..." She looked between the two men. "...never mind. I'll just go." Not getting a response, she left.

Mason told himself to stay cool. Although he hadn't spoken to Trick in years, his old partner had not forgotten how to get under his skin, but Mason refused to be drawn into another inane discussion about his ex-wife. "How about we cut to the chase? Why did you come?"

Trick walked to the couch and sat, holding his mug. Mason stood from his desk and approached Trick, waiting to hear the answer.

Trick sighed. "Chad is dead."

"Who?" Mason rested a hand on the back of the chair.

"Chad Howard. My stepbrother. Rudy's kid. You met him. Remember? Kid used to follow us around like we were superheroes."

Mason recalled a younger version of Trick with long legs and dirty hair, pestering them with questions whenever they were around. "Chip?"

Trick ran a hand through his brown hair, which was almost as long as Mason recalled Chip's used to be. "Yeah. I used to call him that. Kid could eat a bag of chips faster than a pile of racoons." He hung his head. "He grew up, though. Came out here last year for employment with his new wife. Her name's Cissy. Cissy found him dead on their sofa three weeks ago in their living room. She'd gone out for groceries." Trick paused. "He'd been shot in the head."

Recalling Chad, Mason's heart thumped, and he remembered how attached Chad and Trick had been. Even though they were stepbrothers, Trick had considered Chad to be as close as a biological brother. Taking a deep breath, he took a seat in the chair across from Trick. "I'm sorry. I know how you felt about him."

Trick put his mug down. "After you left, we hung out a lot. He thought about becoming a Ranger and made it into the Fort Worth P.D., but ultimately decided it wasn't for him. He became a security consultant and got a lucrative offer from a firm out here. He and Cissy found a place outside of San Diego, and I'd been planning to visit, but just hadn't made it out here yet." He traced a thumb over his jeans. "Maybe if I had…"

"You don't know if you could have prevented it," said Mason. "You likely would have come out and left, and he'd still be dead."

"He had something on his mind. Wanted to talk to me about it." He paused. "I should have paid more attention."

Mason nodded. He understood the pain of regret. "They know who did it?"

Trick rubbed his face. "They arrested Cissy."

Mason dropped his jaw. "His wife?"

Trick stood and paced. "It's absurd, but they insist she did it. They picked her up the day after the funeral. She's the spouse. Has no real alibi, other than she went to the store, came home, and found him. They believe she shot him before she left, and then claimed that it happened while she was gone. Chad was killed with his own gun, but it wasn't a suicide. Whoever did it knew where the gun was, and where he lived. Chad must have let them in because there was no forced entry."

"How do you know she didn't kill him? How was their marriage?"

Trick flicked a pained glance at Mason. "Those two were closer than a couch and my butt during a Cowboy game. Chad met her his first year as a cop. He pulled her over for speeding, and they'd been together ever since. They were happy, and she is devastated by his loss."

Mason studied his hands. "You don't know for sure. They'd been out here for a year, and you hadn't seen them recently. Maybe that's what Chad wanted to talk to you about."

"Hell, no. I don't believe it. They were trying to get pregnant. Chad couldn't wait to be a dad, and Cissy couldn't wait to be a mom." He shook his head. "And even if they weren't happy, Cissy could have easily filed for divorce. She hates guns and doesn't even like scary movies. There's no way she would have shot him."

Mason considered what to say. In his experience, he knew how even the closest spouses could turn on each other. As a medium, he'd seen and heard plenty of examples from those who'd passed on who'd expressed regret over their perceived neglect or unintended abuse of their significant other. And the ones left behind often struggled with how to deal with it.

Trick returned to the couch and sat. "Listen, I know what you're thinking. I'm too attached to this, and I need to let the law take it from here. But you and I know that sometimes the law gets a hold of something and refuses to see any other scenario." He pointed. "I think that's what's happening here. The police suspected Cissy from the start, and they're not even bothering to look for anyone else. And that's just not right." He hesitated. "Cissy deserves her chance to be proven innocent, and Chad's killer needs to be brought to justice."

"Doesn't she have an attorney?" asked Mason.

"She needs more than an attorney, Red." He stared pointedly.

Mason straightened in his seat. "Wait a minute. Is that why you're here? You want my help?"

"I know you do that SCOPE stuff. God knows I didn't understand your woo-woo issues back when we were partners, and I still don't get it, but I also know you were a damn good investigator, and you have a P.I. license out here. Plus, you're bound to have some connections. You have access to people and things that I don't."

Mason put his elbows on his knees. "Are you serious? You want me to help you investigate Chad's death?"

"Hell, yes."

"We haven't worked together in years, and the last time we spoke, you were very specific about where I should put my head."

"And you weren't too kind about what I could do with my mother." Trick sat back against the couch, looking worn and frazzled. "I know I did things I shouldn't have done, and if you ever want to talk about it, I'm all ears, but right now, I could use your help. The past is the past. There's nothing I can do about any of it. If I could take it back, I would. But I need to focus on the here and now, and you're my best bet if I want to find Chad's killer."

Mason held his head. "And if it turns out to be Cissy?"

"Then so be it. At least I'll know the truth."

Mason sighed, uncertain of what to do. "I don't know, Trick. Something tells me this is a bad idea. Maybe it's better if we go our separate ways. I'm sure her attorney can find a good investigator."

Trick went quiet, and Mason waited for the outburst, but none came. Trick just tipped his head and spoke softly. "You owe me, Red."

Mason's heart fell. "Hell. You're gonna pull that card? I figured you screwing my wife made us even."

Trick grimaced. "Whatever. You two were separated at the time, and you'd already come out here, and she was lonely."

"Thank God you were around to make her feel better." He glowered. "I still had hopes she would join me here."

"She didn't want to leave Texas and you know it, so stop blaming me for the loss of your marriage. I wasn't the cause, only the result."

"That's a convenient argument, coming from the man who lied to me."

"I promised her I wouldn't tell you. I honored that."

"What about your promise to me as a friend? What happened to that?"

"I never stopped being your friend. I tried to talk to you, but you wouldn't even give me a chance."

"I tend to do that when people show me their true colors."

"My colors haven't faded one bit. You're just too damn stubborn to see it, or even take a trickle of blame for the giant mess that was your marriage."

Mason's anger bubbled up, and he set his jaw. "This is why we shouldn't work together."

Trick leaned forward. "This is exactly why we should. We have some things to work out. And this is the time to do it. But if you think that your issues with Cara have somehow wiped out your debt to me, then you're wrong. I didn't break you two up, and you know it."

Mason grunted, and he stifled the urge to throw Trick out and leave his past behind, but the memory of his former partner's role in saving his life could not be forgotten, and in some part of his gut, he realized that he'd screwed up when it came to Cara. Taking a heavy breath, he made his decision. "Fine. I owe you." He raised a finger. "But once this plays out and we figure out what's going on, we're even. You got that?"

"I got it. Call me Even Steven."

Mason sighed and fell back in his chair. His days off were no longer off. "Then where do you want to start?"

Chapter Four

MASON SAT AT HIS kitchen table, sipping a cup of tea, and tried to relax. After talking to Trick that afternoon, they'd decided the first thing to do was to visit the crime scene and talk to Cissy. Since Cissy had not yet made bail, they'd headed out to Chad and Cissy's former apartment, which had been released by the police and was now back up for rent.

It had taken an hour to get there, and once they'd arrived, they had found little to help with Cissy's defense. The place had been cleaned and all the furniture removed. The carpets were new and vacuumed and the space was vacant. A leasing agent had even asked if they were in the market for an apartment. A conversation with her had revealed that Cissy and Chad were good tenants. They'd paid the rent on time, going month-to-month, with hopes of buying a house of their own. The neighbors they'd spoken with said they were a quiet couple, but well-liked, and no one had heard any arguments or fights. Most seemed to think they were happy, although none of them knew the couple well. Trick and Mason had asked to see the video footage of the apartment from the morning of the crime, but the office manager had not been in, and they would need to return later to view it.

After a long day, and drive home, they'd agreed to meet again in the morning, and decide what to target next. Chad's business associates would need to be interviewed, plus any friends of the couple. Mason realized, though, that their best source of information would be the crime scene photos, financial records, and personal information collected by the police. That would be required information if they planned to put some pieces into place. How to access it would be his next challenge.

Sighing, he leaned back in his chair, glad that he was in his own place. Not long after being kicked out by his last girlfriend, Joanna, he'd decided it was time to buy a house. He'd been putting it off, mainly because of Joanna, but also because he knew the mental strain of looking for a home would take its toll. Going into other people's residences often meant confronting spirits lingering in the home who wished to communicate. And sometimes, the energy of a home would feel sad or lonely, as if unaddressed regrets hovered.

New builds had been out of his price range, but it didn't matter because they had an emptiness to them, like looking out a window at a brick wall. He preferred an older home, just not the stagnant energy that it could contain.

He recalled the day he'd found this house. Mason had felt the rightness of it the moment he'd entered. It was homey and welcoming; whomever had lived here before had been happy. The space was small but cozy, and that's exactly what he'd wanted. He'd made an offer that day.

Resting his head back, he listened to the soft background sounds of ocean waves playing on his sound system, which helped him relax and clear his head. He thought of Chad, Cissy and Trick, and hoped his old friend would not be disappointed by the outcome of the investigation. In Mason's experience, it was often the spouse who was at fault, no matter how innocent they seemed. His memories of Trick flashed in his mind, and he questioned again if he should have agreed to help. Mason had done his best to let go of his former life, but Trick had brought the memories back.

A loud bang made him jump, and the tea splashed from his mug. Sitting up, he turned in his seat. It had sounded like a closing door. He stood, put the cup on the table and walked down the narrow hall toward his bedroom. Stopping outside the guest bathroom, he paused, seeing the closed door. Had he shut it?

He put his hand on the knob and opened it. The bathroom was dark and empty, but he recalled the door had been left open. A cold waft of air chilled his skin, and Mason realized he wasn't alone. Someone was trying to get his attention. Despite the boundaries he'd erected and tried to uphold, he tuned in, but whatever was there did not engage.

Mason stared into the bathroom, listening and waiting, when his phone rang from the other room, and he jumped again. *Get a hold of yourself, Mason*, he said to himself. *You're tired, and they're sensing an opening*. That was one of the main reasons Joanna had kicked him out and broken up with him. Mason didn't come alone when it came to relationships, and not many women liked to share with the living, much less the dead.

The phone kept ringing, and Mason returned to the living room and grabbed his cell from the side table and saw that it was Mikey. He sat and answered. "Hey."

"Hey," she said. "How are you?"

"Worn out."

"Why don't you go to bed?"

"I will. Just need to unwind."

"You should rest, Mason. Especially now that you're helping Trick."

"Now who's hovering?"

"It's my job to look out for you. God knows you won't do it for yourself."

Mason didn't have the energy to argue. "Fine. I'll go to bed after we talk."

"How'd your day go? Anything interesting?"

Mason told her about the visit to the apartment and subsequent interviews. "We didn't learn much of value. No smoking guns. Maybe we'll learn more after talking to Cissy."

"I can check their social media tomorrow. That might reveal something."

"That would be helpful. Thanks." He stifled a yawn.

"I still can't believe you're doing this after what Trick did."

Mason rubbed his eyes. "Despite our rocky history, I owe him." He picked some lint off his pants. "And as much as I'd like to blame him for his indiscretions with Cara, I know I played a major role in sinking that relationship."

"She was your wife, Mason."

Mason thought back. "Only because of a paper we signed. Cara and I were...I don't know...like the proverbial oil and water. She wanted one thing, and I wanted another, and the more we fought for ourselves, the faster it went down the toilet."

"It didn't give him the right to sleep with her."

"No. Maybe not, but Trick has his own scars, and so did Cara. When I left, it affected them both. They talked and supported each other, and one thing led to another."

"It was still wrong." She hesitated. "And why do you owe him? You were partners. You were expected to help each other. I'm sure you did things for him, too."

Mason chuckled. "I did, but this was a little different." He thought back, remembering two big reasons why he owed Trick. He kept one to himself but told her the other. "We'd been partners barely two months, and I'd inadvertently interrupted a bank robbery. I seemed to have a knack for showing up at the wrong place at the wrong time. I tried to play stupid, but they saw my badge and the robber put the gun to my head. I figured that was the end when Trick walked in. He acted like he knew the man, and they were old friends. It confused the guy enough that he hesitated before shooting, and Trick tackled and disarmed him." Mason recalled that day with fondness and fear. "How do you think he got his nickname?" Mason picked up his tea. "So, yeah. I owe him. You wouldn't be talking to me otherwise."

"Well, when you put it that way…"

Mason leaned back in his seat. "You just steer clear of him, okay? He likes the ladies, and I saw the way he looked at you."

"Seriously? I'm a grown woman. I can take care of myself." She paused. "He is pretty cute, though. He's got that hot cowboy vibe. It's attractive to a young innocent such as myself."

Mason straightened. "Mikey—"

She laughed. "I'm kidding. Well, not about the hotness thing, but don't worry. He's not my type, plus his history with you makes it weird. He's more like a brother than a lover."

"He'd break your heart. He has a history of it. That's the only reason I'm warning you off. You've had enough to deal with. You don't need more."

"Thanks for the concern, but don't worry. I've got something else for you to fret over."

Mason groaned. "I'm afraid to ask."

"I called Remalla. Told him about this case."

Mason gripped the phone. "You what? What for? I didn't want you to do that."

"Why not? Come on. You need information, and Rem and Daniels can get it for you. They're cops and if you want to talk about owing someone, they owe you. Did you forget what you did for them?"

Mason held his head. "I'm sure they have enough on their plates."

"On the contrary, Rem said he'd do some digging for you. He asked if you could meet him and Daniels for lunch tomorrow at that diner where we ate before. Rem loves their grilled cheese sandwich."

Mason hesitated. He hadn't known Rem and Daniels long, but their involvement in stopping Mason's former friend, Victor D'Mato and his ugly activities, had forged a fast friendship between them. "You're sure they're okay with it?"

"You need to learn to ask for help every once in a while. They had no problem asking you when they needed it. It's time to call in a favor or two."

Mason had to admit, the information they could access would be exactly what he needed. "All right. I'll let Trick know and we'll meet them for lunch."

"Good. I'll tell Rem."

"Rem, huh? Not Remalla?"

He heard her sigh. "That's his name. It's what people call him."

Mason nodded, wondering when she'd figure it out. "Fine. If they get busy, though, we can reschedule."

"Stop worrying about it. Let them help, okay? But first, you need to go get some rest. You have a busy day coming up."

He sipped his tea. "Okay. You'll be at the office tomorrow?"

"Bright and early."

"I'll see you then."

"See you."

He hung up and put the phone on the table, thinking about Remalla and Daniels, and wishing they hadn't been pulled into this. While Trick was comfortable calling in favors, Mason was the opposite. Half debating whether he should call and tell the detectives not to bother, he settled back and jumped again when another slam rattled the walls.

Cursing, Mason almost dropped his tea. He put it down, stood, and returned to the hall, finding the closed bathroom door. That cool air returned and prickled his skin. "What the hell are you trying to tell me?" asked Mason aloud.

He tuned in again, but there was no answer.

Chapter Five

Detective Aaron Remalla opened the door to the diner and waved his partner, Detective Gordon Daniels, through. "Age before beauty."

Daniels shook his head. "I'm eight months older, and you've got a mustard stain on your shirt." He entered the diner.

Rem swiped at the yellow blotch. "My jacket's covering the stain. Nobody can see it." He eyed his partner's pressed pants, ironed collared shirt and gelled-back blonde hair. "I'll admit, though, you make a better impression." He pulled up his baggy, worn jeans. "Good thing I'm the brains of this organization."

"That's not the word I'd use." Daniels pointed. "Mason's here."

Rem saw Mason Redstone sitting at a far table, waving them over. "Man's punctual."

"Something I can appreciate."

Rem snorted. "I wasn't that late this morning."

"You got your oil changed on the way to work."

"My car needed it. You'd rather we break down on the side of the road?"

"Then take it after work, not before."

"You're such a stickler for details," said Rem. They walked up to the table, and he pulled out a chair across from Redstone. "Hey, Mason."

"Remalla. Daniels. How are you?" asked Mason.

Daniels took a seat beside Rem. "I think I need a vacation."

Rem sat. "Really? Where do you want to go?"

"I'm going with Marjorie," said Daniels. "You can stay here."

Rem frowned. "Somebody's grouchy this morning." He regarded Mason. "How are you? Better than him, I hope."

"Doing well." Mason reached for some cream and added it to the cup of coffee in front of him. "I appreciate you helping me out."

"Well, after all you did for us, it's the least we could do," said Daniels, picking up a menu from the table.

"We owe you," said Rem, shifting in his seat, the uncomfortable memories swirling. "Mikey said your friend was joining us?"

"Yes," said Mason. "He is. Sorry he's running late. Apparently, Cissy Howard is securing bail this morning. Her parents paid it, and Trick is with them, but he should be here soon." He put his menu down. "There's no need to wait, though. I'm sure you two are busy."

The waitress came over and took their drink orders. "We're fine," said Daniels. "It's actually been quiet today." He knocked on the table. "Knock on Formica. Or whatever this is made of."

"Mikey said your friend lost somebody close and wants you to help him investigate?" asked Remalla. He didn't bother checking the menu. His mouth was watering for the grilled cheese and fries.

"Yes. For the most part." Mason filled them in on his former partner, Trick, and the death of his stepbrother.

"Old partner, huh?" asked Daniels. "You think you two can work together again, or do you prefer being on your own?"

"Especially now that you're, you know, talking to dead people and all that," said Rem. "How's Trick handle that part of the deal?"

The waitress brought their drinks and freshened Mason's coffee, then took their orders and menus.

"It's an interesting dynamic, to say the least," said Mason. "To be honest, I miss certain aspects of a partnership. Someone to bang around ideas with and talk to. We were close once, much like you two."

"We have our moments." Daniels sipped his water.

"Ain't that the truth," said Rem.

"I know. I've witnessed them." Mason looked between them. "You two can bicker all you want, but when the smelly stuff hits the fan, you'd die for each other." He put his napkin on his lap. "Trick and I had that once."

Rem made eye contact with Daniels, recalling plenty of close calls. They'd relied on each other more than once to survive. "I am lucky in that regard," said Rem. "I'd have been dead a long time ago."

"You and me both," said Daniels. "Of course, there was the time you almost killed me." He cocked his head at Rem.

Rem dropped his jaw. "That was a total accident. It's partly your fault, anyway. Why'd you put the rat poison near the sugar container?"

"I didn't think it would be too much to ask of you to read a label," said Daniels. "Especially when it's got a skull-and-crossbones on it."

Rem rolled his eyes. "Anyway," he said to Mason, "outside of the occasional near poisoning, I can understand why you'd miss a partnership." He added sugar and cream to his coffee. "What does Trick say about the paranormal stuff?"

"He accepts it," said Mason, "but don't think he likes it. I'm sure if he saw a ghost, he'd outrun Usain Bolt."

"That we have in common," said Rem. "Too bad we didn't meet you sooner. You could have joined us at his grandfather's house in the lovely town of Dumont. You'd have had your fill."

"You didn't outrun Usain Bolt," said Daniels.

"Because I was too scared to move, plus I had to save your ass," said Rem.

"I suppose," said Daniels.

Mason smiled. "It seems you two did fine. I find most ghosts just want to tell you their story, be heard, and then move on."

"If you're lucky," said Daniels. "How's business? The paranormal world staying busy?"

"It's brisker than you might expect," said Mason. "You'd be surprised how many people encounter spectral problems and are open to mystical solutions, or who just want to reconnect with their loved ones."

"Seems to be the world we live in now," said Rem.

"Seems so," said Daniels.

Mason raised an arm. "There he is."

Rem swiveled to see a tall, narrow-waisted man wearing jeans, a checkered shirt, cowboy boots and hat, enter the diner and approach their table. "Sorry I'm late." He hooked his hat on the back of the chair and sat. Rem noticed his bloodshot eyes and pale pallor. "You must be Red's friends." He offered a hand. "I'm Trick Monroe. Red's former partner."

They shook hands as Mason introduced Remalla and Daniels. "Nice to meet you," said Rem.

"You, too," said Trick. The waitress came over and took his drink order. "You talking about Chad?"

"Not yet," said Mason. "We were catching up." He stirred his coffee. "Did Cissy make bail?"

"She did," said Trick. "Thank God. Her parents mortgaged their house, and they're in an extended stay hotel until we figure out what happens next. Cissy's staying with them."

"Glad to hear it. I'm sure she's happy to be out," said Mason.

"She's a mess. Poor girl doesn't know what's going on." Trick opened his menu. "I just hope we can help her." He grimaced and put the menu down. "I think I'll just stick to coffee."

Mason raised a brow but didn't say anything.

"Speaking of helping, Rem and I did some digging. Mikey gave us some information and we put together a file on Chad's case," said Daniels.

"We also talked to the detectives investigating. Names are Bevins and...Winter?" Rem asked Daniels.

"Winkler," said Daniels.

"Yeah. Winkler. They seem convinced of Cissy's guilt and have their ducks in a row," said Rem.

"It's nonsense. Cissy didn't kill Chad." The waitress came over and filled Trick's coffee cup. Trick sipped from it and Rem detected the slightest shake in his fingers. The waitress asked him about food, but he waved her off.

Rem reached into his jacket and pulled out a folder folded lengthwise. "I guess you guys are going to find out. Here's what we got." He handed the file to Mason. "And remember, this is just between you and us. Got it? I doubt Bevins and Winter—"

"Winkler," said Daniels.

"Whatever," said Rem. "I doubt they'd be too keen on us sharing this with you."

Mason opened the folder and grimaced.

"And maybe you should open it at home." Rem reached over and raised the side of the folder so the neighboring table wouldn't see inside. "I included crime scene photos."

Trick glanced over, and his face turned white. "Aw, shit." He swallowed and his face froze. He slid out of his seat. "Excuse me."

Mason narrowed his eyes and watched him go.

"I know it's his stepbrother, but with your history, I'm sure you two have seen worse," said Daniels.

Mason closed the file and put it on the table. "He's hungover. I could tell the moment he walked in."

"He going to be okay?" asked Rem. "You think he can handle the truth if it turns out Cissy did it?"

"He won't have a choice," said Mason, tapping a finger on the table.

The waitress returned, and Mason asked for a pitcher of coffee. "He'll need it," said Mason. Sighing, he patted the folder. "You learn anything interesting when you pulled this?"

Rem sipped his coffee. "From what we read, it looks pretty open and shut. Chad was alive when Cissy went to the store and dead when she came back. No forced entry. Nobody heard anything suspicious. A couple of neighbors said they heard the shot but thought it was a car backfiring. They couldn't be sure at the time."

"It couldn't have been a suicide?" asked Mason.

Daniels shook his head. "Not based on Chad's position and the weapon. There was no blood or gunshot residue on his hand. Plus, there were no outward signs he was suicidal. He was doing well at work based on the interviews with friends and family. Plus, Cissy had a life insurance policy worth a hundred grand on him."

"What about Cissy? Any residue on her?" asked Mason.

"No," said Daniels, "But Bevins and Winkler believe she wore gloves and changed clothes, then tossed them on the way to the store," said Daniels.

"They think it was pre-meditated?" asked Mason.

"That's what they're going for," said Rem.

Mason sighed. "I still don't see a motive though, other than the insurance policy, which doesn't make her a murderer. From what Trick says, they were a happy couple. They'd just moved out here. Chad was making good money, so why would Cissy need more? God knows she'd get alimony if they'd divorced. And from what Trick knew, they were looking for a house and planning a family."

"Doesn't mean she wasn't unhappy," said Rem. "We've seen people do worse for less. I'm sure you have too."

"But you can usually trace it back to something. A broken home, abuse, an affair. Addiction. I don't see any of that here," said Mason.

"That you know of," said Daniels. "Keep in mind. Your only source of information so far is your friend." He leaned back as the waitress arrived and put his salad in front of him. "And how long's it been since you've seen him?"

Pleased the food arrived quickly, Rem smiled as the waitress set his grilled cheese down. "Maybe you ought to go through the file first before you assume anything. We put phone and credit card info in there, too." He picked up a fry and ate it.

"Thank you. That's a huge help," said Mason. "We'll review it, and re-interview friends and family, plus check out Chad's job. Hopefully, if there's a red flag, it will show up." The waitress gave him a plate of chicken salad. "Let's hope there's something there that's more obvious to us than to Bevins and Winkler."

"And let's hope it points to someone other than Cissy or I sense more hangovers in Trick's future," said Daniels.

Mason glanced back toward the bathroom. "Let's hope."

Chapter Six

AFTER TREATING DANIELS AND Remalla to lunch to thank them for their help, Mason returned to his car, and Trick followed. Reaching the driver's side, he started to open the door, but stopped, his anger bubbling up. He faced Trick. "You want to tell me what the hell happened in there?"

Trick, his eyes sunken and red, glowered. "What are you talking about?"

"You're hungover. You can barely walk straight, and you reek of alcohol. Two detectives whose time is valuable stuck their noses out for me, and got us the information we need, and you embarrass me, walking in there, looking like you crawled out of a beer keg."

Trick put his hand on the car hood. "Oh, c'mon, Red. Since when were you such a sucker for good impressions? You and I closed down plenty of bars back in Texas and had a few rough mornings. You didn't care much back then."

"This isn't Texas, Trick, and we never showed up for something important, looking like hell and smelling worse. You came here and asked me for a favor because I owed you. And what do you do? You get wasted on your first night here." He paused and took a breath. "You want me to help you? Then go have fun when this is over. You aren't a kid anymore. Your appetite for liquor and women isn't becoming. It barely was back then." He gripped his key ring. "Get your shit together or go home. I don't have the time or interest in babysitting you. I did it plenty of times when we were partners, but I don't have to do it now. I don't care what our history is."

Trick straightened, his back rigid. "I don't need a babysitter. Never did when we were partners, either."

"The hell you didn't."

"Stop acting like you were so perfect. Just because you like to get up on that damn high horse and tell everyone else how to live their lives while you go off and live yours however you want, regardless of the consequences, doesn't mean I have to listen." Trick rubbed his head, and Mason could imagine it was pounding. "I know I drank too much, but hell, I needed it."

"Needed it?" Mason scoffed. "People deal with loads of crap every day, and most do their best, go home, manage their responsibilities, and go to bed sober. Why are you the exception?"

"It's been a helluva week...month...actually year."

"Join the club, Trick."

Trick frowned. "Don't give me that holier than thou attitude. I've seen you hit bottom, and you know how deep it went. And you've had plenty of hangovers, plus a few one-night-stands. You're not an angel, either."

Mason held back an ugly retort and realized what Trick was subtly telling him. "Did you hook up with someone last night?"

Trick's face turned paler, and he leaned against the car.

Mason grit his teeth. "That's great. Nothing's changed since I last saw you, has it?"

Trick glared. "Why do you care who I sleep with? It's none of your damn business."

Mason jabbed out a finger. "I told Remalla and Daniels you were helping Cissy's parents bail her out of jail. That's what you told me. Was that a lie?"

"It wasn't a lie. They were bailing her out. I just may not have made it there."

"So you let them down too?"

Trick looked up at the sky. "Shit." He squinted and dropped his head. "Fine. You're right and I'm wrong. Per usual. I screwed up. What do you want me to do? Beg for your forgiveness?"

Mason groaned and tried to think. Closing his eyes, he told himself to stay cool. Screaming at his former best friend would solve nothing. Finally, feeling a little more level-headed, he opened his eyes. "You know what? I think this was a mistake." He pulled the folder Remalla had given him out of his jacket pocket and held it out. "Here's all the info you need. Take it. Go through it and talk to whomever you can. Maybe you'll figure out what happened and it will lead to proving Cissy's innocence."

Trick stared at the folder. "You're serious? You're bailing on me?"

Mason debated how to respond, but chose to be honest. "I'm not that guy from the good ole days, Trick. You and I, we had our fun, got into a few messes, and used our clout as Rangers to get out of them. We did stupid things, got ugly drunk, slept with pretty ladies, and broke a few hearts." He sighed, recalling the past. "We've both had regrets, and God knows, we helped each other out of plenty of hard spots. You've got a slew of shit on me, and I've got a slew of it on you." A car drove by blaring music, and Mason waited for it to pass. "I will always remember those days with fondness and a little shame, but I've let them go. I can't do the work that I do without being at my best, and I can't work this case with you unless you can do the same, and let's be real. You can't."

Trick opened his mouth, but it took a few seconds for him to answer. "I miss those days."

"That's the difference between you and me," said Mason. "I don't."

Trick scraped the toe of his foot along the hard concrete of the parking lot. "I guess I just figured, once we reconnected, and maybe if you forgave me..."

"That we'd pick up where we left off?" Mason chuckled. "No. I've moved on." He paused. "Maybe you should too."

Trick nodded, and he eyed the folder Mason held. "Okay. I hear you."

"Good."

"But I'm still not letting you off the hook." He took the folder. "You and I have unfinished business, and I need your help."

Mason started to argue, but Trick held up his hand. "And before you get all pissy with me, you know I'm right. I'll concede I screwed up. I let my frustration and stress get the best of me and didn't handle it well. I should have been here on time, and I should have been there for Cissy and her parents. I get it, and you're right."

"Trick"

"Just shut up. I admire you for what you've done. I hated it at first. I was mad at you for a long time. We had a good thing going, and you screwed it all up. Cara was angry too, and maybe I used that and her to get back at you. I can be man enough to admit my mistakes, and I'm sorry." He rubbed his neck. "But I can't do this without you. I need your insight and wits. We'll accomplish a lot more as a team than anything I can do on my own. I'll get my shit together and promise to not go on any more benders, but you need to stay on this with me."

"Trick, listen□"

"Just work with me a couple of days. Then we can reevaluate how it's going. If I can take it from there, or if it's obvious Cissy did it, I'll move on and your debt will be paid. But if it isn't, and there's another suspect to consider, then we stick." He waved a hand. "You may not agree with me or my lifestyle, but I can behave long enough to get through this, no matter how much you might look down on me."

Mason stood still, his mind unsettled. "I don't look down on you."

"Yes. You do. I see the judgement all over your face."

"You just don't see what I do. I know the man you are, and the man you could be. I wish you could see it, too."

Trick ticked up a brow. "You let me worry about the man I could be, but I appreciate the thought." He opened the folder, winced, and closed it. "Hell. I can't even look at the photos."

Mason's heart fell, and he cursed himself for giving in. "Okay, Trick. You win. I'll stay. But you avoid the booze. You pull another shitshow like last night and today, and you can choke on the dust from my boots."

"I got it." Trick's eyes softened and his shoulders dropped. "Thank you."

Mason nodded. "I guess we need to go through that folder. You want to start there? We can go back to my office, or your place. Where are you staying?"

Trick fiddled with the edge of the folder. "Well, that's another thing I need to talk to you about."

"Hell," said Mason. "I spoke too soon, didn't I?"

Trick rubbed his stomach, still looking pale. "Me and my lady friend may have gotten a little loud in my hotel room. The people next door called the cops, and we got thrown out, which is probably a good thing, since my credit card is maxed out. Thankfully, the police had some grace when they heard I was a former Ranger, and I stayed the rest of the night at her place."

Mason rubbed his forehead. "What are you telling me, Trick?"

Trick shrugged. "You got an extra room I can bunk in?"

Mason blew out a breath, and wanted to tell his friend what he could do with that folder, but a sudden sharp tingle of cold wiggled up his back, making his stomach clench. Turning toward the lot, he took a few steps and eyed the area. Tuning in, he didn't sense the presence of spirit, and realized he was picking up on the living. The tingle grew, and Mason sensed what had caught his attention. They were being watched.

"It'll only be for a couple of days. You won't even know I'm around," said Trick. "We probably won't be spending much time there anyway, while we're working this."

Mason barely heard him and scanned the parked cars. They were empty from what he could tell. A man on his phone paced outside the restaurant, and a woman holding the hand of a young child walked into a neighboring retail store.

"Red? Somethin' wrong?" Trick came up beside him. "What's got you on edge, other than me?" His gaze followed Mason's.

The tingle flared in Mason's gut. "I think we're being watched."

Trick became alert. "You sure it's not one of your ghost friends?" He studied the lot, then turned and scanned the cars and shops behind them.

"It's not." He continued to watch, as did Trick.

"I don't see anything," said Trick. "You?"

"Nothing. Doesn't mean they aren't there."

"Unless we check every car, there's no way to know." He raised up on his toes to look further back. "You got an admirer I should know about, or are we scrambling up a tree someone doesn't want us to climb?"

"My list of admirers has dwindled." Mason heard a door close and saw a teenager hop out of a car carrying a pizza box.

"Then we might end up having some fun after all."

Mason's hope that Chad's case would be open and shut faded. "You got your stuff? A suitcase?" Another car drove by, but the driver was an elderly woman wearing a flowery hat.

"I dropped it off at your office on the way here. Mikey's got it."

Mason nodded, taking a last look around, but saw nothing that roused more suspicion, even though the anxious tingle remained. He turned and faced Trick. "You do anything stupid, and you're out on your ass."

Trick returned his attention to Mason and smacked him on the shoulder. "I appreciate it. I promise to keep the country music at an acceptable volume."

"Acceptable means off." His heart rate slowing, Mason returned to the car and opened the door. "Get in."

Trick didn't argue, but took a last look around before joining Mason in the front seat. He reached for the seat belt. "I don't know about you, but I'm starting to think we may catch a killer." He grinned. "I'm as excited as an acne-prone teenager on his first date."

"Most teenagers are nervous as hell, especially those with acne."

"Not me." He rapped his fingers on the armrest. "Did I ever tell you about my first date?"

"Mary Hudgins, and yes, I know what happened."

Trick chuckled. "If this case turns out to be as eye-opening as that was, then hold on to your hat, partner."

Mason almost argued that this partnership was temporary, but a nudge of worry stopped him, and he started up the ignition, backed out and drove off.

Chapter Seven

MIKEY CLICKED THE MOUSE, and the screen flicked to a new page. Reading, she made a few notes on her pad of paper and scrolled down, studying the feed.

Hearing the door up front open, she clicked over to the cameras and saw Mason and Trick. She returned to the page she'd been reading as Mason entered the inner office.

"How was lunch?" asked Mikey, adding another scribble to her notes. "Did you get what you needed?"

Mason tossed his jacket over the chair, and Trick took off his hat and put it over Mason's jacket. Mikey noted Trick seemed a little more stable on his feet than he had earlier when he'd dropped off his backpack and small suitcase.

Mason waved a folder. "They came through. We've got a lot to go over."

"Great," said Mikey. "I figured they'd get you the goods." She went back to studying the screen.

"You having any luck?" asked Mason.

"I'm finding a few things," she said. "Not sure if they're going to help clear Cissy though."

"You never know. The smallest clue could make a difference," said Mason. He sat on the couch and opened the folder. Trick sat beside him. "You going to be able to get through this?" asked Mason.

Trick held his stomach. "I think so. I'm feeling better."

"There's a fridge in the back with bottled water if you want some," said Mikey.

"Thanks," said Trick. "But I may help myself to another cup of coffee."

Mason leaned over the file and pulled out some photos. Mikey saw the contents and blanched. "Crime scene?"

"Yes," said Mason. He rifled through the papers and pulled some out. "Here's credit card and phone records."

"Give me the phone stuff," said Trick. "My stomach can tolerate that better."

Mason handed them over, picked up the photos, and studied them. "Nothing surprising here. Shot to the head. He's sitting on the couch. Gun's on the floor beside the coffee table. Nothing else seems disturbed." He narrowed his eyes, and then took out his phone and checked something. "Why is he home on a weekday? Time stamp says it's a Thursday at noon."

Trick looked up from the papers. "Don't know. We'll have to ask Cissy."

"We need to swing by and check the cameras at the apartments today. See who came and went that morning," said Mason.

"Hopefully, the manager will be there today," said Trick.

"Mikey," said Mason. "Can you call and check if we can view the video this afternoon?"

Mikey noted something on the screen. "Sure," she said absentmindedly. She rubbed her jaw. "Huh."

"Find something interesting?" asked Mason, still eyeing the photos.

Mikey sat back in her seat. "Maybe."

Trick lowered his papers. "Don't keep us in suspense."

"I'm checking their social media..." She sat back up and opened a new screen.

"And?" asked Trick.

Mikey typed into the search bar and hit enter. A list of results appeared on the screen. "Well, there's not much to report on Chad. He kept a low profile and didn't post much unless he was pissed when the Cowboys lost."

Trick chuckled. "I believe that. Chad was a huge sports fan. Loved the Cowboys." He shook his head. "What's happened to that team is a travesty."

"Yeah," said Mikey. "He posted something about them not being able to find the end zone with binoculars."

"Sounds like him," said Trick.

"Cissy's a different story, though," said Mikey. "She posted pretty regularly. Almost every day when they moved out here. Pictures of their new apartment, going to the zoo, the wharf, the beach, visiting spots along the coast. They were obviously happy as a couple, all smiley and close."

"I know that much," said Trick.

"Up until about six months ago, and then her posts are less regular."

"They were settling in by then," said Trick. "Makes sense."

Mikey tapped her pen on the pad. "They weren't just less regular, the tone changed, too. No more happy, touchy, feely stuff."

Mason looked up from a photo. "What do you mean?"

"She starts posting quotes and sayings, and a lot of them are whimsical, even sad. As if she missed her old life."

"She was probably missing Texas," said Trick. "That wouldn't surprise me. Her whole family's back there."

Mikey eyed the screen. "Maybe. The posts are a little depressing, though, like something's changed."

"Unless she comes out and says she wants to kill her husband, that's not much to go on," said Mason. "People get sad."

"No, I know," said Mikey. "But this past summer, there was an event at Chad's workplace. I guess they were having some sort of company picnic. Chad and Cissy attended. Pictures were posted online, and Cissy and Chad were tagged."

"Nothing strange about that," said Trick, trailing his finger down the phone records he held.

"Except in one of the photos, Cissy made a comment," said Mikey. She swiveled in her seat. "It's a picture of a group of people smiling, Chad and Cissy among them."

Mason stood and came over, and Mikey clicked over to the window with the picture. "There. See it?"

Mason nodded. "What did she comment?"

Mikey rolled her eyes. "You really need to brush up on your social media skills."

"I'd rather stab myself in the eyes," said Mason. "That's why I have you."

Trick joined them, and Mikey pointed out the comment. "She says 'I see you.'"

"I see you?" asked Trick. "What does that mean?"

"I have no idea," said Mikey. "I did some checking on the people in the picture. I learned one is Chad's boss, a Tony Povia, and his wife. Nothing stood out on his page. It's a big group, and not everyone was tagged, but I checked the ones that were and didn't find much, except for one." She clicked the mouse. "Her name is Lydia Stanford. I found her page with a profile pic, but it's a picture of a flower. There's not much else listed, other than where she works and her birthday. She's about as active on social media as you are Mason." She clicked over to Lydia's page.

"Why does it stand out?" said Trick.

"Seems pretty routine," asked Mason.

"It does until you look a little deeper," said Mikey. "She rarely posts, and there are no personal photos, so I can't tell which one she is from the company photo, but about six months ago, she switched her status to 'In a Relationship.'"

"So?" asked Mason.

Mikey scoffed. "Hello? Aren't you supposed to be smart? Why would a woman who rarely posts, who has no photos of herself or a significant other, suddenly post that she's dating someone? It's odd."

"It's still a stretch," said Trick. "She could just be excited about it."

"I would agree until I saw this." She scrolled and pointed. Mason and Trick leaned in.

"Well, I'll be damned," said Trick.

It was a post of the state of Texas with a red heart and an arrow shot through it like a bullseye.

Mason's brow furrowed. "You think that's a reference to her lover?"

"You're the supposed brains in this organization. What do you think?" asked Mikey.

"Still a stretch," said Mason.

"Probably," said Mikey, "But a week before the picnic..." She scrolled again. "...she posts that her relationship status is back to single."

Trick whistled. "Now that's interesting."

"Is your theory that Chad had a relationship with this woman?" asked Mason. "They broke it off, but Cissy somehow knew about it?"

"And she posted 'I see you' on the photo as some sort of message to Lydia." Mikey clicked back to her search results. "Assuming Cissy was referring to Lydia, I did a search on Lydia's name. I just pulled it up." Mikey scanned the results, stopped on a headline, and dropped her jaw.

"What?" asked Mason.

"Shit," said Trick, reading over Mikey's shoulder.

"What do you see?" asked Mason, bending down.

"Here," said Mikey, tapping the screen. "It's an obituary." Mikey clicked the link, and the story pulled up. "Maybe it's a different Lydia Stanford."

The wheel turned and then the page popped up. A column of text appeared under a banner of a funeral home. Mikey quickly read it. "Hard to say. It's pretty brief, and there's no picture. She was cremated and precedes a mother, brother and sister." Mikey noticed the date. "Crap. If it is her, she died two weeks before Chad, but it doesn't say how." She clicked back over to the search results. "Maybe there's more." She scrolled and read and then stopped. "There." She clicked on the link from a local newspaper.

"What?" asked Mason.

"It's coming up," said Trick.

The page loaded, and the headline stood out in stark black-and-white letters. *Local Woman Found Dead in Swimming Pool.* Mikey scanned the brief story. "It's her. They mention her workplace. She drowned, but they ruled it accidental. Said she hit her head and lost consciousness. Paramedics couldn't revive her." She grunted. "Damn it. Doesn't anyone have a picture of this woman?"

"Don't know that we need it. I think the pieces are coming together." Trick stepped back. "Ain't this some shit on a stick," said Trick.

Mason straightened. "Doesn't necessarily mean anything."

"Maybe not, but it's a hell of a coincidence," said Mikey. "If Cissy was referring to Lydia when she wrote 'I see you' and Lydia winds up dead two weeks before Chad..."

"It's not exactly helping her case," said Trick. "I wonder if Bevins and Winter found this, too."

"Winkler," said Mason. "And even if they did, it's all circumstantial, but I agree. It doesn't look good."

"Bevins and Winkler?" asked Mikey.

"Your friends told us they're the detectives on the case who are convinced it's Cissy," said Trick.

"Maybe we're starting to see why," said Mikey.

Trick massaged his temples. "This is all nonsense. Cissy didn't kill Chad, and she sure as hell didn't kill Lydia Stanford." He walked out from behind the desk. "The girl doesn't like killing flies with a flyswatter, and suddenly, she's going to kill two people?"

"Nobody said she killed Lydia," said Mason. "This is pure conjecture. None of this would even be allowed at her trial, which is why we need to be careful of our own assumptions. And why we need to talk to Cissy. Let's hear her side of the story."

"Damn straight," said Trick. He took out his phone. "I'll text her parents. See when we can stop by."

"I'll call the apartment complex," said Mikey. "And try to get you guys in to see the video." She picked up her cell.

"Good," said Mason. "Let's hope somewhere in this mess there's a clue as to who really killed Chad, and that Lydia actually drowned."

Mikey held the phone to her ear and heard it ring. "By accident, you mean?"

Mason cocked a brow at her, glanced at Trick, but didn't answer.

Mason sat at the table and sipped on his glass of water.

"What the hell is taking so long?" asked Trick.

"Stop being so impatient," said Mason. "They don't have to let us see the video at all. We don't have a warrant."

"It must have been my charm that won her over," said Trick. "You see her smiling at me?"

"She's an apartment manager. She smiles at everyone, plus it didn't hurt that you told her you were in the market for a three bedroom with a garage."

"Money smooths the wheels."

"Not when you don't have any."

Trick smirked and was about to make a retort when the door opened to the small conference area, and the manager named Vicki entered carrying a laptop. "Sorry it took so long. I had another prospective client come in, plus I wanted to check with my boss, and make sure it was okay to show you guys this footage. I know the police could see it, but I wasn't sure about a P.I." She set the laptop down in front of Mason and Trick. "He said the police got nothing from it, so he didn't see the harm in you two checking it out."

"Thank you, Vicki. We appreciate it," said Mason. "I hope you didn't go to too much trouble. I'm sure you're busy."

"Smart and pretty lady like you must have clients lined up," said Trick. He flashed a charming grin.

Vicki pursed her lips and flicked a glance at Trick. "My husband would agree with you." She set down a mouse, and the screen winked on.

Mason couldn't help but smile when Trick went quiet, and noted Vicki was not wearing a wedding ring.

"There you go," said Vicki as two images brightened, each of a different view, one from outside the walkway leading to Chad's apartment, and another from the parking lot looking toward it. "This is exactly what the police saw. It's from the morning of Mr. Howard's death up until the cops arrived." She straightened. "Have fun."

"Oh, I'm sure we will," said Mason.

"Let's hope we see something the police didn't," said Trick.

"Handsome and smart as you are, I'm sure you will," said Vicki, the side of her lip rising as she left the room.

"Son-of-a...," said Trick. "I don't think she liked me after all."

Mason chuckled. "The truth hurts. That Trick Monroe swagger has its limits."

"I don't think she's even married."

Mason clicked on the screen. "I think you're right."

Trick shook his head. "Damned if I'm renting a three bedroom from her."

"I think she'll live," said Mason. "Pay attention."

They spent the next hour reviewing the footage, speeding it up when nothing was happening and slowing it down when there was activity. They saw a couple of cars come and go as residents went about their day, but no one approached Chad and Cissy's apartment. At about ten thirty, Cissy left and returned about an hour later, carrying groceries, and within fifteen minutes the first patrol car arrived, and soon after, the parking lot became a sea of police.

Mason flipped off the video. "That wasn't a big help. No one went near their apartment, other than Cissy."

Trick fell back in his seat with a huff. "That doesn't prove anything."

Mason took a last sip of his water. "I don't know what to tell you, Trick. If you want to prove Cissy isn't the murderer, then you're going to have to prove that someone else is at the scene. These videos don't do that."

"Exactly," said Trick. "They don't show anyone entering the parking lot or heading down the walkway. They don't show his front door."

"Anyone heading to his front door would have had to pass these cameras," said Mason.

"True, but who says they passed them that morning? Who says the murderer wasn't already inside?"

"What are you saying?" asked Mason. "Someone was in their apartment, and they didn't know it? Did you see their place? It was a one bedroom. Nobody's hiding anywhere, and I don't recall Cissy saying she had any guests."

"No, you moron," said Trick. "I'm not saying they were inside with Cissy and Chad." He shifted and waved at the screen, "But that walkway leads to other apartments. Who says somebody didn't come from one of them? We wouldn't have seen that on the camera."

Mason held the bridge of his nose and thought about it. "A neighbor was harboring a murderer and didn't bother to mention that to the police?"

Trick's brow furrowed. "You've been out of law enforcement too long. You're assuming all those apartments are rented. What if one of them wasn't?" He waited while Mason considered that. "It's not a bad place to hang out and wait until an opportunity arises. It's also the perfect place to hide until the heat dies down. Nobody's checking out empty apartments while the police are investigating a murder."

Mason realized it wasn't altogether impossible. If there had been a vacant apartment near Chad and Cissy's, someone could have easily shown up several hours, or even days earlier, jimmied the lock and waited, then left when the police did. "We need to talk to Vicki. See if there's an empty apartment down that walkway."

Trick stood. "Took you a while, but you finally made it there. You can do the talking, though. I don't think I hold much clout with her."

"If you'd stop trying to schmooze her, you might get somewhere." Mason closed the laptop and headed for the door.

"Schmooze? What the hell is schmooze? That sounds disgusting."

"Which is why you should stop doing it." He opened the door and saw Vicki at her desk, talking to a young couple. After waiting a few minutes, Vicki stood, shook the couple's hands, and the couple left.

Mason approached her. "Thanks for allowing us to view the videos. The police were right. There wasn't much to see."

"Sorry to hear it," said Vicki. "I wish I could be of more help."

"Actually, you might," said Mason. "Could you check and see if there is a vacancy near that apartment? Or if there was at the time of the crime?"

Vicki straightened her jacket, and Mason could smell her flowery perfume. Trick stayed back and remained quiet.

Vicki appeared to think for a second and then returned to her desk. "Actually, I think there is." She typed on the keyboard and studied the screen. "Yes. It's nine-fourteen, a two-bedroom, just two doors down from Mr. Howard's."

Trick stepped up. "How long's it been vacant?"

"It looks like the tenant moved out a week before the murder." She pointed and read the screen. "It's been rented again, though. Couple moves in next week."

Mason made eye contact with Trick. "You mind if we take a look at it?" asked Mason.

Vicki looked up from the screen. "I thought you were in the market for a three-bedroom?" She glanced at Trick.

"I spoke too soon," said Trick, holding his hat. "A two-bedroom makes more sense. A bed for me and one for anyone not wanting to share it with me." He grinned. "Shocking as that may seem."

Mason almost groaned. "We'd like to see it, if you don't mind."

Vicki offered Trick an unreadable expression, then reached into a drawer and pulled out some keys. "Okay. Suit yourself. Follow me."

A couple of minutes later, Mason followed Vicki down the walkway outside Chad and Cissy's old apartment. They stopped outside a door further down, and Vicki unlocked it and stood aside. "It's all yours."

Mason stepped inside and Trick entered behind him. "And if you really are interested in renting," said Vicki to Trick as he passed, "let me know, and I'll give you some numbers." She looked him up and down, and her cell rang. "I need to take this. I'll be just outside." Waving the phone, she walked out.

"That Monroe magic may be kicking in yet," said Trick. "I think I got her curious."

"More like ambitious. I think she senses potential business, not romance." Mason walked around the empty living room. The carpet was vacuumed, the perfect lines etched into the pile. The kitchen was clean and empty.

"We'll see about that," said Trick. He entered the bedroom. "Nothing in here."

Mason peeked out the large window that led out onto a small porch and slid the sliding glass door open. Stepping out, he could see the other decks of the surrounding apartments, one of them being Cissy and Chad's. A crushed cigarette butt lay on the concrete. Another chilly tendril traveled up his spine, and he tuned in, trying to determine its source. The sensation felt different from what he'd sensed in the parking lot that morning, but it was no less disturbing. He wished Mikey were there. While he could detect and communicate with spirit, Mikey had the empathic gifts in the family. She could walk into a room and tell you if something or someone bad had affected the area. He wondered what she'd get from this apartment, but he sensed it wouldn't be good.

"Mason?" Trick called from inside.

Mason took a last look around and returned to the living room, shutting the door behind him. "Where are you?"

"Bathroom."

Mason walked down the hall, and into a bathroom that was adjacent to a bedroom. "What is it?"

Trick nodded toward the toilet.

Mason grimaced. "If you're going to show me an unflushed toilet, then we have sunk to new lows."

Trick snorted with disgust. "Just look, you idiot."

Mason eyed the bowl and saw two cigarette butts floating in the water. He thought of the one on the patio. "Could be from a maintenance man."

"Could be." Trick hooked a thumb in a belt buckle. "But this state is so anti-smoking, I'm guessing Miss Vicki out there would threaten a smoking maintenance guy with a firing squad."

Mason couldn't argue with that.

"You're the one with all the woo-woo stuff," said Trick. "What's your gut telling you? Don't forget, someone was watching us outside the restaurant earlier. What if they're a smoker?

"I saw a cigarette butt on the patio, too." That tendril of cold became a spike, and Mason couldn't deny Trick's logic. "It's a long shot at best."

"I like long shots. It's when we're at our best."

Mason sighed and stretched his neck. "How about you use that so-called charm of yours to ask Vicki to get us a plastic bag?"

Trick grinned and smacked him on the arm. "You check out that pretty mustache of yours in the mirror. I'll be right back."

Chapter Eight

CISSY HOWARD STARED AT the clock, watching it tick over to the next minute. Rolling onto her back in the bed, she stared at the ceiling. She'd told her parents she'd wanted to take a nap, but she hadn't slept a wink; her mind wouldn't still as she replayed her life over the past year. Chad's new job, the move to San Diego, the initial excitement, the planning for a family, and the fun of discovering a new city, but then circumstances had changed. Chad had begun to work longer hours, leaving Cissy home alone. She'd joined a neighborhood women's group, a local gym, and worked part time at a nearby bookstore, but had failed to make the close, personal relationships she'd missed from home. Everyone was nice, but many of the women she'd met were mothers and their time was spent with their children or other mothers. Her loneliness had caused her to take out her frustrations on Chad, and she'd made him feel guilty.

Looking back now, she wished they'd handled their issues differently. Instead of working through them, she and Chad had become more distant. Chad had chosen to spend more time at the office, and Cissy wondered if she'd pushed him away. But she wouldn't take all the blame. Chad had to shoulder some of it. He'd been the one to stray, not her, even though it would have been easy for her if she'd wanted to. There had been opportunities.

Thinking of Chad, her eyes welled, and she couldn't stop the images from flashing in her mind of her husband dead on the couch, a garish wound in his head, the police arriving and her hysterical sobbing, the questioning of the detectives and seeing the dubious looks on their faces, and then realizing she was the prime suspect. Within a day of the funeral, she'd been arrested, and had sat in a jail cell until her parents had bailed her out. And now there would be the long wait while her attorney and the state prepared to take her case to trial, and either prove or disprove that she'd killed her husband. It was overwhelming. How had she found herself in such a desperate place in a ridiculously short period of time? How had everything gone wrong so fast?

Sniffing, she wiped her eyes and tried to think of something else. Somehow, she'd figure out how to get out of this mess. Other women had faced worse and managed, and she would too.

She thought of Trick, who was on his way over with his former partner turned private investigator. Trick was determined to prove her innocence, and she prayed he could do it. Based on her history with him, she knew he was tenacious and stubborn, but also charming and persuasive. He could be someone's best friend or worst enemy if either worked to his advantage, and if he'd been the least interested in commitment, Cissy might have still been in Texas right now, and not here, facing life in prison.

Hanging her elbow over her face, she took a deep breath and moaned into her arm. What the hell had happened to her?

Mason stood at the door to the hotel room with Trick. After Trick knocked, an older woman with silver-streaked short brown hair opened the door. Her clothes hung loosely on her body, and Mason guessed she'd lost weight from the stress of the last few weeks.

Seeing Trick, she smiled, though sadly. "Hi, Trick."

A tall man came up behind her. His eyes creased when he saw Trick, but he pulled the door wider. "Hey, Trick," he said. "Thanks for coming."

"Hi, Mr. and Mrs. Bennet," said Trick.

"It's Marsha and Dennis," said Dennis. "If you're going to help Cissy through this, please call us by our first names."

Trick stepped inside. "This is Mason Redstone. My former partner."

Mason shook their hands, said his hellos, and noted their tired and worn faces. Dennis' clothes bagged on him, too.

They went into the front room. "Can I get you something to drink?" asked Marsha, holding her sweater around her. "Tea or coffee?"

"Tea, please," said Mason. "If it's not too much trouble."

"I'll take a coffee, black, if you've got it," said Trick.

"Of course. It's no trouble at all," said Marsha. "We've purchased stock in coffee beans. Haven't we, Dennis?"

Her husband chuckled. "The rate we're going, we probably should."

Marsha nodded. "Be right back." She paused in the hallway. "I'll let Cissy know you're here."

"Thanks," said Trick.

"I can't thank you enough for coming to help us out," said Dennis. He sat in a big chair and wrung his hands. "The police here seem damned determined to prove Cissy did this."

Mason and Trick sat on the couch across from Dennis. "I'm happy to help," said Trick. "I know Cissy didn't hurt Chad." He gestured at Mason. "Red and I go back a ways, and we've been through a few rocky cases ourselves. We'll figure out who did this."

Mason listened, questioning whether they would, and wondered what Trick would tell this family if they couldn't find a killer other than Cissy. As Dennis and Trick talked, he figured that would be Trick's problem to handle.

"I understand you're a private investigator?"

Mason looked over. "Yes. I am." He decided it would be best to leave the paranormal part out. "After I left the Rangers, I came out here. My older brother had moved out here first and loved it, plus there were a few other factors that made me take the leap." He chose not to mention Victor.

"It's quite the jump, going from Texas to California," said Dennis. "And from a Ranger to a P.I."

"It's had its share of challenges," said Mason, "but I don't regret it."

"I wasn't too pleased with him," said Trick. "And I'm still not."

"You still with the Rangers?" asked Dennis.

Trick stilled and fiddled with a couch cushion. "No, sir. I'm not."

"I'm surprised. Chad always talked about how much you loved it. I got the impression he idolized you a bit."

Trick nodded.

"What made you leave?" asked Dennis.

Trick hesitated, and Mason waited for the answer, curious himself.

"Hey."

They looked up, and Mason saw a pretty woman with long black hair pulled back into a messy ponytail, wearing jeans and an oversized shirt, standing just inside the room.

"Cissy," said Dennis, standing. "Trick's here."

Trick rose from the couch. "Hey, Cissy. How are you?"

Cissy smiled and walked over. "Hey, Trick. It's good to see you."

The two hugged and Trick held her when she wrapped her arms around his waist. "Thank you for coming," whispered Cissy.

"Of course," he said, pulling back. "I'm not going to let these assholes get away with this. It's damn nonsense. I know you would never hurt Chad."

Mason observed the young woman and tuned in, trying to get a read on her. Her energy was scattered and frail, and her body language denoted a woman on the edge, but was it because she was unfairly accused or trying to get away with murder?

A familiar tingle ran up his arms, and his hair raised. Mason closed his eyes, recognizing the pull of a spirit. Someone was here and trying to communicate.

"This is Mason Redstone. I told you about him on the phone. Red," said Trick. "This is Cissy Howard."

Mason opened his eyes, trying to stay focused on Cissy while a man materialized behind her. Mason held out his hand. "It's nice to meet you. I'm sorry about your husband."

Cissy took his hand. "Thank you. I appreciate you helping Trick. He said you were the best."

Mason flicked a gaze at Trick, but then turned his attention back to the man behind Cissy. "He did, huh?" He tried not to react when he noticed the gaping wound in the man's head, and Mason realized it was Chad. It wasn't often a victim showed himself to Mason with their injuries intact. In his experience, that often meant that the victim had something unresolved regarding their death and was trying to deliver a message.

"Hey, you in there?" asked Trick.

Mason blinked. "Sorry." He focused on Cissy. "My mind wandered." Trick raised a brow at him, but Mason ignored it. "You mind talking to us about what happened?" He shot a glance at dead Chad, who stood quietly behind Cissy.

"You sure you're all right?" Trick asked Cissy. "You need a minute?"

Cissy waved her hand. "No. I'm okay. You came to help me. No point in making you wait."

"You guys have a seat. I'll go help Marsha," said Dennis. He patted Cissy's shoulder. "I'll get you some water."

"Thanks, Dad," said Cissy.

Dennis left the room, and Cissy took his seat while Trick and Mason returned to the couch. Dead Chad remained behind Cissy, but his gaze fell on Mason.

Mason interlaced his fingers. "Why don't you tell us what happened that day, when you found Chad?"

Cissy sighed and wrung her hands, like her father had done. "Okay."

"Take your time," said Trick.

Mason listened as Cissy went through the sequence of events from the morning of Chad's death, telling them how Chad had taken a day off from work, and she'd hoped they'd spend the day together, but Chad had wanted to stay home and watch TV. They'd argued, and Cissy, frustrated, had left the apartment, mainly because she was angry, and decided to go to the grocery store to give herself time to cool off. She'd come home an hour later, and Chad had been sitting on the couch with his back to her, with the TV blaring. She'd yelled at him to lower the volume, but he'd ignored her. That's when she'd walked around to grab the remote and seen his injuries. She'd immediately called nine-one-one, and Chad had been pronounced dead at the scene, and it had only gone downhill from there. Chad's gun had been found on the floor, and both her and Chad's fingerprints were on it. The police didn't believe it was suicide, and neither did Cissy.

"Why were your prints on the gun?" asked Mason.

"I've gone shooting with Chad a few times," said Cissy. "He wanted me to learn how to use it."

"She's a good shot, too," said Trick. "When's the last time you went shooting?"

Cissy thought about it. "Probably a little over a month ago."

"Forgive me," said Mason, "but why don't you think Chad killed himself?" He eyed dead Chad, who continued to stand behind Cissy, as if wanting to hear the story too.

"Because Chad would never do that," said Cissy. "He wasn't depressed. Maybe we were going through a rough patch, but it certainly didn't warrant suicide."

"I agree," said Trick. "Chad loved life. He'd never off himself."

Dead Chad's gaze briefly flicked over to Trick, but then returned to Mason.

"You said you were going through a rough patch?" asked Mason. "What do you mean?"

Cissy took a deep breath and discussed how after their move, Chad had spent more time at work, and less with her, and she'd been lonely and homesick, and she'd taken it out on Chad.

"Cissy," said Trick. "Chad told me he had wanted to talk to me about something not long before he died. You have any idea what it was about?"

Cissy nodded and swallowed. "Yeah," she said softly. "I think so."

For the first time, dead Chad looked at his wife.

"What's that?" asked Mason.

Cissy's eyes filled. "He'd had an affair." She spoke softly and wiped her eyes. "My parents don't know yet. I haven't told them."

Just then, Marsha walked into the room with a tray. "Here we are. Some tea and coffee, and a few cookies." She set it down on the table in front of the couch.

Dennis followed with a large pot. "Black coffee and plenty of it." He added it to the tray and pulled a flask from his pocket. "In case you want to add anything to your drinks." He placed it next to the coffee. "Take as much as you want. I've got more in the kitchen."

"Thank you," said Trick, his eyes on Cissy, who sniffed again.

"Oh, honey," said Marsha. "Are you okay?" She grabbed a tissue from a box on an end table and handed it to Cissy.

"I'm fine, Mom. Thanks." Cissy took the tissue and dabbed her eyes.

Dennis helped himself to a cup of coffee. "C'mon, Marsha. Let's let them talk." He took his wife's elbow. "We'll be in the kitchen." He led her out of the room.

Trick rubbed his palms down his jeans. "You want something, Cissy?" He grabbed a cup.

"Some tea, please," said Cissy.

"I'll get it," said Mason. He grabbed a tea bag and added it to a cup and poured some hot water from a teapot. "Sugar?"

Cissy shook her head, and he handed her the drink and made one for himself. Dead Chad remained quietly behind Cissy.

Trick got himself some coffee. "Are you sure? About the affair? I can't believe Chad would do that to you."

Cissy sipped her tea. "I'm sure."

Mason thought about Lydia Stanford. "Do you know who it was? Who he had the affair with?" He sipped his own tea.

"A woman from work," said Cissy.

"Hell," said Trick, sitting back on the couch. "I just don't understand it." He blew on his coffee. "Did you tell the cops?"

"Yes. Of course. She was my first thought. It made sense. Chad had broken it off, and she'd retaliated. It had to have been her. At least that's what I thought. I figured the detectives would bring her in and question her, and then I'd be cleared. Until they told me she was dead, too."

Dead Chad made his first movement then. He reached up and touched his wounded head and then looked at his bloody fingers as if surprised. Mason tried not to stare.

"You didn't say how you knew he'd been cheating," said Mason. "Are you sure?"

"I am," said Cissy. "I came out and asked him, and he didn't deny it. Said it was over though, and he knew he'd made a terrible mistake, and it would never happen again." Cissy gripped her cup, her eyes narrowed. "He said that he loved me and didn't want anyone else." Her jaw set. "I asked him who it was, but he wouldn't tell me."

Mason made eye contact with Trick, and Trick asked the obvious question. "Then how'd you know who he'd slept with? How could you tell the police?"

Cissy stiffened in her seat. "Because I'm not stupid, Trick. Chad spent most of his time at work, or at least that's what he told me. I assumed it had to be someone from the office." In her first sign of anger, she leaned over and grabbed her father's flask. She opened it and poured some liquid from it into her tea.

"I'll take some of that, too," said Trick.

Mason glared, but Trick glared back. "Give me a break. It's just a shot to take the edge off."

Cissy sipped her tea, squinted, and cleared her throat. "It's whiskey." She handed the flask to Trick.

"Perfect," said Trick, adding some to his coffee. "Red?" He offered the flask to Mason.

A trickle of blood dribbled down dead Chad's forehead, and Mason broke out in chills. He took the flask from Trick. "Maybe just a touch." He added a little to his tea.

"Good," said Trick. "You need to relax."

Mason frowned at Trick. "How'd you find out who it was?" he asked Cissy. He closed the flask and returned it to the tray.

"We went to a company picnic this past summer." Cissy took another sip of her drink. "I'd suspected that he'd been cheating, but I hadn't confronted him yet. I'd gone to the bathroom, and when I came back, Chad was gone. One of the women there told me to check behind the bleachers and gave me a look that told me something was up. I went, and I saw Chad arguing with a woman. I couldn't hear everything they were saying, but it was obvious he was telling her something she didn't like. I walked over, and they instantly stopped talking, and he acted like it was some sort of business issue and she just stood there frozen, and then said something like, 'you'll regret it' before she stomped off." Cissy paused. "I knew then my suspicions were accurate. Chad returned to the picnic, acting as if it was no big deal."

Mason took a swig of his tea and warmth slid down his throat. "Did you make a comment on social media on one of the pictures posted from the picnic?"

Cissy put her tea down with a bang. "I sure as hell did. I wanted that woman to know I knew. I wanted her to know that whatever was going on between her and Chad was over." She sat back. "But I also didn't want to expose Chad and make it messy at work, or make it embarrassing for all of us. 'I see you' seemed enough to get my point across, and she'd know it was meant for her."

Dead Chad didn't move, but continued to watch. Mason wished he could speak with the man but couldn't do it with Cissy and Trick in the room. Mason's acceptance in their circle would likely change once he started talking to the dead out loud.

"You didn't see this woman again after that?" asked Trick. He drank some coffee. "No more contact?"

"No," said Cissy, shifting in her seat. "Once I confirmed she worked with Chad, I talked to Chad's assistant, Daphne, and found out the woman's name was Lydia Stanford. I tried looking her up online just to see what I could learn about her, but that's it." She played with the seam on the chair. "And I checked Chad's phone, but didn't find anything. The detectives said he may have had a second phone." She snickered. "Can you believe that?"

"Did they find another phone?" asked Mason.

Cissy shrugged. "I don't know. I didn't hear about it if they did."

"We should ask about that," said Trick. "Find out what these detectives think they know."

Mason agreed. "If they found a phone, and there's evidence Chad had an affair, then that doesn't help Cissy. It gives her a motive. It doesn't help that the other woman's dead, either."

Cissy's jaw fell. "Why? You think they'll try to pin her death on me, too?" Her eyes widened. "How did she die?"

"Drowned. In a pool," said Trick. "There was no indication of foul play though."

"You don't know that," said Mason.

"If they were going to arrest Cissy for Lydia Stanford's death," said Trick, "they would have done it already."

"You don't know that either," said Mason. He regarded Cissy. "You need to tell your attorney everything you've told us, and if the cops want to talk to you about Lydia Stanford, you don't say a word without your lawyer present."

Cissy's face paled. "You really think I could be a suspect?"

"You had motive. They'll definitely investigate, and if we found your comment online, so will they," said Mason. "And if you did an online search on her name, they'll find that too."

"Oh, God," said Cissy.

"All of that proves nothing, and if that's all they have, no prosecutor worth his salt would take on that case." Trick picked up the flask and added more whiskey to his coffee. "Don't worry about it. Let's focus on Chad." He offered the flask to Cissy and Mason, but they each declined, and he returned it to the table.

"But it begs the question, doesn't it?" asked Cissy. "Did someone kill Lydia? Isn't it a little coincidental that she and Chad both die within weeks of each other?"

Mason wondered about that while dead Chad swiped at the blood on his head and wiped it on his pants, leaving a red smear. "It is interesting." He looked away and swirled his tea. "I'd like to know why Chad stayed home the day he died and didn't want to go out. Who takes a day off just to watch TV?"

"You think he was avoiding someone?" asked Trick. He reached for the coffee pot. "It wasn't Lydia, because she was already dead." He added coffee to his mug.

"That's something to ask about when we talk to Chad's co-workers," said Mason.

Cissy sat up and tucked a leg beneath her. "Could someone from Chad's work have done this?"

Mason sensed dead Chad's anxiety. Was Chad trying to tell him something? Mason tried to stay focused on Cissy. "I'm sorry to ask this, but could there have been someone else? Another woman other than Lydia?"

"Or was Lydia involved with someone?" asked Trick. "Maybe from work? And that person went after her, and then Chad?"

Dead Chad began to pace behind Cissy's chair, and Mason found it difficult not to get distracted.

"Are the detectives on my case going to look into any of this?" asked Cissy. "Or are they just determined that I'm the killer and all that matters is proving it?"

Trick picked up a cookie from the tray and dunked it in his coffee. "That's a question well worth asking, and I'd like to know myself." He removed the cookie and ate it.

"There're a lot of questions to ask and a lot more digging to do," said Mason. "Let's hope we can find people who will talk to us."

"If I have anything to say about it, they will," said Trick. "Chad deserved better. Despite whatever shortcomings he had, he was a good man, and he would have straightened it out with you. He would have been a good husband and father."

Cissy studied her tea and didn't answer. Dead Chad stopped behind her chair and stared at her.

Mason sensed her uncertainty, and Chad's too. He sat forward and put his tea on the tray. "Cissy? Is there anything else we need to know? Anything that might affect our investigation? The deeper we go, the more important it is not to be surprised. Especially if the detectives on this case discover it first."

Chad hovered over Cissy, and she ran her hands over her upper arms and shivered. "It's cold in here." She put her tea down and pulled a blanket off the back of the chair to lay over her shoulders.

"Cissy?" asked Trick.

Cissy adjusted her position on the chair and sat cross-legged. She scratched at something on her jeans. "I wasn't completely honest about something."

Mason held his breath, waiting for the hammer to fall. "What is it?"

"I haven't told anyone. Not even the cops. Or my parents." Cissy stared off at some distant point. "I, uh, I did something stupid."

"Oh, hell," said Trick, sighing. "Did you cheat on Chad?"

"No," said Cissy. "I mean, I thought about it. I was angry with him, but I knew that would only make it worse." She bunched the blanket in her hands. "No, I...uhm...hell...I did see Lydia. I found out where she lived and went to her place to confront her."

More tingles traveled up Mason's arms.

"What happened?" asked Trick.

"I knocked on her door," said Cissy. "She answered, and we argued. She acted dumb about Chad. Said I didn't know what I was talking about. That I was crazy."

Mason's tingles intensified, and he watched in shock as another spirit began to materialize beside dead Chad.

"I yelled back," said Cissy. "Told her to stay away from my husband, or I'd drop kick her ass back into her momma's womb. She just cackled at me and grinned, like I was making jokes. I saw red and told her to either back off, or I'd make her wish she'd never met Chad, much less screwed him."

The spirit began to take shape, and Mason stared with wide eyes. A woman appeared beside dead Chad, her face pale, her lips blue, and her wet hair stuck to her face and neck. Water dripped down from her clothes and skin. Mason forced himself not to react. Dead Lydia had joined dead Chad.

Cissy shook her head. "I should have never gone, I know, but I had to see her, to tell her to leave us alone, but then I realized something was wrong. Something was off about her. Her eyes kept darting around, her hair was dirty, she had a strange empty stare, and her pupils were wide. I think she was on something, and then I wondered if Chad had gotten in too deep." She reached for her tea, her fingers trembling. "He'd slept with a madwoman, and now he had to pick up the pieces after a horrific mistake. It made me question everything about him. What kind of man would do that?" She closed her eyes. "What the hell was he thinking? Was our life that miserable? How could he have had an affair with someone like her?"

Mason tried to stay focused on Cissy but watched in disbelief as the ghost of Lydia Stanford reached down and slapped at Cissy's tea. The cup fell from Cissy's grasp and liquid splashed all over Cissy's lap. Cissy yelped and sat up, pushing the blanket back.

Mason pulled himself out of his shock and stood, but his attention remained on dead Chad and Lydia. Trick leapt up and grabbed for a napkin on the tray.

Cissy swiped at the liquid. "What a mess. I don't know what happened. I guess it just slipped out of my hands."

"Here," said Trick, holding out the napkin. "I'll go to the kitchen and get some towels."

Cissy took the napkin and dabbed at her pants. "I'm such a klutz."

Mason wanted to help, but was riveted by the presence of Lydia, who smiled as Cissy cleaned up, and then her gaze found Mason's. The prickles became shards of ice and anxiety crept up his spine when Lydia grinned, opened her mouth, and began to cackle.

Chapter Nine

MASON SAT AT THE bar, nursing a tequila. A soft country song about a lonely man and his beer played, and he rested his head in his palm, trying to get Lydia Stanford's face out of his mind.

"Can I get you another?"

Mason looked up. "No. Thanks, Charlie. I better stop here."

Charlie nodded and walked away to help another patron at the bar.

After their interview with Cissy, he and Trick returned to the office, and Mason had decided he'd had enough for the day. Mikey had given him a look, but hadn't said anything. Trick stayed to go through the phone and credit card records and Mikey had agreed to drive him to Mason's later.

Mason had returned home and taken a hot shower, but feeling restless, he'd left and come to Charlie's. It was a small hole-in-the-wall bar that played country music, and the customers wore boots and cowboy hats. It was a little slice of Texas in the Golden State, and it soothed him when he needed to clear his head. It had been a while since communication with the deceased had disturbed him so much, and he needed to distract himself.

Mikey had called earlier, telling him she'd dropped Trick off and had used her key to get in. Trick had also called, but Mason hadn't answered. He needed a little time away from his old partner, and if Trick knew Mason was in a bar, he wouldn't hesitate to join him, and Mason didn't want that right now. He told Mikey to let Trick know he'd be home soon, and to make himself comfortable, and he'd left it at that. Trick would be fine, but Mason wondered about his own state of mind. This case was summoning some alarmingly determined apparitions when he was usually adept at warding them off. Now Mason had to figure out how to deal with them. If he was going to help Cissy, he'd have to determine why Chad and Lydia had shown themselves, and why Lydia held enough acrimony toward Cissy to physically knock a cup from her hand. Was Cissy telling the truth about Chad and Lydia? Or was there more to the story? Cissy obviously had a temper, and she had lied about not seeing Lydia. Had she lied about anything else?

Mason sipped on his liquor and looked around the small bar. Two men sat across from him, talking and drinking beers. A man and a woman laughed as they played a game of pool in a small room across from the bar, and a football game played with the sound turned down on a nearby TV. He noticed a woman sitting by herself at a small table in the corner. A drink sat in front of her, her phone was beside her, and she stared out the window. Her sleeveless top revealed smooth, toned bronze skin, and her thick, dark hair ran down her back. Mason had glanced over at her a few times and found himself wondering about her. Her face was round but sculpted, and he'd seen her apply a bit of lip gloss to her full lips to make them shine. Her perfectly arched eyebrows mesmerized him. How did women like that sit alone at a bar? If he'd been in a better mood, he would have approached and offered to buy her a drink.

The door to the bar opened, and Mason spotted Mikey entering with Detective Remalla behind her. Mikey headed to the bar and slid onto the stool beside him. Remalla sat next to her.

Mason grumbled. "Mikey. What are you doing here?"

"Don't give me that look," said Mikey. "I didn't like that tone in your voice when I talked to you. Something's up."

"How'd you know I was here?" asked Mason.

Mikey rolled her eyes. "Because you always come to Charlie's when you need a drink."

Remalla leaned over. "Don't mind me. She dragged me here after we got a burger. Said she was worried about you. I know her well enough not to argue."

Charlie came over. "Can I get you guys something?"

Remalla eyed Mikey. "You want a beer?"

Mikey nodded. "Sure. Thanks."

Remalla ordered, and Mason sighed. "I'm fine," he said. "You didn't have to check on me. I'm capable of taking care of myself."

"Famous last words," said Remalla.

Mikey swiveled in her seat. "Don't give me that crap, Mason. I can tell that something's bugging you. What happened today? Is it Trick?"

Lydia's cackle echoed in his head. "No, although he is a pain in the ass."

"Was he drunk this morning?" asked Mikey.

"Yes," said Mason and Remalla at the same time.

"Sorry about that," said Mason to Remalla. "He tends to play first and think later."

"Considering he puked his way through our meal, I figured," said Remalla. "I know he's your former partner and all, but are you sure you can rely on him?"

Mason tinkered with the rim of his glass. "I hope so."

"That doesn't sound encouraging," said Mikey. "Maybe you should back out of this while you still can."

Mason had been considering the same thing through two drinks. "I can't. Much as I think it might be best for my mental health, Trick and I have too much history and if he needs my help, then I'm going to be there for him. I know, despite our differences, that he'd do the same for me." He leaned over and spoke to Remalla. "I'm sure you get it. I doubt you'd do any less for your partner if you were in a similar situation."

Remalla nodded. "I can't deny it. You go through a few things together, and hell, if he was wanted for murder, I'd help him."

Mikey looked between the two of them. "Even if it meant sacrificing yourselves in the process?"

Mason nodded, along with Remalla. "Admit it, Mikey," said Mason. "You'd help me if I were in a pinch."

"You're my brother, Mason," she said. "There's a difference."

"Not really," said Mason.

"Agreed," said Remalla.

Charlie approached with two beers and set them down in front of Remalla and Mikey.

"I can deal with Trick, though," said Mason. "It's the dead I'm having issues with."

"Wonderful," said Remalla. "Maybe I can get my beer to go."

"Oh, please," said Mikey. "This is hardly news to you. You've been through a lot worse."

Rem shrugged. "You've got a point." He drank some beer.

Mikey spoke to Mason. "What is it? What happened? What are you seeing?"

Dead Chad and Lydia flashed in his mind, and Mason shuddered. Realizing Mikey wasn't going to let him off the hook, he told her about his afternoon with Trick, starting at the apartment complex and then ending with their talk with Cissy. She and Remalla listened, and Remalla's eyes widened when he mentioned dead Chad and Lydia.

Mason took the last swig of his drink and noticed the pretty woman with the bronze skin who was sitting alone looking over at them. When she met his gaze, she looked away.

"Hell. It's a good thing I don't see that stuff. I'd have ended up in a straitjacket." Remalla grabbed a peanut from a bowl and popped it in his mouth. "The cigarette butts are interesting, though. You think someone was waiting in the empty apartment?"

"Don't know," said Mason. "But it's possible. If Cissy didn't do it, it would be the only way to explain how no one is seen on the cameras. I doubt those cigarettes will help much, though. Any DNA on them is likely gone after sitting in that water, unless the one from the porch comes through."

"You want me to get them analyzed?" asked Rem. "They may not be admissible in court, but if there is DNA, it might point to whoever was in the apartment."

"I've bothered you enough," said Mason. "I can find a lab."

Mikey prodded him. "Mason, accept help when it's offered."

"Mikey...," said Mason.

"It's no big deal," said Rem. "I'm happy to do it."

Mason hesitated and wondered where he'd put the cigarettes once they'd placed them in the plastic bag, then realized they were still in his jacket pocket. He pulled them out. "I've still got them. Almost forgot."

Remalla took them. "Okay. I'll take 'em in tomorrow. But it will be awhile before we know."

"Yeah. I figured. Thanks, though," said Mason.

"You're welcome," said Remalla.

"Why do you think Chad and Lydia made an appearance?" asked Mikey. "What were they trying to tell you?"

"I wish I knew," said Mason. "After we left, they disappeared. I tried to reach out afterward, but they didn't return."

"What's your take on it? You think Cissy's innocent or guilty?" asked Mikey.

Mason thought back on the interview. "My gut tells me she's innocent, but my gut's been wrong before. Trick certainly believes in her. Chad did have an affair though, and I saw a glimpse of Cissy's temper. Women can do crazy things when their husbands cheat. Plus, she lied about going to see Lydia."

"You need to check out Lydia," said Remalla. "Find out what her story is. Is she really nuts, or is that just Cissy's story?"

"It's on the list," said Mason, "plus talking to Chad's co-workers. Maybe they can shed some light on Lydia, plus any relationship she may have had with Chad or anyone else." He grabbed a peanut from the bowl. "You think Bevins and Winkler would talk to us about the case?"

Remalla nodded. "I can ask. But they won't tell you everything. They'll keep their cards close to the vest until they're ready to reveal them."

"Yeah. I know," said Mason, chewing the peanut. "Something tells me they're trying to link Cissy to Lydia's death. If they find out Cissy went to see her, it'll be another nail in that box they're trying to seal."

"It will," said Remalla, "which is why you need to get out ahead of this as fast as possible. Obviously, they don't have a smoking gun when it comes to Lydia, or they would have arrested Cissy by now. Confronting her husband's mistress and leaving cryptic comments on a picture aren't enough to convict."

"Let's assume Cissy didn't do it," said Mikey. "Then who's running around killing people? Lydia drowns two weeks before Chad is shot. Who would want them both dead?"

"Chad stayed home the day he was murdered," said Remalla. "Was he avoiding someone? And if he was, it obviously wasn't Cissy, which bodes well for her."

"Or could Cissy be in on this with someone else?" asked Mikey. "Was she lying about having an affair of her own?"

Mason's head hurt. He picked up his glass, drained the rest of his drink, and put the glass down.

"You better check out Cissy too," said Remalla. "I know Trick vouches for her, but he hasn't seen her or Chad in a while. The phone and credit card records will help, but that's just a start."

"I'm getting that," said Mason. "So much for this being a two-day distraction." He eyed Mikey. "I think you may have to push back a few more appointments."

"I can do that," said Mikey. "Serita Avery called back today. Said she saw that man in the mirror again and it freaked her out. I told her you were busy until next week, but she was willing to wait."

"That's fine," said Mason, with a sigh. "You need to check the books for this month. Our finances may take a hit since I'm working for free at the moment."

Mikey finished her beer. "We'll be fine. We can take it, as long as you don't stay pro bono for long. Tell Chad and Lydia to give you some hints about who did it so you can get back to helping other dead people."

Remalla drained his beer. "Thank God I work with the living." He checked his watch. "You ready? I've got an early day tomorrow."

Mikey nodded. "I'm ready. You all right, Mason? You want us to wait?"

"No. Go home," said Mason. "I'll settle up with Charlie and head out. I've got a busy day tomorrow, too."

"I'd offer to leave her here with you if I could," said Remalla, "but she drove." He ticked a brow at Mikey. "Which may be a good reason to find another ride." He shot a thumb at Mikey. "You ever feel you're taking your life in your hands when you're in the car with her?"

Mason noticed the woman from the corner table watching, but she looked away again when he glanced over. "Every time."

"Hey," said Mikey. "There's nothing wrong with my driving."

Remalla shot out a hand. "You almost ran that guy off the highway and took his bumper with you. He followed us, and if I hadn't flashed my badge, you'd have had to use those karate skills of yours to survive."

"Karate skills?" asked Mason. "What karate skills?"

Mikey swatted him on the arm. "I told you I was taking a self-defense class. I started it last week."

"You did?" asked Mason.

Mikey huffed. "You have the worst memory. Why do I tell you anything?"

"Sorry," said Mason, pulling out his wallet. "I've been preoccupied. How was your class?" He put bills on the counter.

Mikey slid off the bar seat. "Pretty good. That marshmallow man was toast once I finally got away from him."

Remalla chuckled.

"Marshmallow man?" asked Mason.

"The guy with all the padding," said Mikey. "I kicked the shit out of him."

"I almost feel sorry for him," said Remalla, standing and throwing some cash on the bar. "I'll get those cigarettes to the lab, and I'll ask Bevins and Winkler about talking to you. And if you need anything else, let me or Daniels know. To be honest, I'm a little curious to see what you find out."

"I appreciate that, and I'll keep you posted," said Mason.

Mikey touched Mason's arm. "You sure you're okay? I'm just going to drop Rem off and head home, so if you want to talk, you can call me."

Mason smiled. "Thanks, but I'm better. I just needed to sit and be on my own for a bit. Once I get some sleep, I'll be good to go."

Mikey eyed him, as if gauging his truthfulness. "Then I'll see you tomorrow."

"See you tomorrow," said Mason. "And thanks for the help, Rem. Daniels, too."

Remalla waved. "You're welcome." He walked to the door and held it open for Mikey. Charlie took the cash from the bar, and Mason sought the woman with the bronze skin, hoping to talk to her, but her table was empty. She was gone.

Chapter Ten

TRICK EMERGED FROM THE shower, wiped down with a towel and wrapped it around his waist. He left the bathroom and headed into the small bedroom off the hall. The house was quiet, and Trick assumed Red hadn't returned. Knowing his friend, Trick guessed Red was nursing a drink somewhere, and wanted to be alone. Not much had changed since their Ranger days; Red had done the same when a difficult or gruesome case got to him, and Trick knew to leave him be and let him have his reset time.

Trick's ways of escaping were a bit more raucous. He'd get drunk, party, find a woman, and deal with the aftereffects for the next twenty-four hours. Forty-eight, now that he was older. Stopping at a mirror, he stared at himself. His jaw was shaded with stubble, his eyes drooped from the lack of sleep, but his lanky, muscular frame was still holding it together, although he may have lost some weight since Chad's death.

He dropped the towel, threw on some sweats, and headed into Mason's kitchen, hoping to find some food. Thinking there had to be a game on somewhere, he returned to the living room, but didn't see a TV. "What in the..." he muttered to himself. He checked Mason's room, too, finding it neat and tidy, but no television. "Well, I'll be damned," said Trick to himself. "Who the hell doesn't have a TV?"

After finding his phone, he returned to the kitchen and found a music station. A George Strait song filled the silence, and he opened the fridge, immediately seeing a couple of beers on a shelf. "He's not totally insane," he said, grabbing a beer. He also saw what looked like leftover chicken and grabbed that, plus some cheese, mayo, and a tomato, and closed the fridge.

Listening to the music, he made himself a sandwich with some bread from the counter and drank his beer. The events of the day flickered through his mind, and he thought about their plans for the next day. They would talk to Chad's boss and co-workers, and Mikey would do some digging into Lydia Stanford. He hoped to speak to the detectives investigating Chad's murder, but unless someone had a smoking gun and was prepared to reveal it, Bevins and Winkler would likely offer little insight into proving Cissy's innocence.

He held out some hope that if Lydia Stanford had a history of mental instability, and possibly violence, then maybe there was someone in her past that they could target as another potential suspect that would allow a jury an inch of reasonable doubt. He'd like to think Bevins and Winkler would be checking that angle as well, but if their sights were set on Cissy, then they could also find a way to use those issues against her.

His sandwich made, he returned the items to the refrigerator, grabbed his beer, and sat to eat. His mind wandering, he thought of his own future. Once this case was done, and Cissy was either incarcerated or free, he'd have a decision to make, and it wouldn't be an easy one. Remembering where he'd been a few weeks earlier, his belly tightened, and his appetite waned, but he hadn't eaten much that day, and considering the weight he'd lost, he forced himself to finish the sandwich.

At least the phone and credit card records didn't incriminate anyone, he thought to himself. That was one small bit of good news in a sea of bad. But then he thought of Chad having another phone, and his hope dwindled. Recalling his last conversation with Chad, he suspected his stepbrother had a second cell because when Chad had called him, the number had come up as unknown. Trick had asked him about it, but Chad had said it was a work phone. Work phone or not, if Chad used that phone to talk to Lydia, and the cops had it, then that wouldn't help Cissy. Although a good defense attorney would say those conversations made sense because they worked together, the prosecutor could seed doubt, especially with corroborating evidence of Chad's affair. His only hope was that Lydia, or someone else, could have left something incriminating on the phone, either a message or a photo that could link them to Chad's death, but there was no way to know. Had Lydia threatened Chad before she died? Could she have hired someone to hurt Chad?

Trick pushed his plate back and took a long pull on his beer as Johnny Cash began to sing the next tune. Trick picked up his cell, stared at it and checked the time. Red would be home soon, and his heart thumping, he debated making the call he was tempted to make. Cursing, he stood, picked up his plate and put it in the sink, then turned and leaned back against the counter. He thought of Chad and how much he missed him, and recalled some of their exploits together. Although they'd seen less of each other since Chad had moved, and Trick had made some stupid mistakes, he'd still considered Chad family and believed Chad had felt the same. Trick couldn't help but think of Red, too, and how losing his partner had cracked something inside him, and he'd been trying ever since to glue it back together, but the glue hadn't held, and he'd lost the only job that had ever mattered to him.

Sadness and depression loomed, and he considered grabbing another beer from the fridge, but he'd told Red he'd keep it together on this case, and he was determined to do it. The last thing he needed was to scare Red off.

More ugly thoughts joined the others, and Trick wondered if it was worth all the effort. Maybe if he'd had the guts, he could just end it all, then he wouldn't trouble anyone anymore.

A door slammed, and Trick jumped. The ugly thoughts vanished when he shifted into protective mode. Had someone entered the house? He didn't have a weapon, and he steeled himself for a potential confrontation. The slam had come from the direction of the hall, and he waited and listened. The house went quiet again, and Trick moved silently out of the kitchen and into the living room. Nothing was out of place. The windows were closed, and he couldn't determine the source of the noise. He entered the hallway, peered into his room, and was about to enter it when he noticed the bathroom door was closed. Had he closed it?

Trick approached and put his hand on the cold knob. Did someone enter the house to use the facilities? Trick almost chuckled and pushed the door open. The light was off, and he flicked it on. The bathroom was as he'd left it. The shower was damp, the toilet seat was up, and the hand towel he'd used still hung from the side of the sink. He picked it up and slid it into the towel holder on the wall. It must have been a draft, he said to himself, although he wondered from where. He flicked the light off, left the door open, and returned to the kitchen.

He eyed the phone still lying on the table and sat. A LeeAnn Rimes tune began to softly play, and Trick forgot about the door. Leaning over, he held his head and murmured to himself, wishing he wasn't so stupid. He thought of where he was, where he had been, and where he wanted to be, and shook his head. "Fuck it," he said. Sighing, he turned off the music and recalled the number he'd memorized. His fingers shook, and he kept an eye on the front window, watching for Red's return.

He dialed and listened as the phone connected and rang. It was answered on the first ring, and he heard her pensive voice. "I hoped you'd call."

Trick swallowed. "I shouldn't have, but I wanted to talk to you. I miss you, baby."

Cissy's breath caught. "Oh God, Trick. I miss you, too."

Chapter Eleven

MASON SAT IN A chair outside the office of Chad's boss, Tony Povia, and Trick sat in the chair next to him. They were on the top floor of a large building overlooking the city, and the view was stunning. An assistant sat at her desk across the room and spoke on the phone.

Trick flipped through a magazine, closed it, and tossed it on the coffee table. He stared out the window. "I had no idea there was so much money in security."

Mason admired the view. "I don't think this is the type of security that patrols the grounds on a golf cart."

"I'm guessin' not. More like *Mission Impossible* stuff."

"Mission what?" asked Mason.

Trick snorted. "Never mind."

The assistant hung up the phone and stood. "He's ready," she said. "Come on back."

Mason and Trick stood and followed her to a large wooden door, which she opened. Mason entered, seeing a spacious office with big windows and glass furniture. A man walked on a slow-moving treadmill with a workspace attached. Ear buds were in his ears, and his black, slightly tousled hair sported a wind-blown look. He wore dark jeans and a long-sleeved collared shirt with no tie. When he saw them, he pulled out his ear buds, stopped the treadmill, and hopped off.

"Thanks, Jenna. You must be Chad's friends. Come in. Can we get you something to drink? Water? Coffee?" He extended his hand.

"Thank you for seeing us," said Mason, shaking his hand. "A water would be great. Thanks."

"Coffee. Black," said Trick.

"I'll get it. Be right back," said Jenna, who closed the door behind them.

Tony shook Trick's hand and gestured. "Have a seat."

A large, beige leather couch with a multicolored rug beneath it sat off to the side, and Mason and Trick went to sit. Tony sat across from them in a shiny chair. "I understand you're here to talk about Chad," said Tony, his face falling. "Such a tremendous loss. He was an excellent addition to our staff. Chad could have sold our services to Fort Knox. He was that good." He smiled, and Mason noted Tony's pearly white teeth.

"What kind of services do you offer, Mr. Povia?" asked Mason. He looked around the room. "This is an impressive setup you have here." Although they'd already done some digging into Chad's workplace, Mason wanted to hear Tony's description.

Tony sat back. "Ah, well, our main goal is to provide management security for major businesses. We come in, see what your goals are, and make suggestions as to how to best protect your assets, and then once we have a plan, we help implement it. Pretty boring stuff, actually, unless you own a million-dollar company." He grinned. "You guys own one of those, by chance? I've got a state-of-the-art video and surveillance system if you're interested. Real cutting-edge stuff. No one will come within a ten-mile radius of you without being shot between the eyes with a high-powered laser." He chuckled.

Trick stared, and Mason squinted.

Tony's chuckle faded. "Sorry," he said. "My poor attempt at humor during an uncomfortable moment." He rested an ankle on his knee. "So, how can I help you? I assume you have some questions about Chad?"

"We do," said Trick.

"We already spoke to the police. Answered all their questions," said Tony.

Mason leaned in. "We were hoping you might talk to us as well. Trick here is Chad's stepbrother and, as I told Jenna on the phone, I'm a private investigator. Since Chad was murdered, we were hoping to get some information about his role here, and who he was working with. Maybe talk to his co-workers."

Tony nodded. "But I thought they'd arrested his wife." He paused. "Are you saying she didn't do it?"

"She didn't," said Trick. "No way."

Mason shot a look at Trick. "We're just doing our own investigation to be sure," said Mason. "Your cooperation would be helpful."

The door opened, and Jenna returned, holding a water bottle and a cup of coffee. She placed them on the table in front of Mason and Trick. "Here you go."

"Thanks, Jenna," said Mason.

"Thanks," said Trick.

Jenna left and closed the door.

"Well, I can't offer any information about his clients. That's privileged and would violate our privacy policy," said Tony.

"Of course," said Mason. "But what about Chad himself? Did you work with him closely?"

Tony pursed his lips. "Not every day, but I saw him frequently. He was friendly, personable, and hard-working. He was good with clients, and they liked him. No complaints from them or office staff."

"Did he seem stressed or not himself in the days before his death?" asked Mason. "Anything stand out?"

Tony stared off. "I'd mentioned to the police that he'd had an argument in the cafeteria. A few weeks before he died."

"An argument?" asked Trick. He picked up his coffee. "With who?"

"It was with the cafeteria manager. Apparently, Chad was upset because there were no mashed potatoes. We were offering a lovely roast that day, with green beans, and salad." He paused. "Our cafeteria is stellar. Only the best for our staff." He smiled. "Anyway, apparently we'd run out of potatoes. Chad threw a fit and made a scene. The manager came out, and it almost came to blows."

"Chad was pissed about potatoes?" asked Trick. "That doesn't sound like him."

"I didn't think so either," said Tony. "He was normally very laid back. That's why he was so likable. It was hard to ruffle his feathers." He interlaced his fingers.

"I talked to him though, and he realized he'd overreacted. He apologized, and all was well in the cafeteria world, although our manager made sure to stock up on potatoes." He shook his head. "When Chad gets mad, he's a bit intimidating. I wouldn't want to be on his bad side."

Mason picked up his water. "When was this argument?" He cracked the bottle open.

"Oh, I looked at the dates for the police." He tapped his chin and looked down. "It was around ten days, maybe two weeks, before he died." His brow furrowed. "You think this has something to do with his death?" He grinned. "Did the cafeteria man kill Chad over the potato incident?" He waved his hand. "Eureka. I've solved the crime."

Trick put his coffee down. "Listen, Tony▢"

Mason put his hand on Trick's elbow, and Trick went quiet. The last thing Mason needed was for Trick to get in Tony's face, or this discussion would be over before it started.

Tony grunted. "I'm sorry. I did it again. Bad joke at a bad time." He settled back. "I can't think of anything else of consequence. Why? Do you think his death had some connection to his work?"

Mason debated how much to say. "What can you tell us about an employee named Lydia Stanford? Did she work with Chad?"

"Lydia Stanford?" Tony asked, his eyes narrowing. "The woman who drowned?"

Mason nodded.

"Tragic accident," said Tony. "At least that's what I heard. Are you saying Chad and Lydia's deaths are related?"

"We don't know," said Trick. "That's why we're here."

"Now I'm intrigued," said Tony. "Let me think. I didn't really know Lydia that well. She worked in accounting. I'm sure Chad knew her, though. We're a tight-knit bunch around here. We try to provide lots of employee enrichment opportunities. We have a gym, childcare center, walking trail, ice cream store▢"

"I'm sure it's a wonderful place to work," said Mason. "We saw online that you recently had a company picnic."

Tony smiled again. "It was fantastic. There were games and rides, and we provided barbecue for lunch. Stuff for the kids. Plus, we divided into teams and played baseball and hired a band. It was a hit."

"Chad and Lydia were there...," said Trick.

"...along with everybody else, including Chad's wife, if I recall," said Tony. "Cissy. Nice woman. A little quiet, though."

"Nothing stood out from the picnic?" asked Mason.

"I wouldn't be the one to ask," said Tony. "I spent my time making the rounds and talking to everyone. I saw Chad briefly and probably Lydia too."

"Did the police ever ask you about Lydia?" asked Mason.

"No," said Tony. "They didn't, which is why this is so interesting."

"Figures," said Trick. "Could we talk to Chad's coworkers? Anyone he worked closely with?"

Tony nodded. "He had an assistant. Daphne. They worked together. She was devastated when he died. She's only been back to work recently, I think. Still trying to cope."

"We'd love to speak with her," said Mason. "Is she here today?" He almost crossed his fingers. Tracking down Daphne would only add more time to this burgeoning investigation.

Tony rubbed his jaw. "To be honest, I'm not sure."

"That she's here or if we can talk to her," said Trick.

"Oh, she's here," said Tony, "but she was quite upset when the police questioned her before. I'd hate to do that to her again."

"We'll be careful. We don't want to upset her either," said Mason.

"I can tell this is important to you." Tony hesitated. "Maybe we can work something out."

Trick tensed. "What do you mean?"

Tony flicked a gaze at Trick, but then eyed Mason. "I'm in the security business, Mr. Redstone. It's my job to check people out. So, when I heard you and Mr. Monroe were stopping by to talk to me, I did my homework."

Mason nodded, anticipating what was coming.

Tony leaned in and put his elbows on his knees. "I understand you have an interest in investigating the paranormal?"

Trick put his coffee on the table. "Ah, hell."

Mason didn't see the point of deflecting. "I do."

"And you're a medium as well?" asked Tony.

"I am," said Mason.

"Shit," said Trick, rubbing his face.

"Fascinating," said Tony. "I admit. I'm a novice when it comes to the paranormal, but I've always been intrigued by it." He studied his hands. "I checked your references. You come highly recommended."

"I'm not a charlatan, Tony. I stand by what I do," said Mason.

"I can see that," said Tony. "I like a man with confidence." He rested back against his seat. "I could use a man like you in my business. You looking for any extra work?"

Mason began to wonder that if this investigation continued the way this conversation was, he might need it. "I'm doing fine at the moment, but thanks for the offer."

"Can we get back to Daphne?" asked Trick.

Tony raised a finger. "In a sec." He stood and walked to the window. "Do you really talk to dead people, Mr. Redstone?" He looked back. "No bullshitting."

Mason didn't hesitate. "Yes. No bullshitting."

Tony put his hands in his pockets and turned to face them. "Then I'll make you a deal. You want to talk to Daphne? Then I'll personally call her up and you can talk to her here, in my office and in private."

"In exchange for...?" asked Trick.

Tony paused. "In exchange for a reading." He paused. "My mother died recently, and I want to talk to her."

Trick stood. "Are you serious? You're going to bribe him?"

Mason held his head. "Trick□"

"No, Red," said Trick, his anger building and his voice rising. He pointed at Tony. "What kind of business are you running here?"

Tony remained by the window. "It's the business of two professionals. You want something, and I want something. Why not work together?"

Trick glared. "This is ridiculous."

Mason stood. "It's fine. I'd be happy to provide a reading."

Trick dropped his jaw. "You don't have to do this."

"It's okay." Mason sighed. "You know how it goes. We've done it before, remember? You scratch my back..."

"...and I scratch yours," said Tony. "I can't imagine you're not familiar with it, Mr. Monroe?"

Trick wanted to knock the smug look off of Tony's face, but knew he'd been defeated. "He does this, and we talk to Daphne today? In this office?"

"And in private," said Tony. "That's the deal."

"What if Daphne decides otherwise?" asked Mason.

"I suspect if you tell her you're trying to help Chad and solve his murder, she'll be more than willing to help." He shrugged. "But if not, then I'll pay you your standard rate for the reading. Sound fair?"

Mason nodded. "Okay." He eyed Trick. "You'll have to wait outside."

"You've got to be kidding," said Trick.

"Privacy issues," said Mason, "unless Tony is okay with you staying."

Tony waved. "It's fine. He can stay."

Trick raked a hand through his hair. "I can't believe we're doing this."

"It is a little unconventional," said Tony, returning to his chair and standing beside it. "But I've learned that a little give-and-take in business has its perks." He tipped his head at Mason. "Don't you agree?"

"Red, are you sure about this?" asked Trick. "We can find another way…"

"It's okay. And another way will only take longer," said Mason. He gestured. "Have a seat, Tony, and get comfortable."

Tony sat and settled back. Mason sat, too, and Trick remained standing, until Mason and Tony looked at him with impatience, and then he sat on the couch with a grunt.

Mason shifted and got comfortable. "Let me start by saying that I can't promise who will come through. I'll only open myself up and see what happens. I can ask for your mother, but if she chooses not to communicate, that's out of my hands."

Tony's expression didn't change. "You don't know my mother, Mr. Redstone. I'm surprised she's not here already."

Trick watched as Mason closed his eyes. In their years of partnership, Trick had been aware of his friend's abilities, although it had taken Mason some time to confide in his partner. Trick had, at first, thought Mason needed psychological help, but it hadn't taken long for Trick to realize that Mason had a gift. He'd known things and seen things that Trick could not explain, and he'd told Trick a few things about Trick's own family, which only a few were privy to. Mason's abilities had been a fun novelty until he'd told Trick he was leaving the Rangers and moving to pursue his calling. Then it hadn't been so fun anymore.

Mason took a deep breath and let it out, while Trick and Tony waited. Tony seemed nervous and bounced his knee. Trick hoped Tony's mother would show herself and scold her son for holding this reading over their heads, or he at least hoped Mason would tell Tony as much.

Several seconds passed quietly until Mason shook out his hands and opened his eyes. "There's an older woman here. Black hair with silver roots. Thin. Almost too thin. She's got a shawl wrapped around her shoulders and a silver clip holding her hair back." Tony sat up in his seat, his eyes wide. "She doesn't like that shirt you're wearing."

Tony's eyes widened. "Holy—." He pulled on his sleeve. "She always hated this shirt."

"She's impatient," said Mason. "Wants to know what you want. She's got things to do."

Tony shook his head. "Some things never change. What the hell is on her schedule? She's dead."

Mason frowned. "She doesn't like your tone. Says you're the one that's dead. Not her."

"What?" asked Tony. "What does that even mean?"

Mason went quiet and stared off at a fixed point. Trick looked in the same direction, but only saw Tony's desk, and a wall of books, plaques, and awards.

"You should spend more time with your family," said Mason, looking back at Tony. "You work too hard. You don't enjoy life. Stop making money and start making memories."

Tony paled. "She said that to me on her deathbed." He swallowed and sat up. "Is she okay?"

Mason scowled. "Of course, I'm okay." He closed his eyes. "Sorry. She's speaking through me. She's a feisty one, but I like her. I'm going to let her talk."

Tony nodded, although he seemed uncertain. "Okay."

Mason blew out his breath. "I'm with your grandfather. Your grandmother's around here somewhere, but she's probably flirting with Frank."

Tony sucked in a breath. "Frank? You don't mean...?"

Mason kept his eyes closed. "Yes. Sinatra. She's still a huge fan."

"I don't believe this," said Tony. "My grandma Trudy loved Sinatra."

"He still has those blue eyes. Handsome as ever," said Mason.

Tony gestured at Trick. "You guys didn't do some sort of background search on me, did you?"

Trick chuckled. "Yeah. Like we care about your background."

"Stop being so damn cynical, buster," said Mason. "I'm here, and I'm fine. Is there something else you need?"

Tony stared. "Buster," he whispered. "That's what she called me when I was little. I don't believe it."

"Yeah, well. Red's an overachiever," said Trick. "Be careful what you ask for, 'cause you'll get it."

"I can see that," said Tony. He watched Mason, who continued to sit with his eyes closed. "Mom?"

"Yes, Buster?" said Mason. "Spit it out."

Tony chuckled. "I just wanted to say I'm sorry. I should have been there more than I was." His voice stuck, and he cleared his throat.

"You did fine," said Mason. "You're still doing fine, but you can do better. I didn't need you as much as I told you I did. I was yanking your chain most of the time. I liked control, and I used it to make you feel guilty. But I'm over it now and see things differently. You're a big boy, Buster, and I'm proud of you. But you don't need to make the same mistakes I made. Don't let your family slip away and then get mad when they're gone. It's a lonely life."

Tony sniffed, and Trick tried to hide his own swelling emotions. The woman made some solid points.

Tony wiped a finger over his shiny eye. "I miss you, Mom."

"Hogwash. I'm right here," said Mason.

Tony smiled. "Can I talk to granddad?"

Mason paused and tipped his head. "Let me see...he's enjoying a cocktail..."

Trick waited, and then Mason straightened and spoke in a different tone. "Hey Busterballs."

Tony laughed. "Holy shit. Hey Grandpa."

"Watch your language, son," said Mason.

"You know I hated it when you called me that," said Tony.

"You'll live," said Mason.

Trick watched as Mason continued to channel Tony's loved ones as they had a lively discussion about Tony and his other relatives, both living and dead, and had to admit he was astonished at Mason's abilities. While he'd seen Mason in action before, it had never been during a reading as he interacted casually with the dead. He listened in disbelief as the reading continued, but could see the signs as Mason began to tire.

"I think we need to wrap this up," said Tony's mom through Mason. "Our conduit needs his rest, and you've got work to do."

Tony blotted his eyes with a tissue. "I know. It was good to talk to you, Mom, and Grandpa too."

"You can talk to us anytime," said Mason. "Where do you think we are? Oz? You don't need anyone's help, either. You just need to do a better job of listening. Not just to us, but to your family, too."

Tony nodded. "I hear you. Thanks, Mom. I love you."

"I love you, too, Buster. Now go change that shirt." Mason's eyes creased and opened, and he blinked. "She left."

Tony reached for another tissue from a box on the table. He already had several crumpled in his hand. He dabbed his cheeks and blew his nose.

"You okay, Red?" asked Trick.

Mason's eyes were weary, and his shoulders slumped. "It's not often I let them talk through me. It saps my strength."

Tony put his elbows on his knees. "That was by far the most impressive thing I've ever seen, Mr. Redstone. I'm paying you double your rate, in addition to your talk with Daphne." He rubbed his puffy eyes. "Let me get Jenna to call her." He stood and left the office.

Mason picked up his water and drained it.

"You remember any of what you said?" asked Trick.

He massaged his temples. "Bits and pieces, but most of it is fading fast."

Trick tried to come to terms with what he'd witnessed. "He's right. It was damned impressive. I knew you had your gifts, but now...well, now I've seen the goods." He scoffed. "If I ever doubted you before, I apologize."

"You doubted me all the time," said Mason. "Most do. It comes with the territory. I didn't take it personally, though."

"As usual, I let my idiot side out and didn't trust you."

"Your idiot side is the dominant one. You couldn't help yourself." Mason put his water bottle down. "It's fine, though. Idiot Trick is a lot of fun, although a bit tiresome."

"He's also getting a little old," said Trick. He paused and thought back on their history. "You've pulled me out of a lot of messes, and I blamed you for most of them. I'm sorry about that."

Mason studied him. "It wasn't that bad. I didn't mind picking up a few of your pieces. You picked up a few of mine, plus put up with a paranormal partner. Most men would have run from that, but you never did."

"Believe me. I wanted to. You freaked me out on more than one occasion."

Mason smiled. "Sometimes on purpose. You know you shriek like a woman when you're scared."

"Not all the time."

"Most of it."

Trick chuckled along with Mason.

A few quiet seconds passed, and Trick picked at the edge of a cushion. "If I haven't said it before, I screwed up with Cara. It was a dumb mistake. I shouldn't have done it, but I let my anger and disappointment justify it. But I know it was wrong."

Mason went still and took his own second. "I could have done better myself. I can't put all the blame on you or her. I think I just expected you two would be happy with my decision to completely uproot my life and would adjust to it. I didn't think through how it might uproot your lives, too, and how hard it would be. I apologize for that."

Trick smiled. "Funny, isn't it?" he said. "It's just like us to have our come to Jesus moment in Tony Povia's office."

Mason sighed softly. "I guess it's better than during a high-speed chase. Remember when you tried to apologize for losing my hat?"

"I figured you were distracted with keeping your eyes on the road, so it was the perfect time. And that wasn't totally my fault."

Mason gave him a dirty look. "You lost it during a poker game."

"That guy was cheating▫"

The office door opened, and Tony returned. "Good news. Daphne is on her way up."

Chapter Twelve

MASON SPLASHED COLD WATER on his face in Tony's private bathroom and grabbed a hand towel. He dabbed his skin dry and stared at himself in the mirror. His eyes looked a little bloodshot, but his cheeks had some color, and his energy levels were decent, although he knew as the day progressed, that would change. Allowing a spirit to speak through him taxed his mental and physical strength, which is why he rarely did it. But in this instance, it seemed the logical approach, and he'd been in a hurry. He didn't want the reading to drag out, which they often did if the connection was strong, so he took the chance and let Tony's mom and grandfather in.

"Red." Trick called his name, and with a last look, Mason returned the face cloth, straightened his shirt, smoothed his mustache, and left the bathroom.

Trick stood beside a woman near the couch. Heavyset with round cheeks and bright eyes, she fiddled with her fingers. She was already holding a tissue, and Mason thought she might burst into tears the moment he said hello.

He took a breath and hoped for the best. "You must be Daphne." He held out his hand.

"It is," said Trick. "Daphne Stewart, Chad's assistant, and apparently his right-hand woman."

"Hello," said Daphne. She took Mason's hand in a delicate grasp. "Tony said you wanted to talk about Chad." At the mention of his name, her eyes welled, and she dabbed at them. "I'm sorry," she whispered. "It's still difficult."

Mason's guilt bloomed. "Are you sure you're up for this? We can arrange to meet at another time."

Trick frowned at him, and Mason shrugged.

"No, no. I'm okay." Daphne sniffed. "I want to help." She walked around and sat on the couch.

Trick sat beside her, and Mason took the seat Tony had occupied.

"Tony said you're a private investigator?" she asked.

"Yes, I am," said Mason. "And Trick here is Chad's stepbrother."

She glanced over at Trick. "I'm so sorry."

"Thank you," said Trick. He shifted toward her. "Did Tony tell you why we wanted to speak with you?"

"Not really, no." She wiped her nose. "But I already talked to the police. Does this have to do with his death?"

"Yes, it does," said Mason. "I assume you know they arrested his wife?"

Daphne's face drooped. "It's awful. Poor Cissy. Such a nice woman, at least she always was to me. I can't imagine she'd do that to Chad, no matter what they might have been going through."

"Were they going through something?" asked Mason. "That you know of?"

She played with her tissue. "Every married couple does. I should know. I've been divorced twice."

"Can you tell us anything about their relationship?" asked Trick. "I don't believe Cissy hurt Chad, and I'd like to find out what happened."

"Yes. Of course." Daphne stared off. "Chad confided a little in me, but not too much. I know he was at work a lot, and a few times I heard him on the phone with Cissy, and he sounded frustrated."

"Was he spending more time at work because he had to, or was he avoiding home?" asked Mason.

"I suppose a little of both," she said. "But again, it's just based on my observations. He didn't tell me specifically. We were busy, though. That much was true. Business was booming, and Chad was a hard worker. We spent more than one several-hour days together."

Trick nodded. "Did he work with anyone else besides you?"

"Well, yes. I could name several people. There are a lot of meetings around here."

"We mean someone who he might have spent more time with outside of the office," said Mason. "Without his wife knowing." He raised a brow.

Her mouth fell open. "Like an affair?"

"Yes," said Trick.

"Chad? Seriously?" asked Daphne.

"If anyone would have insight into that, it would be you," said Mason. "You saw him the most, and probably knew him best, other than Cissy."

"I...I don't know," she said. "Let me think." Her eyes darted away and back. "Did you have someone in mind? I mean...off the top of my head, no one comes to mind."

Trick looked at Mason. "Did you know Lydia Stanford?"

Her mouth dropped open again. "Lydia Stanford? You can't be serious. Why do you suspect her?"

"We have our reasons," said Trick. "But again, we can't be certain, which is why we need to ask. Did Lydia and Chad work together?"

Her eyes filled, and she swiped at them. "You realize Lydia died, too, just before Chad? Horrible." She shook her head.

"Yes, we know," said Mason. "And we have to consider a possible connection between the two deaths, which is why we wanted to talk to you."

Daphne held her head and closed her eyes. "Dear Lord. This is too much." She opened her eyes. "You think Lydia was murdered, too?" Her eyes widened. "Do the police think Cissy killed them both?"

"It's possible," said Trick, "which is why the faster we figure this out, the better."

"Poor girl," said Daphne. "I mean, I saw her get upset with Chad once or twice, but I'd never suspect her of doing anything violent."

Mason perked up. "Upset? When was she was upset?"

"Umm...well...she came into the office one day, and Chad was out. I told her I didn't know where he was, and I could tell she wasn't happy. I texted Chad and told Cissy to wait in his office. He came in about thirty minutes later, and they spoke for a few minutes before they left together, but I saw her face and heard her ask where he'd been. He'd told her he'd had a client meeting, but I knew his schedule, and the meeting had ended that morning."

"Could he have been with Lydia?" asked Trick.

"I have no idea," said Daphne. "Maybe he had an impromptu meeting, and it didn't get added to the calendar."

"When was this?" asked Mason.

"Oh, gosh. It's been a while. Last summer," said Daphne.

"And you told the police this?" asked Trick.

Daphne nodded. "I think so, yes." Her face paled. "Oh, dear. Did I implicate Cissy?"

Mason reached for the fresh bottle of water Jenna had brought him before Daphne arrived. "Don't worry about it, Daphne. That's not enough to convict anyone." He didn't tell her it could still be used against Cissy at trial, doubting Daphne could handle it. He sipped his water. "But I'd like to get back to Lydia. What was Chad's relationship with her?"

Daphne twisted her tissue. "Well, Lydia worked in Accounting. She'd occasionally come up if she had a billing or expense question, and she'd be in department meetings on occasion with Chad." Her fingers tightened on the tissue. "I didn't know her all that well, and to be honest," she lowered her voice. "I didn't like her that much. She was a little odd."

"Odd how?" asked Trick.

"Umm, well...she seemed easily distracted. We'd be in a conversation, and she'd just stare off, as if she was going through her to-do list or something. And she could shift moods in a second. Be all business in one moment, and then impatient and angry over the smallest error the next. I thought it was me, and that maybe she just didn't like me. And then when we spent that weekend together□"

Mason leaned forward. "Weekend? You spent a weekend with Lydia?"

"I thought you said you didn't know her that well," said Trick.

Daphne touched her forehead. "Oh, dear. I'm sorry. Yes, I did, and no I didn't." She shook her head. "I'm getting confused."

"It's okay, Daphne. Take your time," said Mason. "Tell us about the weekend. Did Chad know about it?"

Daphne offered him a smirk. "Well, yes. He was there too."

Mason tried not to show impatience. "When and why were you two spending a weekend with Lydia?"

Daphne sighed. "Gosh. It was last spring. We had a system crash. It was a huge mess. Chad lost a lot of billing information and expense reports, and we had to re-enter a lot of data that couldn't be recovered. I told Chad maybe we should be securing our own files, as well as we secure our clients." She bit her lip. "He laughed but agreed." Swallowing, she dabbed her eyes. "Anyway, Lydia said we had to get it re-entered as quickly as we could and agreed to help us. It took a full weekend, and Lydia offered her home for us to meet and work, which was probably convenient for her because she didn't drive. We could spread everything out on her dining table and just knock it out. It took the full two days, but we got it done."

"Lydia didn't drive?" asked Trick.

"No," said Daphne. "That was another one of her odd quirks. She rode her bike or the bus to work." Her face fell. "I remember going to her house. She lived in one of those areas that used to be upscale but was now a little run down. The grass was uncut, and the paint was peeling. I figured with the real estate prices around here, that's what she could afford, and one of the reasons she didn't want a car." She sighed. "She had a small pool in the back, the one she later drowned in. The wall was crumbling, and it didn't look well maintained. I've wondered if that's how she fell and hit her head." She paused, and her breath caught. "So tragic."

Trick reached for his refilled coffee. "Did Chad spend any time over at Lydia's on his own?"

"I don't know," said Daphne, "but it's certainly possible."

Mason regarded Trick. "That's something to look into."

"Definitely," said Trick. "Anything else you can think of where Chad and Lydia might have spent time together? We heard they had an argument at the company picnic."

"Argument? At the picnic?" asked Daphne. "I hadn't heard that. I just saw them talking, and then Cissy got upset."

Mason clasped his hands together. "You saw Chad and Lydia at the picnic together?"

"Well, not together together, if that's what you mean," said Daphne. "They were having a conversation, and then they walked off. Cissy came back and had asked where Chad was, but I didn't know. Then she disappeared, and I tried to help Linda - she's a co-worker - clean up, and maybe sneak some leftovers. That beef brisket was delicious, and so was the potato salad."

"Did you see any of them again?" asked Trick.

"Yes. Chad and Cissy returned, but Chad was quiet, and Cissy sullen." Daphne leaned in. "I think they'd had an argument."

"And you didn't see Lydia?" asked Mason.

"Not that I recall."

Mason paused. "Was there anything else about Lydia you noticed that, as you say, seemed odd?"

"Again, I didn't know her well," said Daphne. "Except for her temper."

Mason felt another chunk of his energy dwindle. "Temper? Lydia had a temper?"

"Didn't I mention that?" Daphne held her chin. "Gosh, yes. I remember she got a phone call when we were working at her house. She went into another room to talk, but I could hear her yelling. Whoever it was, they weren't making Lydia happy. She was very upset, and I heard some harsh language."

"Did you ever see her mad at Chad?" asked Trick.

"No," she said.

Mason remembered the potato incident. "We heard Chad yelled at the cafeteria manager a couple weeks before Lydia died. Tony said he had to intervene. You know about that?"

Daphne tipped her head. "If I recall, Chad wanted potatoes, and they were out."

"Had Chad done that before?" asked Trick.

"Certainly not," said Daphne. "I guess he was just hungry. We all have our days."

Mason grunted, giving up on that line of questioning. "Let me ask you about this." He pulled out his cell and opened the picture Mikey had texted him. "This picture from the picnic. Which one is Lydia?" He held out the photo.

Daphne didn't look. "Oh, she's not there."

"But she was at the picnic," said Trick.

"She was, but Lydia never wanted her picture taken. It was another one of her strange phobias, if that's what you'd call it. She won't be in any of the pictures. People suspected that's another reason why she didn't drive."

Trick scratched his head. "Why's that?"

"Because she didn't want her photo taken, you know, for a driver's license." Daphne huffed, as if it was obvious.

"Well, that's a new one," said Trick.

"Let's add it to the list," said Mason. He put his phone away and considered his next question. "What about the day Chad died? He stayed home in the middle of the week. Did he say why?"

Daphne's face paled. "I hate thinking about that day." Tears welled up again and spilled over her lashes. "He just called and said he'd be out of the office. He didn't elaborate, and I didn't ask. I just assumed he wasn't feeling well." Her breath caught. "Maybe if I had..."

"It's okay," said Mason. "There's nothing you could have done, Daphne."

Daphne wiped her tears, and Trick handed her another tissue from a box on the table. "Did you ever hear Chad and Cissy argue, other than the time Cissy showed up unexpectedly at the office and the picnic?"

"I wouldn't call them arguments. They weren't yelling, but I sensed the tension between them." Daphne played with her frayed tissues, and another tear slipped down her face. "I feel like I'm betraying Chad."

Trick patted her hand. "You're not. He'd want us to know the truth. And he certainly wouldn't want his wife to go to jail for a crime she didn't commit."

Daphne sniffed. "I just feel so bad. I mean, I keep wondering if I should have known something or could have prevented this in some way. Maybe if I'd talked to Chad, especially after I overheard that terrible fight..." She dabbed her cheeks.

Mason held back a groan, and Trick took a deep breath. "Fight?" asked Trick. "I thought you said you didn't see either Lydia or Cissy arguing with Chad."

"I didn't *see* anything," said Daphne. "I heard it." She blew her nose and took another tissue. "I told those detectives about it, and now I feel bad. Maybe I should have kept it to myself."

"What happened?" asked Mason, keeping his voice light. "What did you hear?"

Taking a moment, Daphne pressed the tissue to her lips. "It was just before Lydia's death. I'd been working late with Chad one night, and I had just left. Chad said he'd be right behind me, but when I got to the car, I realized I'd forgotten my wallet. I'd left it in my drawer, so I went back to get it. When I got to my desk, I saw Chad's office door was closed and so were the blinds, which was strange because they were always left open. I almost knocked when I heard yelling. It was Chad and a woman. I couldn't make out most of it, but I caught a few things."

"Like what?" asked Trick.

Daphne nibbled her bottom lip. "I heard the woman call him a liar. Then she said things like 'you should have told me,' 'you must think I'm stupid,' and 'she's not worth it.' Chad yelled too, but not as much. I heard him say 'you're wrong' and 'that's not what I meant,' but then she yelled back that he'd be sorry, and he'd duped the wrong woman." Daphne let go of a weary sigh. "I felt like an intruder, and I got out of there. I didn't want Chad to know that I'd overheard. He'd have been so embarrassed." Her breath caught again, and she wiped a tear that had slid down to her jaw. "Lydia was dead a few days later."

"You don't know who the woman was that Chad was arguing with?" asked Mason.

"No, I don't," said Daphne. "The voices were muffled, and I couldn't see anything. It was hard to be sure. It could have been Cissy, and I suppose I assumed it was, but now, based on what you're telling me, it could have been Lydia." She put her hands over her eyes. "I think I told the police it was Cissy. Oh, dear. What have I done?" She dropped her hands. "Have I accused the wrong person? Do they think she did it because of me?"

Trick, his face solemn, sat back. "There's no way to know, Daphne, but I suspect there's more to it than that." He sipped some coffee and put the cup back on the table. "The problem is, Lydia died before Chad, so she couldn't have killed him. So, if Cissy didn't kill Chad, then who did?"

"It does give us something else to consider, though," said Mason.

"What's that?" asked Daphne, her eyes wide.

Trick groaned, and Mason suspected Trick knew what Mason was about to say. "What if Chad killed Lydia?"

Daphne sucked in a breath, dropped her jaw, and burst into tears.

Chapter Thirteen

MIKEY OPENED THE PAPER bag and pulled out the food she'd picked up on the way to Mason's. "Your noodles." She handed a box to Mason. "And here's your Chow Mein." She gave a box to Trick. "And here's mine." She pulled out a carton, took off her jacket, and sat. "I'm starving."

"Thanks, Mikey," said Trick.

Sitting at the table, Mason took the food, put it in front of him, and held the bridge of his nose. "Thanks."

Mikey noticed. "I'll get you some aspirin." She stood and eyed Mason, feeling that familiar constriction. "Did you do a reading today? You're not usually this beat." She grimaced. "I can feel your tension."

"I'm okay," said Mason. "But I'd love that aspirin."

"He did a hell of a reading for Tony, Chad's boss," said Trick, opening his food and grabbing his chopsticks. "Blew Tony's mind. Even let Tony's mom speak through him. It was an eye-opener."

Mikey put a hand on her hip. "What? Why the hell are you doing readings for Chad's boss, much less letting spirits channel through you? You know what that does to you."

Mason glared. "Thanks, Trick."

Trick dug through his Chow Mein with his chopsticks. "Any time."

"You should know better, Mason." Mikey walked to a cabinet in the kitchen and grabbed a bottle of aspirin. She shook out two tablets, returned the bottle and brought them to Mason. "Here."

Mason sighed and took them. "Thanks."

"You know your day's shot, don't you?" said Mikey, returning to her seat. "You're worthless until you get some rest."

"I'll be fine," said Mason, opening his food. "Eating will help. Let's go over what we know."

"Why? So you can stare aimlessly and try to stay awake while we talk? That'll be helpful." She opened her carton of chicken fried rice.

"Mikey, please. Right now, the only thing sapping my strength is you," said Mason.

"Now I know you're tired. You get cranky." Mikey opened her chopsticks.

"Let him be. If he wants to fall asleep in his food, it'll make for a great picture, which I can share with my friends," said Trick.

"What friends?" asked Mason.

"Ouch," said Trick. "You are cranky."

"Can we please get back to the investigation?" asked Mason. "Before I end up like Cissy–accused of murder?"

Trick picked up a bite of food. "You'd never make it to trial. I'd haunt you to death."

"Me too," said Mikey.

"What trial?" asked Mason. "I'd plead guilty just to get some rest."

"I'd haunt you in your cell," said Trick.

"Me too," said Mikey, taking a bite of her fried rice.

"It seems I'm screwed either way," said Mason, opening his noodles.

"You are," said Mikey. Chewing, she reached down and pulled out a pad and pencil from her backpack and set them on the table. "But since you insist on acting like you're capable, let's go over your interviews, and I'll let you know what I learned about Lydia."

"Finally," said Mason, grabbing some noodles with his chopsticks.

They spent the next hour discussing the talks with Tony and Daphne while they ate and Mikey took notes. Mikey had bought an iced tea, and she sipped from the straw and reviewed her scribbles. "Let's see what we have here." She put her cup down. "If we put this into some sort of timeline, then I think it starts last spring with Daphne and Chad meeting at Lydia's to fix a system crash. Not long after that, Lydia posts that she's in a relationship." She scratched her head. "So, does Chad start his fling with Lydia during this weekend?"

"Maybe," said Trick. He scraped at the bottom of his carton with his chopsticks. "Seems likely."

Mikey went back to her notes. "Then during the summer, Cissy says Chad is becoming more distant, and their relationship suffers. Her social media reflects that. At some point, she shows up unexpectedly at Chad's office, but he's not there and she's not happy. Supposedly, he's at a meeting that's not on the schedule. Could he have been with Lydia?"

"Maybe," said Mason. He leaned his head back against the seat and closed his eyes. "Most likely."

Mikey continued. "Daphne dislikes Lydia and thinks that Lydia is strange. Believes she's odd and easily distracted and maybe has a mood disorder. Also, Lydia doesn't drive and doesn't like her picture taken."

"Don't forget the temper," said Trick. "Daphne overheard Lydia's overheated conversation during their working weekend."

"That's right. Lydia's temper." Mikey made a note on her pad. "Then comes the company picnic at the end of the summer. Lydia and Chad talk and then disappear. Cissy looks for him and sees Chad arguing under the bleachers with a woman, who we assume is Lydia."

"Makes sense," said Mason, his head still back against the seat.

"Lydia is angry and leaves when Cissy shows, and Chad says it's no big deal. Cissy isn't buying it."

"Nope," said Trick. "Can't blame her."

"Then Tony posts pics from the picnic, and Cissy replies with a comment directed at Lydia that says 'I see you.' She knows now that Chad is having an affair."

"Wait a minute," said Mason, his eyes still closed. "Cissy confronted Chad about it. Was that before or after the picnic?"

"Good question." Mikey flipped through her notes. "I think it was before."

"It was after," said Trick. "She'd only suspected before the picnic." He sipped his soda.

Mason cracked an eye open at Trick, but then closed it again.

"Okay," said Mikey, writing. "Cissy makes that cryptic comment, although if Lydia was actually aware of it, no one knows. She's not very active on social media."

"There's still some hope for the world," said Mason, interlacing his fingers and resting them against his stomach.

Mikey ignored him. "Then Cissy confronts Chad, who doesn't deny the affair, but won't tell her who the woman is, and tells Cissy the affair is over." She paused. "Now it gets interesting. Cissy believes it's Lydia. Finds out where she lives and knocks on her door. They argue, and she thinks Lydia's strange, too, which would back up Daphne's claim that Lydia's odd and has a temper."

"Let's not forget Cissy has a temper too," said Mason, his head still back.

After scraping his carton clean, Trick put it down. "You can't blame her for confronting her husband's mistress. Most women would."

Mason cracked another eye open. "I'll grant you that, but it's a bold move. Plus, we have no idea what actually happened during that altercation, or what was said."

"I might have some insight into that," said Mikey, "but we'll get to that in a sec." She flipped a sheet of paper over. "Moving on. Cissy confronts Lydia, who laughs at her. Cissy questions how her husband can sleep with someone who's crazy, and his sanity."

"Which leads us to Lydia's background." Mason lifted his head. "Does she have a history of mental illness?"

"Again, we'll get to my stuff in a minute," said Mikey. "Let's finish this." She tapped her pencil on the paper. "Just before Lydia's death, Chad loses it at the office over mashed potatoes, which indicates he's stressed, and Daphne overhears an argument in Chad's office between Chad and another woman, whose identity is a mystery. Is it Cissy or is it Lydia? Daphne can't be sure." She made a note. "Lydia dies soon after in a supposed accidental drowning, then two weeks later,

Chad takes an unexplained day off, and is murdered when Cissy goes to the grocery store. Video shows no one coming or going, but you two find cigarette butts in a vacant nearby apartment." She looked up. "Rem called, by the way. He dropped the cigarettes off at the lab."

Mason nodded. "Great."

Mikey resumed. "So, who is the murderer waiting in the apartment for Cissy to leave? Because it's not Lydia."

Trick tossed his empty box in the food bag. "And was Lydia's death an accident?"

"And could Chad have killed Lydia?" asked Mason. "And then someone retaliated and killed him?"

Trick scoffed. "Chad couldn't have killed anyone any more than Cissy could have."

"In the heat of an argument, anything can happen," said Mason. "You know that. Chad could have gone to talk to her. They meet by the pool, things get overheated, and he either hits her, or she trips. Lydia falls, hits her head, and ends up in the water. Chad panics and takes off."

"That could easily be answered by finding out where Chad was the night of Lydia's death. Same goes for Cissy," said Trick. "If they're both at home, we're good to go."

Mason sat up. "Hardly. Cissy could say they were at home, or Chad went out, but without Chad to corroborate, it's worthless. A good attorney will accuse her of lying to protect herself. Unless they were somewhere with plenty of witnesses, it won't help."

"Then we'll find out," said Trick.

Mikey flipped the papers back. "Hell. This is a mess." She eyed Trick. "I hate to tell you, Trickster, but this doesn't look good for Cissy. Based on this, a jury could obviously see that she found out her husband was having an affair, argued with the mistress, killed her, and then killed her husband." She picked up her iced tea. "I can see why Bevins and Winkler are after her."

Trick tapped a finger on the table. "Trickster," he said. "You haven't called me that in a long time."

"Mikey's right," said Mason. "You have to consider the probability that Cissy is guilty. The simplest solution is usually the correct one. That's Ranger Rule one-o-one."

Trick ran his hands into his hair. "I'm sorry, but I don't buy it. There has to be another explanation, and until we've exhausted all possibilities, I won't stop looking. I have to be sure, and I'm not yet."

Mikey shot a look at Mason, who shrugged. Taking that as consent to continue, she pulled out a small spiral-bound notebook from her backpack. "Okay, then. Here's what I've learned about Lydia."

Trick expelled a frustrated grunt. "Any chance she spent time in a mental institution, and someone overheard her hiring someone to kill Chad?"

"No such luck," said Mikey. "But Lydia has her issues." She flipped through the notebook. "I found Lydia's mom after getting her name from Lydia's obituary. I sent her a message via social media, and she replied. We talked on the phone this afternoon."

"That was fast," said Trick.

"Mikey could find Jimmy Hoffa if I asked her to," said Mason. He reached for a fortune cookie.

"Maybe one day when I have some free time," said Mikey. "Anyway, her name's Michelle, and she's...well...different."

Mason opened his wrapper and cracked the cookie. "How so?" His weary eyes told Mikey he wouldn't last much longer and would need to lie down soon. He took a bite of cookie and read the fortune.

Mikey flipped a page. "Well, for starters, I'm pretty sure she was drunk when I talked to her, or else she's got a speech impediment and she's way too relaxed with strangers and her personal information."

"That might work in our favor," said Mason.

"I can't deny that," said Mikey. "Considering her daughter recently died, she didn't act terribly grief stricken. Complained about Lydia more than anything, and the more I tried to discuss her daughter, the more she wanted to talk about herself, but I still got some information out of her." She sipped from her straw and studied her notes. "Lydia has two siblings, who Michelle didn't seem too thrilled with, either. A younger brother named Bradley and a younger sister named Shay. Lydia and Bradley had the same father, but their dad died from a drug overdose when Lydia was eight."

"Drug overdose?" asked Mason. "Or suicide?"

"You be the judge," said Mikey. "Michelle didn't elaborate." She trailed a finger down her notes. "After her first husband died, she remarried a man named Douglas, who had money, but was boring, didn't satisfy her in the bedroom, and snored."

"Seriously?" asked Trick.

"Told you she was different." Mikey flipped the page. "They divorced, and she remarried Pablo, who, in her words, was the best lover she ever had, and he didn't snore."

"Good for her," said Mason.

"Shay was born a year later, but once there was an infant in the house, Pablo couldn't keep the goods to himself. He liked to share his loverly skills with other women. Michelle kicked him out and raised Shay on her own. Pablo came around to see his kid, but not often." She paused. "Then Michelle met and married Richard..."

"Jeez," said Trick.

"Richard lasted two years, but he had a temper and yelled and screamed at her, and yelled and screamed at the kids, too. She put up with it for a while because she liked how the kids behaved when he was around."

"I bet she did," said Mason. "Let's hope all he did was just yell and scream."

Mikey tipped her head. "It may not have been. She caught him looking at Lydia in a way that he used to look at her. Said she couldn't handle that, and booted him, too."

"Before or after he abused Lydia?" asked Trick.

"I don't know," said Mikey. "Again, this wasn't about Lydia, this was about her." She went back to her notes. "Then she met and married Von. They're in their eighth year of marriage, and she's happy, at least for now."

"What about her kids?" asked Mason. "How'd they handle the revolving door of fathers?"

"From what I gather, not too well." Mikey looked up from her notes. "They don't talk much. They occasionally connect during the holidays, but they're not close. She did tell me that during Lydia and Bradley's childhood, she tried to get them counseling, especially after their father died, but it didn't last. Lydia was introverted and shy. Bradley was insecure and always trying to prove himself. Shay keeps to herself, too, and, according to Michelle, drinks too much. Which is ironic, considering. Her father, Pablo, died last year and left Shay some money, and now Shay rarely comes around. Lydia started taking anti-depressants when she was a teenager, and it didn't stop there. Lydia apparently had quite the medicine cabinet. In Michelle's words, the 'girl was never quite right in the head.'"

"Nice of her to say," said Mason.

"She did tell me that Lydia moved out at eighteen and put herself through college. Michelle took credit that Lydia was smart and graduated at the top of her class," said Mikey. "So, despite whatever pills she was taking, Lydia wasn't that out of it."

"Was Lydia ever married?" asked Mason.

Mikey flipped through her notes. "Not that Michelle said, although there was a man in her life, but apparently it was a disaster. She didn't give me any more details than that."

"Could that have been Chad, or someone else?" asked Trick.

"She didn't say," said Mikey. "Michelle kept wanting to talk about her men, and not Lydia's. It was hard enough to keep her focused on the subject. It annoyed her because she says all the kids want to blame their problems on her, and she's had enough."

"But Lydia's dead," said Trick. "She didn't offer anything on that?"

"Said that wasn't her fault, either. Lydia had issues, and when Michelle offered advice, or suggested rehab, Lydia would get furious and tell her to stay out of it."

"Can't imagine why," said Mason.

"Based on the amount she was slurring by then, I can." Mikey tapped on the paper with her pen. "She did say she was angry that Lydia was cremated. Apparently, that was Bradley's decision."

"What's his story?" asked Trick.

Mikey flipped the page again. "Not much better than Lydia's. According to Michelle, he's a lost cause. In and out of jail for a variety of issues. Petty theft, public lewdness, check fraud, and a few other things. Never has any money, drinks, and does drugs. Michelle thinks he asked for the cremation just to piss her off. Apparently, Lydia designated him as the executor in her will, much to Michelle's dismay."

Trick perked up. "Did he get anything else? Did she leave him any money? Did Lydia have any life insurance?"

"It's a good question, but Michelle didn't offer any information on that," said Mikey. Mikey sipped her tea and sat back. "It's something to check into, though."

Mason took a bite of his cookie. "Anything else?"

Mikey nodded. "She gave me the phone numbers for Shay and Bradley. I called Shay and left a message. Bradley answered."

Trick straightened. "What'd he have to say?"

"Not much. He sounded like I'd woken him up, even though it was late in the day. He at least seemed a little more distraught about Lydia's death than her mother. Said he missed his sister. He told me they'd been estranged for a few years when she started dating that loser, his words, and they got in a big fight. But once she broke it off with the loser, they'd reconnected and been close."

Mason forced back a yawn. "I'm guessing this loser is the disaster Michelle referred to. Is it Chad?"

"Nope," said Mikey. "It's an old boyfriend." She pointed at her notes. "Name's Kyle Morrow. Lydia dated him after she was out of college. Bradley and Shay hated the guy. Said he was possessive, but Lydia loved him and wouldn't break up with him."

"Figures," said Trick. "Where is this guy now?" He pointed. "If he's still hanging around, we could have another suspect. Do we know if he was abusive?"

"It's possible," said Mikey. "Lydia never talked to Bradley much about Kyle, though, so he couldn't say for sure, but he suspected." She read through her notes. "I asked about Shay and Lydia, and if they were close. He said his sisters had a love-hate relationship but stayed in touch."

"Interesting," said Mason. "Now we need to dig into Kyle. See what we can find." He eyed Trick. "He may be our missing clue."

"Bradley, too," said Trick. "If he benefited from Lydia's death, he's on the list. Did you ask about that?"

"No, I didn't, but I'm working on Kyle and Bradley's history," said Mikey, scribbling in her notebook. "I'll see what I can learn about Bradley's money situation. If he's bought any fancy cars or real estate lately, maybe Shay can fill me in once she calls me back."

"More likely, he'd stock up on drugs and booze if his track record is accurate," said Mason.

"You're already on Kyle's trail?" asked Trick.

Mikey shifted and grabbed a fortune cookie. "Sort of."

Mason's weary eyes widened. "I know that look. What are you up to?" He took another bite of his fortune cookie. "I'm not going to like it, am I?"

Mikey put her pen down. "No, you're not, but too bad. When Rem called about the cigarette butts, he asked about our progress. I told him about Kyle..."

"You didn't," said Mason. "Mikey..."

"What's the big deal?" asked Trick. "We helped a few people out when we were cops."

"He offered. I didn't ask," said Mikey. "I think he wants to know himself. He's curious. Said he'd call me once he did a check on Morrow and Bradley."

"Hell, Bradley too?" asked Mason. "Daniels and Rem are not our staff. They are busy detectives, and we can't keep asking them for favors."

"He didn't mind," said Mikey. "Besides, you know eventually there will be some case they'll need help with, and we'll return the favor. And if Rem didn't want to do it, he wouldn't have offered."

"You and this Rem fella are pretty close," said Trick. "You two dating?"

"Not yet," said Mason.

Mikey shook her head, exasperated. "We are not dating. We are just friends."

"Famous last words," said Trick, finishing his soda. "If you ever do date him though, just keep in mind, a cop's hours suck, and you'll spend every day worrying about whether he's coming home." He opened a fortune cookie.

"Sounds like you have some experience," said Mikey. "There's no one special in your life?"

Trick didn't answer, and Mason broke the silence. "I think the smart thing would be to warn Remalla about you." He pointed. "If anyone needs to worry, it's him."

Mikey smirked. "Ha ha. Very funny. But I keep telling you. We're just friends."

Mason rubbed his neck and yawned. "For now."

"Mason□" Mikey's phone rang, and she picked it up. "It's Rem."

"Speak of the devil," said Trick.

Mikey rolled her eyes and answered. "Hey, Rem."

Rem's voice traveled over the line. "Hey. I got some info on your Kyle Morrow you might find interesting. And a few things on Bradley Stanford."

"Great." Mikey grabbed her notebook. "What is it?"

Rem filled her in on what he'd learned, and Mikey wrote it down. Mason and Trick waited until Mikey thanked Rem. He told her to be careful and hung up.

"Well, what is it?" asked Mason. "Don't keep us in suspense."

Mikey reread the notes. "Bradley has indeed been in and out of prison, but only one incident was violent. He got charged for assault after a bar fight. He's done time for the other things I mentioned, plus did a stint in rehab. Bradley was right about Kyle, too. Lydia took out a restraining order against him after an altercation at her home. Police showed and arrested Kyle, but they dropped the charges after Lydia refused to prosecute."

"Well, well, well," said Trick. He regarded Mason. "What do you think about that?"

Mikey recalled what else Rem had mentioned. "Rem also said that Bevins and Winkler are willing to meet with you guys. Said you could stop by tomorrow after twelve. He'll text you the address to the station."

Mason fiddled with the small paper with his fortune on it. "Looks like we've got some more people to talk to, and another busy day ahead of us." He offered Mikey a dubious look. "Did Rem happen to give you□?"

"□Morrow's address?" asked Mikey. She waved the notebook. "Got it right here."

Mason sipped from his water. "I owe Remalla a big drink."

"Get him a steak, too. He'll love that," said Mikey. She reached for a cookie.

Trick waved his fortune. "Looks like my luck is changing." He read from the paper. "It says 'A pleasant surprise is waiting for you.'" He smiled. "Maybe it's Kyle or Bradley." He stood. "Be right back. Gonna use the facilities." He left the table and headed for the bathroom.

Mikey read hers and chuckled.

"What's it say?" asked Mason.

"You'll love it. It says 'An important person will offer you support.'"

"Important, huh? That's one word for it," said Mason.

Mikey rolled her eyes again. "If you weren't my brother..." Mason held his own fortune, and Mikey leaned in. "What does yours say?"

Mason looked at it and handed it to her. Mikey read it out loud. "A dubious friend may be an enemy in camouflage." She frowned, an uncomfortable chill running up her spine. "Let's hope that's not true."

Mason shifted and rested his head back. "Let's hope."

Chapter Fourteen

LATER THAT NIGHT, MASON yawned and sat up on the couch, his mind dull and weary. He'd tried to lie down after Mikey had left, but couldn't relax. Unsettling images of dead Chad and Lydia from their interview with Cissy swam in and out of his head and then, after dozing, he'd dreamt of his mother and had startled awake. Hearing a car door close, he stood and opened the front door as Trick walked in with groceries. Mason closed the door behind him, noting the number of bags. "How long do you plan on staying? Should I prepare some paperwork for you to sign?"

Trick snickered. "You need food, Red. Real food. And something to drink. It's bad enough you don't have a TV, but my stomach doesn't have to suffer, too." He opened one of the bags. "Did you get some sleep?"

Mason recalled the dream of his mother. "No. Not really. Couldn't settle."

"I can't imagine why not. Between you and your spooky companions, I'm surprised you sleep at all."

Mason watched him put away beans, tortillas, and jalapenos. He shook his head. "Did you have enough money?"

Trick pulled out some taco shells. "I'm not completely destitute."

Mason eyed the time. "I'm going to take a shower and go to bed early. Hopefully, I can sleep, and we can start fresh tomorrow."

Trick waved the box of shells. "I bought stuff for tacos. You want them tonight or tomorrow?"

"Let's save them for tomorrow, when I can appreciate them more."

"Will do." Trick held up a couple of six-packs. "We can have these with them."

Mason almost chuckled. "You're missing Texas, I see."

"I'm missing Texas food, that's for damn sure." He pulled out some shredded cheese and salsa. "I bought plenty, so if you want to invite Mikey and even those detective friends of yours, that's fine. We owe them."

Mason nodded. "It's a good idea. I'll let Mikey know." He covered a yawn. "I'm calling it a night. Feel free to hang out, but keep the music down, will you?"

"Sure thing. I'll sit out on your patio, make a few phone calls. I won't be up late, though."

Mason nodded. "Let's plan on visiting Lydia's ex in the morning, and then hit Bevins and Winkler in the afternoon. Sound good?"

"Sounds good."

Mason spotted a box of brownie mix Trick removed from a bag and shook his head.

"Hey," said Trick, holding the box.

"No brownies for me tonight," said Mason, with a wave.

Trick put the box down. "Not that. I just wanted to thank you. You're putting up with a lot, and this is taking more time than you thought, and I'm sort of a thorn in your side."

"Not a thorn. More like an annoying, festering splinter."

The side of Trick's lip rose. "I just appreciate you doing this for me. You could have walked away."

"Almost did," said Mason. "What was I thinking?"

"Should have gone with your gut," said Trick.

Mason paused. "I did."

Trick reached for a bag, but stopped.

"Listen," said Mason. "You and I have had our ups and downs, but some of my best times were the two of us working together." He paused. "It's good to see you and to work with you again. I've missed it."

Trick smiled. "I've missed it, too." He picked up the brownies. "We'll have these tomorrow too." He wiggled his brows and set them aside.

"You just keep your nose clean, okay? I know how quickly a case can go south if you don't."

"You don't have to worry about me," said Trick. He shot a stare at Mason. "I'm glad to see you're doing the same."

Mason held his gaze. "Have been for a while now. Don't intend to stop."

"Good." Trick grabbed a bag of chips and put them in the pantry.

Mason rubbed his tight neck. "See you in the morning."

"See you."

Mason walked out of the kitchen and into his bedroom. Unbuttoning his shirt, he walked into his bathroom and flipped on the shower. The water shot from the nozzle, and Mason sighed in anticipation. During moments of mental fatigue, just sitting under a hot spray did wonders to help shed some of the weariness. He pulled off the rest of his clothes, threw on a robe, and stared into his mirror, waiting as the water heated. Staring at himself, he noted his tired features. His eyes were red, and his pallor a little gray. The day had taken its toll, and he couldn't wait to get into bed and crash. Closing his eyes, he hung his head, thinking of his dream, and praying he could sleep. Sometimes his mind wouldn't relent, and he would end up staring at the ceiling, worn and frustrated. Determined to rest, though, he looked back in the mirror, and seeing his haggard features, he opened the medicine cabinet.

A loud slam, followed by a high-pitched shriek, made him jump, and his hand hit a shelf and almost knocked everything down. After righting the items, he closed the cabinet, ran out, and threw the bedroom door open. Looking down the hall, he saw Trick sitting on the floor outside the hallway bathroom, his hand on his heart and his breathing coming in short gasps. The bathroom door was closed.

Mason ran over. "What happened? You okay?"

Trick stared, his face pale. "That damn door slammed on me. I was about to go in, and it...it...just closed. Hard. Right in front of me."

Mason turned, recalling the door shutting the other night. He opened up his senses, trying to figure out what presence was getting its kicks out of scaring him, and now Trick.

"It happened yesterday when you were out," said Trick. "I thought it was a draft."

"It's not a draft," said Mason, approaching the door.

"I'm getting' that. Scared the shit out of me."

Mason put his hand on the ice-cold knob and opened it. The door creaked, and he looked in but saw just the dark interior. Nothing was out of place.

"What the hell is going on, Red?" Trick stood and came up behind Mason, breathing hard.

"I don't know," said Mason. "It's happened to me too. A few nights ago. I think someone's trying to get our attention."

"Someone? What do you mean?" Trick sputtered. "Like a ghost?"

"Yes. Like a ghost." Mason checked behind the door and then stepped back, leaving it open.

Trick's eyes were wide. "Are you kidding me?"

"No." Mason took a deep breath and felt for whatever spirit was around, but couldn't pick up on anything. "I am not kidding you."

Trick's jaw hung open. "Well, that's something you might want to include in your welcome brochure."

Mason shrugged. "It's no big deal. I think it's gone now." He headed down the hall toward his room.

"Wh...What?" Trick followed him. "Wait a minute. Where are you going?" He kept an eye on the bathroom.

"To the shower. The water's running. Then I'm going to sleep."

Trick's eyes rounded. "You're going to bed? After that?"

"Yes. Why not?"

Trick pointed. "Because there's a damn ghost in the house. Doesn't that bother you?"

"No." Mason shrugged. "There're ghosts all over the place. Not just this house. The majority are harmless. Don't worry about it." He turned toward his room, but Trick grabbed his elbow.

"Are you trying to tell me we're not alone? There are other ghosts here besides the bathroom man?"

"It actually feels female to me, and yes, there are others hanging around." He patted Trick on the shoulder. "But don't worry. You'll get used to it."

"Used to it?" yelled Trick.

Mason stopped at his door. "If you're going to stay with me, it comes with the territory. I broke up with my girlfriend because of it. She didn't like it either. They kept pulling her covers off at night."

Trick's jaw fell. "Can't you do something?"

Mason hesitated and rested his hand against the doorframe. "What would you like me to do?"

"I don't know. You're the one who talks to 'em. Tell them to back off. I'm a virgin in these woods."

Mason almost laughed. "You screamed like a kid. You keep doing that, and they'll either keep scaring you because they get a kick out of it, or they'll stop because you're scaring them too." He chuckled. "Most singers can't hit the note you hit."

"Can you blame me?" Trick's gaze darted around the hall. "I'm creeped out."

"Well, you can sleep in your car if you want, but I suspect the bed will be more comfortable." A clock on the wall chimed softly and Trick jumped. "Just relax. It'll be fine."

"Didn't the mom in *The Exorcist* say that to her daughter?"

Mason started to shut the door. "I'm going to take my shower."

"You expect me to use that bathroom?"

"There's always the great outdoors. Your choice. Good night." He swung the door and closed it.

Trick yelled from the hall. "If I'm cranky tomorrow, it's your fault."

Mason yelled back. "I'll take the risk." Smiling, he couldn't help himself and yelled again. "There are extra blankets in the closet if a ghost takes yours."

"Red..."

Laughing, Mason dropped his robe and got in the shower.

The next morning, Mason knocked on the apartment door and waited.

Trick stood beside him, yawned, and leaned against the wall. "Morrow's probably at work. We should have called first."

Mason knocked again. "I prefer the surprise visit. If this guy did have something to do with Lydia's death, I'd rather not give him time to prepare."

"If he did kill Lydia, I'd hope he'd be expecting a visit like this. Guy should have his story ready by now. Besides, I like for them to sweat if they know we're coming. Messes with their heads."

"Maybe so..." Mason knocked again. "I guess we'll have to come back later."

A door down from Morrow's opened, and a woman stepped out, wearing a fitted blue suit that stopped just above her knees and emphasized her narrow frame and full cleavage. Her smooth blonde hair blew softly and grazed her cheeks. Closing her door, she spotted them and smiled. "You looking for Kyle?" she asked.

Trick straightened and smiled back. "Yes, ma'am." His gaze didn't hide his appraisal of her. "You know where he might be?"

She locked her door, swung her purse over her shoulder, and walked over. Her gaze met Trick's, who stood in his jeans, boots, and cowboy hat, and she appraised him as well. "I just might, Cowboy." Her mouth crooked up. "Where you two from?" She studied Mason, who also wore his cowboy hat and boots. "Obviously not around here."

"The great state of Texas, ma'am," said Trick, tipping his hat at her.

Mason almost groaned.

"I like Texas," she said. "Hot, though." She fanned herself but held Trick's gaze.

"You're beautiful enough to be from Texas, ma'am, if you don't mind me saying so." Trick took his hat off.

She fiddled with the strap of her purse. "I don't mind at all." Her cheeks turned pink.

Mason tried to get back to why they were there. "Do you know Kyle, Mrs...." He waited.

She never took her eyes off Trick. "Miss...," she said. "Monica Renfro." She held out her hand and Trick took it. "Nice to meet you."

"You too, Monica," said Trick. He introduced himself and Mason, and finally let go of her hand.

"Kyle's a friend," she said. "We occasionally...um...hang out." She paused. "He's at work, though. Probably be back around four."

There was a moment of quiet as Trick and Monica stared at each other. Mason half-expected Trick to reach down for a piece of grass and start chewing on it. "I guess we'll come back later then," said Mason, raising a brow at Trick.

"Guess so," said Trick.

"Listen, just in case he's not here," Monica pulled her purse around and dug through it, "and you need to find him," she pulled out a card, "just call me." She handed the card to Trick. "Anytime." Her cheeks turned redder, and she smiled sheepishly.

"Thanks, Monica. I'll do that," said Trick. He took out his wallet, added her card, and pulled out his own. "And if for any reason you need to reach us, here's my number."

"Thanks," said Monica, taking the card. "I'll hold on to it."

"I hope so," said Trick.

"I better go," said Monica. She stepped between the two of them and waved. "Good luck in your search." She giggled. "Maybe I'll see you around sometime."

"I think you will," said Trick. "You have a nice day, Monica." He put his hat back on and winked at her.

Mason half-expected Monica to trip over the stairs, but she found her footing and waved again. "See you."

"See you," said Trick.

Mason and Trick watched her walk away. "What the hell are you doing?" asked Mason, as Monica made it to her car and got in.

Trick grinned. "What do you think I'm doing?" He waved a hand as Monica drove off. "That's a pretty lady."

"You're not here to date," said Mason. "We've got things to do."

Trick crossed his arms. "I know that, but she's friends with Morrow. Can't hurt to see what she knows."

"You think Morrow confided in his neighbor and told her he killed Lydia?"

Trick shrugged. "Maybe. Can't be sure till we ask. She may tell us something Kyle doesn't. It's worth a shot, don't you think?"

Mason adjusted his hat. "Doesn't hurt you either, does it?"

Trick cocked his head. "You're just mad she wasn't looking at you." He turned and headed down the sidewalk.

Mason followed. "She's not my type."

Trick looked back. "Who exactly is?"

They got to the car, and Mason went to the driver's side. "Depends. It's not about one thing with a woman. It's about her energy." He opened the door and slid in.

Trick got into the passenger seat and closed the door. "Gorgeous legs don't hurt either." He tapped his knee with his hand. "Did you happen to see Monica's?"

Mason checked his phone. "I did."

Trick grinned. "See. You were looking."

Mason put the phone down. "I'm not dead." He thought for a second. "How about we grab some food, then head over to talk to Bevins and Winkler? We'll stop by here again on the way home."

Trick nodded. "Sounds good. Maybe somewhere along the way, I'll call Monica." He took off his hat. "Make a date."

Mason smirked at his friend, started the car, and drove off.

Mikey sat at the sandwich shop and sipped some coffee. After spending the morning trying to find out more about Kyle Morrow, Bradley, any possible insurance policies, and checking into Cissy's background, she decided to head out, get some fresh air, and check out the bookstore where Cissy had worked. She'd thought about calling, but Mason had told her that sometimes, a face-to-face interview was better. It was easy for people to dodge questions on a phone call, but harder to do it in person, and you could read their body language.

After stopping in, she'd learned from the man behind the counter that he was new and didn't know Cissy, but that another employee would be coming in later, and he thought she would know more.

Mikey had thanked him and now sat at the sandwich shop, waiting and thinking. She'd texted Mason, who was on his way to speak to Bevins and Winkler. She told him she might be a little late to dinner, depending on when she would be able to talk to Cissy's co-worker. She'd invited Rem and Daniels for tacos, and they would be meeting them at the house later.

Adding some sugar to her mug, she thought about her progress. She'd talked to Cissy's parents and had tracked down and talked to a couple of ladies from the women's group that Cissy had joined. None of them could shed much light on Cissy's activities prior to Chad's death. Kyle Morrow's background was oddly bland. There were no other red flags regarding him and domestic abuse, or angry girlfriends. Lydia appeared to be the only one who'd filed a complaint against him. She'd also failed to determine if Lydia had left money to Bradley. She supposed she could call Bradley and ask, and see how he responded, but decided to talk to Shay first and see if Lydia's sister might reveal something. Mikey debated calling Shay again since Shay had not returned her call, when her phone buzzed, and Shay's number popped up on the display.

Mikey answered. "Hello?"

"Is this Mikey?" The voice was high and nasally.

"Yes. Shay Stanford?"

"Well, close enough. That's my mom's last name."

Mikey recalled Shay had a different father than Lydia. "Thank you for calling me back. I hope I'm not bothering you."

She heard a sniff on the line. "It's fine. I would have called sooner, but I'm dealing with a horrible cold." Mikey heard her blow her nose. "I'm guessing you want to talk about Lydia?"

"Is that okay? I just have a few questions."

"I suppose. Is something wrong? I thought her death was ruled an accident."

Mikey thought about Lydia's drowning and wondered how much to push. "No. Nothing's wrong. I'm just looking into the death of her co-worker, Chad Howard. Did you know him?"

There was a pause. "The man who was murdered? What would Lydia have to do with...?" Mikey heard a snort. "Oh, no. Is that the man Lydia was sleeping with?"

Mikey perked up. "You know she was sleeping with someone?"

"I did, but figured it was another loser. Lydia was a mess. If she wasn't on her meds, or rather, if she wasn't correctly on her meds, she made stupid choices, which was most of the time. Girl had the eye of a tiger and the sense of a mule."

"We know she and Chad worked together, and that Chad spent some time at Lydia's. Chad's wife suspected him of seeing someone, and we suspect it was Lydia, but then Lydia drowned right before Chad passed."

She heard a sharp inhale of breath. "What are you saying? That Lydia and Chad's deaths are related?"

"We don't know, which is why I'm calling around to talk to Lydia's friends and family to see if they know anything that might help." She pulled out her notebook and opened it. "Can you shed some light on Lydia's mental state and what you know about her relationships?"

Shay sneezed.

"Bless you."

"Thank you." She sniffed. "Well, good luck finding any friends. If Lydia had any, I never met them. And if you talked to our mother, then you already know what a waste of time that was." She paused and Mikey thought she heard Shay drinking something, and recalled Michelle suggesting that Shay was an alcoholic.

"Lydia and I, we had our good days and bad. It depended on what she was taking, and when."

"Lydia took a lot of pills?" asked Mikey.

Shay laughed. "She's been taking something since I was in diapers. Mom drugged her up to keep Lydia quiet and calm. Nothing much changed over the years. Lydia was always smart, though. She went to school and graduated. Made good grades and got a decent job. Dated real losers, though. Between that and the pills, her life was a wreck."

"What about Bradley?"

"Bradley?" She paused. "You talked to him?"

"I did. Yesterday."

She snorted again. "He's the worst of all of us. I'm surprised he was coherent enough to speak. I'm guessing you know his background?'

"Some. He's been in and out of jail. Has been in rehab. He said he'd been estranged from Lydia for a while but they'd reconnected."

"Yeah. I know. Because of that damned Kyle Morrow. Lydia's ex. We all stayed away while she dated him."

"Was he abusive?"

"He was possessive of her. Didn't like her spending time with anyone but him. They had terrible fights, and Lydia always caved. Me and Bradley tried to tell her to leave him, but she never listened, until finally she got smart and dumped his ass."

"How long ago was this?"

"Oh, I think about a year ago."

"And then she started seeing someone else?"

"Yeah. Not long after. She went from sad and depressed to active and energetic. Personally, I think she was bi-polar, but don't think she was ever diagnosed."

Mikey scribbled on her paper. "She never mentioned Chad to you?"

"Not by name."

Mikey nodded and considered her next question. "Do you know anything about her financial situation?"

"Financial?" Shay paused. "Like salary and shit? I think she made decent money. Nothing to write home about. I know she helped Bradley out a lot, and mom a time or two."

"How was her relationship with Bradley?"

Shay grunted and sniffed. "Depended on the day. They had their moments, just like me and her, but I think she felt sorry for him and tried to help when she could."

"Your mom said Lydia named Bradley as the executor of her will. Do you know if she left him any money or if she had a life insurance policy?"

Shay coughed. "Excuse me a second." Mikey heard more coughing and then Shay returned. "Sorry about that. Life insurance? Not that I'm aware of." Mikey heard her drink something again.

A new question popped into Mikey's head. "Did you find it odd that Lydia had a will and she made Bradley the executor? She seems young to be thinking about that."

"Lydia? Hell, no. She was always thinking ahead. And I think she chose Bradley because she liked him more than me. And she certainly wouldn't consider our mother." She paused. "Personally, I think she made Bradley the executor because she knew it would piss mom off, although I doubt she expected he'd actually have to do anything, and certainly not this soon."

"Do you mind if I ask about her will? How did she leave things?"

Shay hesitated. "You're asking a lot of questions about Lydia, but I thought you were investigating this Chad fella?" There was a pause. "Why is that?"

Mikey debated how to answer. "Chad was murdered two weeks after Lydia drowned. Chad's wife is a suspect in his death..."

Shay's stuffy voice raised. "You think she killed Lydia, too?"

Mikey rubbed her head. "We're not sure. We just thought it was very coincidental, and we're wondering if..." She stopped before she mentioned other suspects, not knowing how to word it.

"You're trying to prove that one of us killed Lydia?" She laughed loudly. "What, so you can take the suspicion off that wife of his?"

Mikey gripped her pencil. "We just want to get to the truth."

"The truth, huh?" She sniffed. "How about this for some truth?" Mikey heard the irritation in Shay's voice. "Lydia confided in me about an argument she had."

"Argument?" asked Mikey.

"With the wife of the man she was seeing. I didn't know it was Chad, but now that I do, it must have been Chad's wife that showed up at Lydia's door."

Mikey sunk in her seat. "Lydia mentioned that? What did she say?"

"Said that bitch was crazy. Told Lydia to leave her husband alone, and if she didn't, she'd be damn sorry. She'd make Lydia wish she'd never laid eyes on her husband, and she knew how to take care of problems that didn't go away."

Mikey wrote furiously.

"If Lydia's death wasn't an accident, and you're looking to find a murderer, I'd start at your own back door. Our family may have our issues, but that doesn't make us killers. You should think twice before accusing any of us. You got that, honey?"

Mikey nodded. "I got that."

"Good." And with a cough, Shay hung up.

Chapter Fifteen

MASON AND TRICK SAT at the four-top table in the cafeteria, waiting for Bevins and Winkler, who were getting a late lunch.

"They're a couple of cool customers," said Trick, hooking an arm over the back of his chair. "Did you see how Winkler was looking at me? I think she's immune to my charms."

"She's a detective with a wedding ring. Not someone you'd call one-eight-hundred-BABE to talk to," said Mason.

"Still," said Trick. "Her partner isn't much better."

Mason watched the two detectives at the register, each holding a tray. Winkler was of average height with curly brown, short hair, but had the muscled body of a woman who spent a lot of time at the free weight section of the gym. Bevins was taller, but rounder, with thinning reddish hair, a loosened tie, and a perpetually tired look. It was the face of a man who'd been at the job too long and had seen everything. Mason was familiar with that look, and it didn't bode well for Cissy. The detectives paid for their food and headed over.

"Just take it easy, will you?" said Mason. "We need to grease the wheels with these two, not throw down spikes."

"Fine. Whatever." Trick sat up as the detectives approached.

"Sorry to keep you waiting," said Winkler. "We got caught up with a case and never had lunch." She put down her tray.

"You sure you two don't want anything?" asked Bevins. He put down his tray and sat.

"We ate, but thanks," said Mason. He picked up his water and sipped it.

Winkler pulled out a napkin and put it in her lap. "You two know Daniels and Remalla?"

Mason nodded. "Yes. I worked with them on a case not long ago. Good detectives. You know them well?"

"Getting to," said Bevins. "We just transferred over from another division. Chad's case is our first over here."

"You two been partners long?" asked Trick.

"Ten years," said Bevins. "I heard you two were Rangers back in Texas." He popped open his can of soda. "I bet you saw a few things." He gestured toward their hats that hung on the back of their chairs. "Everybody wear those where you're from?" He smiled.

Mason figured they'd done enough of the required small talk, and sensing Trick's edginess, he got to the point. "Sure." He rested a hand on the table. "We were hoping to talk to you about Chad's case."

"What about it?" asked Winkler. She opened a small carton of milk and drank from it.

"You two seem damned sure Cissy killed him," said Trick. Mason tensed and shot a side glance at Trick.

"And you aren't?" asked Bevins, eating a chip from a bag he'd opened. "Have you seen the evidence?"

Trick sat up. "You two should□"

Mason put a hand on Trick's arm. "What evidence? Would you mind telling us why you're so sure?"

Winkler made eye contact with Bevins. "Where should we start?" She took a fork and poked at her side salad. "Chad had an affair. Cissy knew about it and confronted him, and his mistress." She dunked some lettuce in a side of dressing. "Yes. We know about Lydia, and we know Cissy went to see her." She let the extra dressing drip off the bite of salad. "And we know there was an altercation at Chad's office with a woman we believe was Cissy. Lydia died shortly after that altercation." She paused. "By accident, supposedly." She ate the dunked lettuce.

"Wait a minute," said Trick. "How can you know it was Cissy that Chad was talking to in his office?"

Mason had a sinking thought. "Were there cameras? Did you see her on video?"

"There were cameras," said Winkler. "but we couldn't see who entered or left his office. Chad's door was just out of view, but his hallway leads to a stairwell which exits to the parking lot."

"So?" asked Trick.

Bevins sipped his soda. "Whoever it was, avoided the parking lot cameras, and obviously knew where they were, so it was someone familiar with the lot and office area. Cissy obviously was, since she'd been there several times."

"Anyone who works there would know about those cameras," said Mason. "Including Lydia."

"Lydia's dead, which makes her hard to accuse," said Bevins.

"You mean it doesn't fit the story you're trying to create for a jury," said Trick. He leaned in. "You know damned well it could have been Lydia in that office."

"Listen," said Winkler. "We have to follow where the clues lead us. Either way, whether it was Cissy or Lydia, Lydia is the one who is dead. And that points the finger toward Cissy."

"And Lydia's death, although ruled an accident, is suspicious." Bevins spoke through a mouthful of sandwich. "Woman had a blood alcohol level worthy of Santa after his Christmas eve run, a busted head and water in her lungs, so she likely fell, hit her head and drowned, but we can't rule out she was pushed."

"And if she was, could it have been Cissy? Did they have another fight? Maybe," said Winkler. She took another bite of salad.

"But even if we can't get her on Lydia's death, we can sure as hell get her on Chad's," said Bevins. "No alibi. No witnesses, other than a camera showing her come and go from the scene. Plenty of motive and familiar with handguns, particularly Chad's handgun."

"She had no residue on her," said Trick.

Winkler put her fork down and picked up her own sandwich. "Easy enough to prevent if you've planned ahead. All she had to do was wear gloves, shoot Chad, then take the gloves off, along with the clothes she's wearing, rinse off and change, go run her errands, and dump the clothes and gloves somewhere in between. Easy enough. Plus, Chad used to be a cop. Cissy would have known about residue and how to hide it."

"Have you found these dumped clothes?" asked Mason.

"No. But it doesn't matter. It makes sense, and a jury will likely agree," said Winkler.

"What about a second phone?" asked Mason. "Did Chad have one?"

"He did," said Winkler. "A work phone, but we never found it. We figure it was dumped with the clothes."

"And before you ask," said Bevins. "We checked the phone records on it. He'd made calls to both Cissy and Lydia, and before you get worked up that he spoke to Lydia, we know it was a work phone and they were co-workers. No big shakes there."

"And if he had a second phone, he hid from his wife," said Winkler. "We never found it. Probably dumped by Cissy, too."

"You two sure do make a lot of assumptions," said Trick.

"We have all the evidence we need when it comes to a conviction," said Bevins, settling back in his seat.

"That's exactly what scares me." Trick set his jaw. "Have you done any investigating into Lydia Stanford?"

"Other than trying to put Cissy at the scene of her death? No. What for?" asked Bevins, taking another bite of food.

"Because maybe there's more to this," said Trick, rapidly tapping his fingers on the table. "And I think you two are more interested in your supposed conviction instead of the truth."

"Trick...," said Mason.

"It's okay," said Winkler. "I can tell you're frustrated. She's your sister-in-law, and it can be hard to see a loved one go down this road." She dunked more lettuce in her side of dressing. "Why don't you tell us what you think happened?"

"This ought to be good," said Bevins.

Mason frowned but didn't respond.

"If you'd bothered to look, you'd know Lydia had a slew of issues," said Trick. "Her family is a mess, her brother's picture is posted beside the definition of hoodlum, her mother and sister are alcoholics, and her old boyfriend harassed her. Any one of them could be responsible for her death and could have killed Chad, too."

Bevins chewed his food, and Winkler sipped her milk. "You got any evidence to support that?" asked Bevins with a belch. "Excuse me."

"Did any of them threaten Lydia or Chad?" asked Winkler. "Any links to Chad's gun? Do any of them have a history of violence? Did they have a motive to kill Chad? Were they at Chad and Cissy's place on the day of the crime?"

"Not according to the video," chuckled Bevins.

"That's another thing," said Trick. "There was a vacant apartment near Chad and Cissy's. An assailant could have hidden there before and after the crime, while you two wandered around, scratching your asses."

Mason sighed and closed his eyes.

"We found cigarette butts in that room," said Trick. "Someone was hanging out in there, and if you'd bothered to check, you might have found them yourselves."

Bevins wiped his mouth with a napkin. "Cigarette butts?" He raised a brow. "I'll call my captain. You've broken this case wide open. Who do they belong to?"

"Any DNA on them?" asked Winkler.

"Unlikely," said Mason, realizing this visit was a mistake. "One was on the patio and two were in the toilet."

"Much like your theories," said Bevins.

"Without DNA, they're worthless. They could have been smoked by the last tenant for all you know." Winkler ate one of Bevin's chips.

"The point is, there is reason to look for someone else outside of Cissy," said Trick.

"We go where the evidence takes us, Cowboy," said Bevins. "I'm sure you two did the same when you were Rangers." He bit into his sandwich.

"We did our job as Rangers and followed all the evidence," said Trick. "Not just the ones that supported our assumptions and solidified a conviction."

Winkler calmly chewed and swallowed a bite of food. "You seem pretty sure."

"Cissy wouldn't kill anybody," said Trick. "That I know."

"We'd just like to rule out any other possibilities," said Mason. "If Cissy's going to get a fair trial, it's important."

"Is that the plan, then?" asked Bevins, picking up his soda. "For her defense? Try to make us look like idiots?"

"If the shoe fits," said Trick.

Mason wanted to punch Trick.

"Then be careful," said Bevins with a smile.

Something in Mason's gut churned. "Why, exactly, do we need to be careful?"

Winkler wiped her fingers with the napkin from her lap. "We're all on the same side here, fellas. We should be working together, and we're happy to help, but if you choose to go down that path, well, it works both ways."

Suspecting the path they were on, Mason held his breath.

"You got nothing on us," said Trick. He turned and grabbed his hat. "And this meeting was pointless. C'mon, Mason."

"When we knew you two were coming to talk to us, we did a little checking," said Bevins to Trick. "Your superiors were hesitant to speak, but we finally found someone willing to talk and learned enough to know that you got yourself a hot head, Cowboy." He grinned and ate a chip.

Trick deflated. "You called Texas?"

"We called Texas," said Winkler. "You punched your sergeant. On top of getting rough with a suspect, which cost you the case and landed him back on the street. Is that what got you fired?"

Trick stared in disbelief.

Mason sat up, his anger growing. "You two don't play nice."

"We're just getting started," said Bevins. "I hear you speak to the dead. I'm sure Cissy's defense attorney would be happy to mention that to the jury. Maybe you can tell them how you talked to Chad, and he told you who was hiding in the parlor with the bloody knife the morning of the crime."

Mason couldn't believe his ears.

Trick stood, putting on his hat. "I think we're done here."

Mason stood too and grabbed his hat. "I agree."

"You two cowboys have a nice day," said Bevins, raising a chip.

Winkler smacked Bevin's arm. "Stop it, Bevins."

Trick held still, and Mason took his arm. "Forget it. Let's go."

Trick pointed. "I'll accept your apology when we prove you wrong."

"You pull that off, and I'll buy myself one of those nice hats," said Bevins. "And eat it."

"Good to know," said Trick. "I'll happily check to see if they have one to fit the size of your head, which is as almost thick as your ass."

Bevins stopped in mid-chew.

"C'mon, Trick." Mason grabbed Trick's elbow and pulled him out of the cafeteria.

Mikey stepped inside the bookstore and looked around. It was small; the main area was filled with rows of books, and there was a smaller area in the back that looked to be a children's section. A large table at the front displayed the latest bestsellers, and Mikey picked up a book and flipped through it. One customer stood at the register, while a woman with short, spiky, pink hair, skin-tight jeans, and a chunky sweater checked him out.

The purchase made, the customer took his bag and left, and the woman at the counter studied a nail.

Mikey approached, and the woman looked up from her fingers. "Can I help you?"

Mikey nodded. "Yes. I hope so." She thought about what to say, and assuming this was the woman who'd worked with Cissy, she just dove in. "I'm investigating the murder of Chad Howard. Did Cissy Howard work here?"

The woman's eyes widened. "Yes. She did."

"You're a friend of hers?" asked Mikey. "Do you mind if I ask you a few questions?"

"Oh, dear." The woman put a hand to her face. "Am I in trouble?"

Mikey put her hand on the counter. "No. Of course not. I'm just□"

"Oh, God. You're that detective, aren't you?"

Mikey frowned. "Detec□"

"Detective Winkler, right? I'm so sorry. You called a few times, and I didn't call you back." She came around the counter, looking like she'd stolen a book and was terrified she'd been caught. "I meant to call. Really." She wrung her hands.

Mikey tried to keep up. "Listen, I'm not□"

"Please don't bring me in. I know I have that unpaid parking ticket. I'll pay it. I swear." She held her head. "What do you need to know? I'll answer any questions. And I won't lie."

Mikey went quiet, trying to think. This woman thought she was Detective Winkler. Her mind raced, and she read the woman's name tag. "Carla, right?"

"Yes. Carla Bellaveena. I was going to call yesterday, but it just got busy, you know?" She laughed, but her eyes didn't show any humor, and Mikey didn't believe for a second that the bookstore had been busy the previous day.

Mikey debated, and making a decision, hoped Mason wouldn't yell at her later. "What can you tell me about Cissy, Carla? How well did you know her?" She pulled out her small notepad and a pencil.

Carla bit her lip. "Not that well. We just worked together. But we were friends. Sort of." She crossed her arms. "I mean, not best friends, but friends."

Mikey scribbled on her paper. "When did you last see her?"

"Umm, well, at her husband's funeral, and then after, at the reception. Didn't really talk to her much, though. She was pretty upset."

"What about before then? When was the last time you saw her before Chad died?"

Carla chewed on her lip. "Umm, the day before. She came in as I was leaving."

"How did she seem?"

"Seem?"

Mikey nodded. "How was her mood? Anything that stuck out? Was she her normal self?"

"I...I think so. I didn't notice anything different."

"And what about before then? Did you know Chad?"

"No. Not really. He came in once or twice. I said hi, but that's it. Nothing weird."

Mikey adjusted her purse strap. "Did you see anything between them that might have indicated they were unhappy? Did Cissy ever confide in you about her relationship?"

"Oh, jeez. I don't know. We had lunch a few times, and I told her about my dickless boyfriend, and she complained about Chad, but that's it. It was just girl talk."

"What did she complain about?"

Carla swallowed and scratched her neck. "Standard stuff. He didn't spend enough time with her. He worked too much. She was lonely."

Mikey held Carla's gaze. "Do you think she killed him?"

Carla's mouth opened. "I...I...don't know. She never struck me as someone who would do that." She waved her hands. "I mean, come on. It's crazy. Course, I once pulled a knife on Dickless, but unfortunately, he's still alive." She chewed a nail.

"Right," said Mikey, disappointed that this interview was going nowhere. "Did Cissy ever say anything to you about Chad cheating on her?"

"Chad? Cheating?" She snorted. "Figures. Just like Dickless." She messed with her spiky pink hair. "I guess they're all alike." She pointed at Mikey. "I like your pink highlights and your nose piercing. I didn't think cops could do that."

Mikey touched the post in her left nostril. "Yeah, well. Regulations have been relaxed recently."

"That's cool. I wish I had the guts to do my nose. I'm a wimp, though, when it comes to pain."

Mikey tapped the pencil on her paper. "Yeah." She tried to think of anything else to ask. "So, nothing about Cissy made you think she'd hurt Chad or could have something to do with his death?"

Carla leaned back against the counter, looking more relaxed. "I like Cissy. She was always nice to me. I guess she was the same with others, too. But if he cheated on her, then who knows?" She scraped her foot over the carpet. "Sometimes, people do stupid things."

Something about her tone caught Mikey's attention. "I know. I've been there. I've had a few dickless men in my life." She straightened, thinking back. "And I've done a few stupid things."

"Yeah," said Carla, still looking down.

Mikey spoke softly. "Did Cissy do anything stupid? I mean, outside of maybe killing Chad?"

Carla went back to nibbling her lip.

"Carla?"

Carla looked up. "I don't know. Maybe."

Mikey's heart picked up its pace. "What?" Carla hesitated and Mikey had a thought and took a chance. "How about I take care of that parking ticket for you?"

Carla sucked in a breath. "You serious?"

"You bet." Mikey asked for forgiveness in her head. "It never existed."

"Okay. Well..." Carla sighed and fiddled with her fingers. "I can't be sure about what I saw. I mean, it was from a distance."

Mikey gripped her pencil. "What did you see?"

Carla pursed her lips. "At the reception after the funeral, I snuck out, you know, to get a smoke. I'm tryin' to quit, but it's hard."

"I'm sure."

"I stepped out into some trees, trying not to be too close. Everyone gets so pissy nowadays if they smell cigarette smoke. People are uptight." She rolled her eyes. "Anyway, I was smoking, and I heard talking. It was distant, but I walked deeper into the woods, and I saw Cissy."

Mikey held her breath. "Wasn't she at the reception?"

"I guess she snuck out for a minute. There was a storage shed or something, and she was behind it. She was talking to some guy."

"Guy? What guy?"

"I don't know. I didn't recognize him. And I only looked for a second, because it seemed private."

"Were they just talking?"

"Yes, but..." Carla groaned. "I finished my cigarette, and was about to leave, and then I peeked one more time, and...and...they were kissing."

Mikey almost dropped her notebook. "Kissing? Like on the cheek?"

Carla shook her head. "No, Detective." Her eyes told Mikey it was much more than a peck on the lips.

"What'd he look like?" Mikey's fingers trembled as she held the pencil.

"I don't know. It was so fast, and then I freaked out, and left." She hugged herself. "It was just a glance."

"Tall? Short? Fat? Thin?" asked Mikey.

"Tall and slim, with brown hair. Handsome."

"Would you know him if you saw him again?"

"Probably not. Like I said. It was from a distance. If he was wearin' that cowboy hat, though, then maybe."

Mikey froze. "Excuse me?"

"That I remember." Carla pointed at her head. "He was wearing a cowboy hat. You know, like those rodeo guys from Texas."

Chapter Sixteen

MASON SAT AT THE bar and nursed his second drink. After a completely worthless day, he debated ordering a third, but knew he had to get home. Trick would be making tacos, and Mikey, Daniels and Remalla would be arriving soon.

He reviewed their afternoon again in his head. After the ugly meeting with Bevins and Winkler, they'd returned to their car and argued–Mason about Trick not telling him about his past and getting kicked off the force, and Trick about how Mason played too nice with Bevins and Winkler.

They stopped only because Trick's phone had rung, and he'd answered. It had been Monica, and Trick had stepped out of the car, leaving Mason to ponder whether he should drive off.

A few minutes later, Trick had returned with a grin, saying Monica had called to let them know that she'd talked to Kyle, and he'd be working late that day, but he'd be happy to talk to him and Mason in the morning, and she'd asked Trick to have a drink with her after she got off work.

Feeling a headache coming on, Mason recalled the conversation.

"Drinks?" he'd asked. "You're supposed to be making dinner tonight."

"I told her that," said Trick. "I won't stay long, but it's worth it to talk to her about Kyle, don't you think? Would you rather I wait and drag this case out longer?"

Mason had to agree. "Just be back in time for our guests. You embarrass me again, and I'll put ketchup in your tacos."

"I'll be back in plenty of time. Why don't you go get a drink yourself, and then meet me back at the house? You look like you could use it."

"You want another drink?"

Mason startled and jumped to the present, seeing Charlie behind the bar. He shook his head. "No, thanks. I can't stay much longer. Got to be somewhere."

Charlie nodded. "This is your second time in here this week. Must be a helluva week."

"You could say that," said Mason with a huff. "Could I get some water?"

"Sure thing," said Charlie. He stepped away and grabbed a glass.

Mason checked the time, reached for his wallet, and felt a hand on his shoulder. A woman spoke in his ear. "You mind if I sit?"

Mason turned and stilled. It was the beautiful woman with the bronze skin from the previous night. Her dark round eyes watched him, her thick hair ran down her back, and she smelled like flowers. He was momentarily tongue-tied.

Not waiting for his answer, she slid onto the stool beside him and put her small red purse on the bar. She wore a fitted, v-cut blue t-shirt and jeans, and silver earrings sparkled from her ears. "My name's Valerie. Valerie Vain."

Mason swallowed. Her effect on him was immediate. Her looks were one thing, but her energy was on a whole other level. She exuded a magnetism he'd rarely felt from anyone. "Mason," he finally spoke. "Mason Redstone." He held out a hand and she took it, briefly holding it in hers. "Nice to meet you, Valerie."

She smiled and swiveled in the seat to face him. "I saw you in here the other day."

"I saw you too, sitting at the back table," said Mason. Charlie returned with his water and set it beside him. "Can I buy you a drink?"

His phone buzzed with a text notification from Mikey, and he punched at it. It said *We need to talk.* He closed it and set his phone aside.

"It's tempting, but no," she said. She smiled and her pearly white teeth glimmered. "I can't stay."

He sighed. "Too bad, but actually, neither can I. I'm supposed to be somewhere."

"Maybe another time then," she said.

"I hope so." Mason picked up his water. "You come in here often?"

"No. The other night was the first time. I followed you here."

Water caught in his throat, and Mason coughed. He picked up a napkin and dabbed his mouth. "Excuse me?"

She put an elbow on the bar. "I'm from Texas, Mason. Like you." She paused. "And your friend Trick."

Mason put the napkin down, and his skin prickled. "How do you□?"

"I'm a private investigator, only... the normal kind." She grinned like she had four aces up her sleeve. "I prefer to investigate the dead," she leaned in, "not talk to them."

Mason put his water glass down and picked up his alcoholic one. This week was getting better and better. "What do you want, Valerie?" He shot back the rest of his liquor.

"I want to talk."

"So talk." He checked the time. "But make it fast." He pulled out his wallet and threw down some cash for Charlie.

"You're investigating Chad Howard's death," she said. "So am I."

That got his attention. "Who hired you?"

"That's not important," she said. "But what is important is what I've learned, and what I think you should know."

"Let me guess. You think Cissy did it?"

"Probably."

He sighed and rubbed his temple. "That's old news, Val. Tell me you've got something more than that, or I'm going to think you're following me just for my good looks." A memory flickered, and he scowled. "Was that you watching us? In the parking lot outside the diner the other day?"

"Maybe," she said. "I was following Trick, but don't think I haven't noticed your good looks." She whispered. "I especially like the mustache. I think it's sexy as hell." She looked him over. "Your butt's nice too. Something about a man in jeans and boots..."

Mason almost forgot why she was there. "You sure you don't want that drink?"

She chuckled. "Maybe once this case is solved..."

"So that's a no then."

"I think we're closer to solving this case than you think."

He was amused to hear her say 'we.' "What do you know, Val, that you think is so important?"

She shifted closer, and Mason smelled her flowery scent. "You're a smart man, Mason, but you've missed what's right in front of you."

"And you're going to tell me what that is?"

"I wouldn't be sitting here otherwise." She smiled softly. "Unless, of course, you'd bought me that drink the other day."

Mason drank some water. "I guess we'll never know."

Her right eyebrow rose. "You should be careful who you trust."

He put his water down and slid off the stool. "I've got to go."

"What do you know about your friend, Trick?"

That stopped him. "What do you mean?"

"He got fired from the Rangers. Did he tell you?"

He snickered. "I know."

"Did he tell you why?"

"He slugged a superior and manhandled a case. So what?"

Her face fell. "He also slept with that superior's wife. Did he tell you that? And showed up drunk to work on more than one occasion."

Mason didn't answer.

She slid off the stool and faced him. "Your boy, Trick, has a thing for the ladies."

"Also old news."

"Except for one lady in particular. Cissy Howard."

Cold crept up Mason's spine, and she grinned. "I thought that'd get your attention. Your good ole' friend dated her before she ever met Chad, and, if you ask me, still has a thing for her. I did some checking on dates and Cissy's not the only one with a lousy alibi. Your pal was fired a week before Chad's death. Then he goes on a bender where he's thrown out of two bars and almost gets arrested before disappearing off the face of the map two days before Chad's death. Then he mysteriously reappears in some crappy hotel in Arizona two days after when he gets the phone call that Chad is dead, and races to California, or maybe I should say back to California, to comfort his old girlfriend, whom he now obsessively defends. The question is why?" She tipped her head. "Is it because he knows she didn't kill Chad since he did, or because they killed him together, and now he's trying to prevent her from taking the fall?" She stepped closer. "And if it's the latter, how long do you think it will be before Cissy points the finger at Trick? Love only goes so far when you're facing life in prison."

Mason stood in disbelief, his mind darting in a thousand different directions. "You don't know what you're talking about. Trick would never☐"

"Wouldn't he?" she asked. "How long's it been since you've seen him, or really, even talked to him? A lot can happen in a few short years."

"That's a big cliff to jump off of, even for Trick."

"People take flying leaps all the time. In your line of work, I'm sure you know that. I suspect there's a few dead people you've spoken with who've done worse? And if he wasn't your partner, I think you'd buy that ticket without thinking twice."

Mason thought back on his history with Trick. Had he missed the signs? "What do you want, Valerie?"

"I want your help. You know him best. If anyone can get him to talk, it's you. At least get his side of the story before he takes you down with him." She pulled a card out of her pocket and tucked it into Mason's shirt pocket. "Then call me, and we'll decide where to go from there. I haven't said anything to Bevins and Winkler. Not yet, anyway. But with a little digging, it won't take them long to learn what I did, and if Cissy talks, well then, it'll be out of my hands."

Mason tried to think. "And if she doesn't talk?"

Valerie shrugged. "I want the truth, like you, Mason. I just thought you should know. You don't strike me as a man who likes surprises." She picked up the small purse she'd laid on the bar and walked to the door. "Call me when you know." And with a sideways glance, she left.

Chapter Seventeen

TRICK ADDED THE GROUND meat to the hot pan, and it began to sizzle. "Red should be here soon. He yelled at me not to be late, so he better not be." He stirred the meat with a spatula. "There's beer in the fridge. Help yourself."

"Thanks." Daniels opened the refrigerator and took out two beers and handed one to Remalla. "Can I get you one?"

"Please," said Trick. "I had one at the bar, but I'm ready for another."

"Bar?" asked Remalla, opening his beer.

Trick put the spatula down. "Yeah. I met a pretty lady today and had a drink with her before coming here." He took a beer from Daniels and opened it.

"We could have rescheduled," said Daniels.

"No way. Red would have shot me." Trick filled them in on meeting Monica Renfro and her connection to Kyle Morrow.

"Did she know anything?" asked Daniels. He sat against the edge of the kitchen table.

"Not really," said Trick. "I get the impression they're friends with benefits, but she didn't act like he was mean to her, or violent, and if he was possessive, it certainly didn't stop her from seeing me."

"Interesting," said Rem. "Maybe she's trying to make him jealous."

"It's possible. Red and I will talk to him tomorrow. Maybe I'll let it drop that I had a couple drinks with Monica, and we'll see how he reacts."

"This case of yours seems to be going in a lot of different directions. You find anything that points to a different killer?" asked Remalla. He drank from his bottle.

"Lydia Stanford and her family are a treasure trove of possibilities, but have we found a smoking gun? No." The meat began to brown, and Trick turned down the heat.

"Well, for Cissy's sake, I hope you figure it out," said Daniels. "Even if she did it. At least you'd know."

"She didn't do it," said Trick, his voice low. He caught the glance between the two detectives and changed the subject. "How long you two been partners?"

Daniels snorted. "Long enough to consider my own mental soundness."

"What are you talking about?" asked Remalla. "Never mind your mental soundness. Your physical soundness would have suffered far worse."

Daniels smiled. "I can't argue with that."

"Not that it doesn't go both ways," said Remalla.

"Can't argue with that either," said Daniels.

"I bet you two have seen it all, and been through it, too." Trick reached for a bag of tortilla chips on the counter and opened it.

The two eyed each other. "We have," said Daniels.

"You could say that," said Remalla, rubbing his chest. His eyes widened. "You got chips and salsa?"

Trick dumped the chips in a bowl and put out the bowl of salsa. "Sure do. Normally I'd make my own salsa but didn't have the time. This brand's a good one though. Help yourself." He put the salsa and chips on the table with some napkins.

"You now know the key to Rem's secrets," said Daniels. "Give him a taco, chips and a beer, and he'll spill his life story, and tell you who killed Kennedy, if he knew." Daniels grabbed a chip and ate it.

"Oswald acted alone," said Remalla, dunking a chip into the salsa.

"What'd I tell you?" Daniels, grabbing a chip.

Trick smiled wistfully. "You two remind me of me and Red when we were partners. We had fun too."

"How long did you two work together before he came out here?" asked Remalla, dunking another chip.

"A little over two years. We were a good team and making a name for ourselves, but I could tell it was taking its toll on Red. His weird abilities were getting in the way. I tried to sway him to stay and push through, and so did his family. They didn't want him to leave either."

"You were close to his family?" asked Daniels.

"Yeah. I remember meeting Mikey. She was a spitfire, and still is. She used to call me Trickster. She used that nickname yesterday, and it brought me back." He chuckled. "She was the one I knew best. Margaret was weird and Max had moved by then, but I'd met him a few times. Mason had a best friend named Victor. I never liked that guy, though. He gave me the creeps."

Remalla stopped in mid-chew.

"Red wouldn't listen to me, though," said Trick, "and Victor and Max, and Red's cousin, Eddie, all convinced Red to move out here. Mikey followed soon after." He stirred the meat again, thinking back. "I'll admit. It didn't sit well with me. I sort of considered Red's family to be mine, too." He added some spices to the meat. "I heard Victor got caught up in some crazy cult and that got him and Eddie killed. Served Victor right, as far as I'm concerned, but it's terrible about Eddie."

Remalla set his beer and uneaten chip down and sat at the table.

Trick looked over. "Did I say something?" He noted Rem's pale face. "Is the salsa bad?"

"No. It's fine. Don't mind me." Remalla patted his stomach. "Sensitive gut. It'll pass." He raised a brow at Daniels, who handed Remalla his beer. Remalla took it and Daniels patted him on the shoulder.

Trick nodded. "Anyway, Red and I didn't really keep in touch the way we should've, and when his mom died, well, he seemed to take it personally. We barely spoke at the funeral, and then he was gone again, back to California. I stayed with the Rangers and got paired up with a new guy. He was good, and it was fine, but it wasn't the same. Then I left the job just before Chad ended up dead, Cissy got arrested, and here I am, suddenly working with Red again." He turned up the heat and mixed in the spices. "Am I rambling? Sorry. I tend to talk a lot. Drives

Red nuts." He checked the time. "Where the hell is he? He should be here by now."

The front door slammed, and Trick stepped back from the stove. "Is that him?"

Mason walked into the kitchen, his face taut and his body rigid.

"Where the hell've you been?" asked Trick. "And you tell me not to be late?"

Mason gripped the counter.

"You okay, Mason?" asked Daniels.

Mason glared at Trick. "What the hell are you hiding?"

Trick put the spatula down. "What are you talking about?"

"I'm talking about Cissy Howard," he said, his voice raising. "Did you know her before Chad? Did you have a relationship with her?"

Trick's heart slammed against his chest. "Oh, shit."

"You're damn right, oh shit," said Mason. "And did you sleep with your sergeant's wife? Go to work drunk? And then get kicked off the Rangers just before Chad wound up dead?"

Trick held his breath, picked up a towel, and wiped his hands. "Who the hell are you talking to?"

Daniels and Remalla eyed each other, looking as if they ought to be somewhere else.

"Is it true?" yelled Mason. "Have you been lying to me this whole time? Did you have something to do with Chad's death?"

Trick almost dropped the towel. "Are you crazy? No. I had nothing to do with that, and you shouldn't have to ask."

"Did you sleep with Cissy?" asked Mason. "Did Chad know?"

Trick tossed the towel on the counter, trying to think of how to explain. "I knew her, yes, before Chad ever did. We dated, but it ended, and then Chad met her. We never told him because we didn't see the point. It was over between us."

"Was it?" asked Mason. "Or were you two still in love? Is that why you are so vociferously defending her? Did you two pick up where you left off?"

Trick stood stunned in the room. The accusations flying at him made it hard for him to know where to start. "Red. I can explain..."

The front door opened and slammed again, and Mikey stormed in. She dropped her purse on the counter. "Carla Belaveena says she saw you and Cissy kissing at Chad's funeral. You care to confirm or deny that before I kick your ass back to Texas?" She narrowed her eyes. "And don't you dare lie."

"What?" yelled Mason.

"Carla who?" asked Trick.

Remalla stood, holding his beer, and walked to the kitchen counter. "Looks like you've got some explaining to do, Trickster."

Mikey put her hands on her hips, waiting for a response from Trick, who stood there looking like he'd rather be standing in his underwear at the North Pole.

"What is going on, Trick?" asked Mason, his voice low and steady, and Mikey gave silent thanks he wasn't mad at her.

Trick shook his head. "Listen, it's not that bad□"

"If it's not that bad, then tell us," said Mikey. "I can't wait to hear it."

Daniels raised his hand. "Umm, we can go if□"

"No. Stay," said Mason. "You can pull me off of him when I wring his neck."

"Works for me," said Remalla.

"Okay. Give me a sec." Trick ran a hand through his hair, closed his eyes, and took a deep breath. "Let me just think."

"By all means, take your time," said Mason.

Trick opened his eyes. "Okay, here it is. Cissy and I did date before she met Chad. I broke it off with her, and six months later, she met and fell for Chad. She didn't know Chad was my stepbrother and when I went to meet Chad's new girlfriend, we both clammed up when we saw each other and didn't say anything. When we finally talked, we agreed to keep it quiet. Chad didn't need to know about what didn't matter anymore."

"But did it matter?" asked Mason.

Trick groaned. "I'll admit, seeing her with Chad kinda made me wish she and I had gone down a different road. I freaked out when we'd started to get serious. You know how I am about commitment, Red. I didn't act on my impulses, but I couldn't help but wonder if Cissy felt the same. Not that it mattered because she ended up marrying Chad, and I let it go, but then I got a call from her when Chad started acting distant, and we talked a few times."

"A few times?" asked Mason. "How much is a few times?"

Trick hesitated, his eyes pensive. "Enough that by the end of the summer, she was using a different phone. She didn't want Chad to know she'd been talking to me."

Mason deflated.

"You stupid idiot," said Mikey. "Where is that phone?"

"Once Chad told Cissy his affair was over, Cissy told me she had to try with him, and we stopped talking. That was about a month before Chad died. I assume she got rid of the phone."

"And what happened when Chad died?" asked Mason, his face stern. "And with the Rangers?"

"I screwed up," said Trick. "I'd stopped talking to Cissy and started drinking too much. Some of the guys got in my face about it, and I got in a few fights. I went to a bar one night, had a one-night-stand, and it turned out to be the Sarge's wife. Then I punched a fellow officer at work and got rough with a suspect. Before I knew it, I was fired." He took a long pull on his beer. "I disappeared for a while." He eyed Red. "Like I did when my grandmother died. Remember? Just got in the car and drove. I'd stop and drink, sleep in the car, then go somewhere else. It was all a blur. Next thing I remember is I'm waking up in some seedy motel, and my phone's ringing. It's Cissy. She's hysterical, telling me Chad's dead, and I try and sober up and head out to California.

"What happened between you two at the funeral?" asked Mikey.

Trick hung his head. "It was stupid. We were stupid."

Mason took a step forward. "Did you sleep with her?"

Trick looked up. "She was upset, and so was I. We snuck out to talk. She told me what happened, and I listened. Next thing I know, I hugged her, and we started to kiss." He paused and closed his eyes. "After the funeral, she came to see me. I told her it was a bad idea. I knew that as the spouse, she was a logical suspect, but one thing led to another, and we...well...we..."

"Rekindled the romance?" asked Remalla.

"You egotistical jackass," said Mason. "You slept with her after Chad's funeral?"

Trick held his head. "It just happened."

"Guess what's going to happen if Bevins and Winkler find out?" asked Remalla.

"I'm surprised they haven't already," said Daniels. "Have you seen Cissy since she made bail?"

Mason grunted and Mikey held her breath.

"God, no," said Trick. "Other than when Red and I talked to her, and...and...I called her."

"You called her?" yelled Mason, his face furrowed. "When?"

"That night when you were at the bar. She got another phone and snuck the number to me when we talked to her□"

"You stupid son-of-a□," said Mason.

"It was just a phone call," said Trick. "That's it."

Mason gritted his teeth, and Mikey worried he might have a stroke. "Do you have any idea what you've done?" asked Mason. "You've jeopardized her entire case, and you lied to me, and to Mikey. If those detectives find Cissy's phone, or learn about you and Cissy, which apparently won't be hard because Carla saw you two together, you're screwed. And Valerie Vain's been following you."

"Valerie Vain?" asked Trick.

"What have you done, Trick?" asked Mikey. Her mind whirled, and she had to consider the obvious, and based on the looks Rem and Daniels were exchanging, she wasn't the only one thinking it. "Did you kill Chad?"

Trick glowered. "You can think whatever you want about me. Yeah, I'm a damn mess, and yes, I'm an idiot, but I did not kill Chad." He met Mason's furious gaze. "I swear it on my grandmother's grave, Red."

Mikey didn't respond and waited to see how Mason wanted to handle this. Rem and Daniels didn't say anything, either.

After a few seconds, Mikey prompted her brother. "Mason, what□"

"Get out," said Mason. "Get out of my house."

Trick's mouth fell open. "Red, you have to believe me. I didn't□"

"I don't know what I believe. You lied to me, and to be honest, I don't know if you're still lying to me."

"Red, you know me," said Trick.

"No, I don't, Trick. Not anymore." Mason stepped aside. "Get out. Now."

Trick's shoulders and face drooped, and he put his beer down. "Fine. If that's what you want, I'll go." He walked past Mason and headed into the front room, and grabbed his keys. "I'll stop by tomorrow to get my things." He opened the door and left.

Mikey stood in silence, along with Mason, Daniels, and Rem. Mason studied the door for a second before leaving the kitchen. "Mason..." She followed him.

He whirled. "I don't want to talk about it, Mikey. As of now, I am off Cissy's case. Call my clients and start booking appointments. I'm back at work tomorrow." He eyed Rem and Daniels. "Sorry about the interruption, fellas. You guys finish the dinner. I'm going to bed." He turned, went to his bedroom, and slammed the door.

Mikey stood in disbelief, staring at Mason's closed door.

Daniels and Remalla stood in the kitchen until Rem put his beer down. "Well, I still want tacos. Guess I'll finish the meat."

Mikey turned and went into the kitchen. "I can't believe this."

Rem grabbed the spatula, adjusted the heat, and stirred. "You want to warm the taco shells?" he asked Daniels.

"Sure. Why not?" Daniels put his beer down and grabbed the box of shells from the counter.

Mikey tried to think.

"You guys sure know how to throw a dinner party," said Rem. "This is better than any I've had at Daniels' place."

Daniels adjusted the oven and searched the kitchen for a pan. "Next time I suspect you of murder, I'll be happy to invite everyone over, then reveal all your secrets before the appetizers. It'll be a blast."

"I mean, what do you two think?" asked Mikey. She sat at the kitchen table. "You think Trick did it? Do you believe him?"

Rem looked over. "Let's just say it's a good thing this isn't our case."

"And that we like you more than Bevins and Winkler," said Daniels. He found a pan and put it on the counter.

"You think Mason should stay on the case?" asked Mikey.

Rem and Daniels made eye contact. "He'll stay on it," said Daniels. He opened the shells and placed them in the pan.

"Yup," said Rem. "He's pissed, but it's his partner. You always help your partner, no matter what."

"Yup," said Daniels. "I'd hold off on making any appointments until Mason cools off." He pointed at the fridge. "You want a beer?"

Watching from her car on the road, Valerie Vain spotted Trick Monroe leaving Redstone's house. Based on his posture and his stomp across the grass, he wasn't a happy man. Trick got in his car, pulled out of the driveway, and, with a squeal of tires, took off. Valerie started up her vehicle, and smiling, followed.

Chapter Eighteen

MASON PULLED UP OUTSIDE Kyle Morrow's apartment, and for the thousandth time that morning, cursed at himself. He'd planned to go straight to the office and figure out where to start his day. He'd postponed too many appointments already, but when he'd gotten in his car, he couldn't help but think of Trick and his friend's stupid situation. Trick had done some ridiculous things in his history with Mason, but this one took the top prize as by far the dumbest, and Red believed if Bevins and Winkler kept digging, that his former partner might end up in prison.

That thought bothered him, and the appearance of Trick's grandmother standing in the kitchen beside Trick while he tried to defend and justify his actions hadn't helped. She'd smiled at Mason, as if knowing Mason would help her grandson, no matter how mad Mason might be. That perhaps had made him the angriest.

Sitting in the parking lot, he picked up his phone and called Mikey, who answered on the first ring. "Mason?"

"Mikey, forget what I said last night." He paused. "Hold off making the appointments."

"Don't worry. I haven't called anyone. You at Morrow's?"

"How'd you know that?"

"Just a hunch." She paused. "You want me to call Cissy? Get her side of the story?"

Mason nodded. "You up for that?"

"You bet. I figure she might confide in me more so than you. We can commiserate over our poor choices in men."

"That's true."

"You didn't have to agree to that so quickly." He heard a rustling of papers. "Have you heard from Trick?"

"No. And I don't expect to."

"What if he went to see Cissy last night?"

Mason laid his head back. "Then God help him. There's only so much I can do if he keeps digging his hole. I'm not a miracle worker."

"Okay. I'll let you know what I find out."

"Meet Cissy for coffee. Don't talk on the phone. Trust that gut of yours to see if she's telling the truth. And one more thing. Check online and see what you can find on Valerie Vain. I need to know what we're dealing with here."

"Good idea on both. And good luck with Morrow."

"Thanks. I'll see you."

"See you."

Mason hung up and got out of his car, still thinking he should forget this whole thing and let Trick find his own way out of this mess. He approached Kyle's door and knocked.

The lock jiggled, and the door opened. A man in his early thirties with razor-cut blonde hair, a muscular build, and wearing sweats studied him. Mason held out his ID. "Kyle Morrow? I'm Mason Redstone, a private investigator looking into the deaths of Lydia Stanford and Chad Howard. Do you have a few minutes to answer a few questions?"

He opened the door wider and frowned. "What? You too? How many of you are there? I just talked to some other guy an hour ago."

Mason squinted. "Tall man, with a stupid grin, and a cowboy hat?"

"That's the one. Can't you two compare notes?"

Mikey hung up and found Cissy Howard's phone number. Dialing, she felt a sliver of worry tingle in her belly when she imagined Trick answering. A woman picked up, though, and Mikey sighed in relief. They talked and Cissy agreed to meet Mikey in a nearby coffee shop.

Thirty minutes later, Mikey sat at a table with her cup when Cissy walked in. Mikey waved and Cissy stopped at the table. "Let me get a coffee."

Mikey nodded and waited until Cissy returned.

"Thanks for meeting me," said Mikey.

Cissy sat across from her. "You said it was urgent." She traced the lid of her drink with a finger. "Your brother is a nice man," said Cissy. "I hope he can help Trick clear my name."

"He's nice, but he has his moments." She leaned in, debating where to begin. "About Trick□"

Cissy spoke softly. "You know, don't you?"

Mikey picked up her coffee. "Yeah. We do."

Cissy pressed her fingers over her mouth. "It was stupid. I know it."

"I'm not here to judge you."

"You should be."

Mikey gave Cissy a second to adjust. "When did you talk to Trick?"

"Last night. He called."

Mikey nodded. "He didn't come by, did he?"

"No. God, no."

"Good."

Cissy stared off. "How'd you find out?"

"Carla saw you two at the funeral."

Cissy closed her eyes and groaned.

"And once those detectives talk to her, they'll know too, which is why we need to get ahead of this." Cissy's eyes shined as they filled with tears. Mikey handed her a napkin. "Hey, you're not the first woman to do something stupid with a man."

She sniffed. "I think this goes way beyond stupid. I thought I was in love with him."

"And now you know you aren't?"

Cissy shook her head. "I was just lonely and liked the attention. He's good at that, you know?"

"He can be a charmer."

"After the funeral, I...I...I don't know what I was thinking. We just had a moment of...of...weakness...or need? It felt good to be wanted." Another tear threatened, and she wiped it away. "It was dumb."

Mikey let her drink some coffee and compose herself. "What did he say last night when you talked to him?"

She dabbed her nose with the napkin. "He broke it off. Told me we couldn't talk or see each other anymore. He'd keep working to prove my innocence, but we couldn't be together. Ever. I didn't argue because I knew he was right. I just never had the courage to say it, but he did." She chuckled softly. "He asked for one thing, though—Chad's cowboy boots."

Mikey frowned. "Doesn't Trick already own a slew of them?"

"Of course, but he gave Chad a pair of brown and white Justins before we left Texas. Chad wore them to the ground. They're beat up, but Trick wants them, I guess for sentimental reasons." She wiped away another tear. "I actually went to look for them this morning. That's where I was when you called. My parents put everything in storage, but I can't find the damn things."

"I'm sure they'll turn up," said Mikey. She thought of her other question. "Cissy, did you have a separate phone to talk to Trick?"

Cissy paled. "I did. But I got rid of it. After I talked to Trick last night, I tossed it in a dumpster."

Mikey wrapped her fingers around her coffee. "You need to tell your attorney everything. He doesn't need any secret affairs coming out at trial. For all we know, those detectives may already be aware of it." She paused. "It's obvious Trick cares for you and is hell bent on proving your innocence. But after learning about you two, Mason and I, we had to question Trick's involvement in all of this..."

Cissy's face tightened. "Trick would have never hurt Chad. I don't care how he felt about me."

"You two talked a lot during the summer. Did you do anything else?"

Cissy squeezed her cup. "No. We did not. I hadn't even seen him since moving until the day before the funeral."

"Do you know where he is now?"

"No. I have no idea. Said he was going to figure this out, no matter what he had to do, and then he hung up."

Mikey held eye contact with Cissy, using her empathic gifts to gauge Cissy's truth telling. Nothing negative sparked, and Mikey sat back. "So, if you didn't kill Chad, and neither did Trick, then who did?"

"I don't know." Cissy held her head. "I just don't know. But whoever it was, they knew exactly what they were doing, didn't they?"

Chapter Nineteen

VALERIE VAIN SAT OUTSIDE in her car, watching the diner. After leaving Red-stone's, she'd followed Trick to a bar. Before entering, though, he'd sat behind his wheel and talked on the phone. Valerie had seen him through her binoculars, and the conversation appeared intense. She suspected he was talking to Cissy Howard. Disappointed that he hadn't gone to see her in person, she pulled out her camera and snapped a few photos. She'd bide her time, knowing he'd eventually crack and meet her.

After the conversation, he'd sat for a while, looking lost, and she'd snapped a few more photos before he'd finally exited and walked into the bar, where he'd remained for several hours. It wasn't until midnight that he'd emerged, crossed the street, and rented a room at a crappy motel.

Val had stayed and half-slept, leaving only to use the bathroom and grab some snacks from a vending machine in the hotel's crappy lobby. She didn't want to miss it if Trick left to go see Cissy, or if Cissy showed to see him, but neither had happened, and Trick hadn't emerged until mid-morning, when he'd left the motel, jumped in his car, and drove off. She'd followed him to an apartment complex, where he'd parked. Valerie parked too, and watched as Trick left his car, approached an apartment, and knocked. A man had answered, and Valerie had snapped a few photos. Trick disappeared inside for about twenty minutes, reemerged, and returned to his car. Valerie followed him back to the motel where Trick parked in the same spot as before, but instead of going back to his room, he'd crossed the street and entered a small diner.

A while later, still sitting and waiting, she wondered what Trick was doing. The lunch crowd, what there was of one, had come and gone and Val had the sinking feeling that he'd left out the back and she'd missed him, although his car remained in the parking lot.

Tapping at the steering wheel as more time passed, her worry got the best of her, and she popped the door open and got out. Checking the traffic, she crossed the street and approached the diner. Glancing inside the windows, she didn't see much, and she walked inside. Spying a lunch counter and a few empty tables and booths, she looked for Trick, but didn't see him.

"Can I help you?" An older woman emerged from the back, her gray bun covered by a hairnet. "Get you something to eat? You can sit wherever."

"I'm looking for a man. Tall, with a cowboy hat?"

"Yeah. He was here," said the woman. She shot out a thumb. "There's a small room in the back. He sat there to eat. I think he left, though."

Val cursed and ran to the back of the restaurant. There were only a few tables and chairs, but they were cleaned and the room was vacant. "Damn it." She kicked at the back of a chair.

"You must be Valerie Vain," said a male voice.

Valerie whirled to see Trick Monroe standing behind her, leaning against the wall, holding his hat and smiling.

The woman with the hairnet peeked out from behind a door to the kitchen. "How'd I do?"

Trick grinned. "Just fine, Miss Charlotte. You're a pro."

The woman blushed. "I'll get you some of that pie you like."

"Thank you, Charlotte. You're a peach too."

Charlotte laughed and went back into the kitchen. Trick straightened and waved his hat. "Have a seat, Miss Vain. Let's talk."

Mason sat on the sofa in his office with a grunt. After the upsetting confrontation with Trick and his restless sleep, his body protested. He took off his hat and dropped it on the cushions, hearing his stomach growl and wishing that he'd at least taken the time for breakfast.

Hearing the outer door open and close, he waited as the inner door opened and Mikey walked in, carrying a bag and two drinks. She dropped her stuff in a chair and held out the bag. "Here. It's lunch."

Mason stared at it. "How'd you☐"

"Because I know you, Mason. You don't eat well when you're stressed."

Mason took the bag. "Thanks." He opened it and pulled out two sandwiches. "How'd your meeting with Cissy go?"

"It was interesting. How'd your meeting with Kyle go?"

Mason opened a sandwich. "It was interesting."

Mikey placed the drinks on the coffee table. "You first." She sat on the sofa beside Mason and grabbed the other sandwich.

Mason took a bite and almost sighed. "Tuna." He chewed. "It's good."

"I like this place. Their sandwiches are almost as good as Mom's."

Mason sighed through a mouthful. "Almost." He took a sip of his drink. It was iced tea. "This isn't, though." He grimaced.

"It's hard to find good iced tea, especially like Mom's, unless you're in Texas."

"True." He took another sip. "I meant to ask how dinner was last night? Did Daniels and Rem stay?"

"They did. I'm surprised you didn't hear us and come out."

"I was done." Mason picked up his sandwich. "Trick took the stuffing out of me, and I crashed."

Mikey picked up her drink. "It's okay. We ate the tacos and had some beer, and I filled them in on what I knew about the case. They're just as flummoxed as we are."

"Great. At least we're in good company."

"I thought so. So, tell me about Kyle. Any red flags?"

Mason pulled a napkin from the bag. "Quite the opposite, actually."

"What do you mean?"

"He dated Lydia for a while. Said they got along fine. He knew she had some issues, but she took her meds, and they did okay. Then, something happened that flipped a switch in her. He met her family. Everything went to hell after that. Her mom drank almost as much as her sister. Her brother was a tool who didn't like Kyle, but he started coming around, asking Lydia for money and Lydia would give it to him. Shay would call and she and Lydia would get into screaming fights. Lydia started going off her meds and then began accusing him of being possessive. Then she started disappearing for a few days, and she'd come back, acting like it was no big deal. One time, he'd gone looking for her, and when she'd returned, out of the blue, she yelled at him for following her. She got furious and started hitting him. He couldn't figure out what was going on. A neighbor heard the commotion and called the cops, and the next thing he knew, Lydia was accusing him of assault, and he'd been hauled off to jail, but was released the next day." Mason wiped his fingers on the napkin. "A few days later, he got served with a restraining order, which amused him because he had no intention of going near her again."

He grabbed another napkin and handed it to Mikey, who took it. "Assuming he's not lying," said Mikey, "then it was Lydia who went off the deep end, not him, and Kyle had no reason to kill her."

"He didn't kill her," said Mason. "I believe him. He hasn't even seen her since their fight. Plus, he's got no record or history of abuse, and Monica definitely likes him too."

"Monica?"

"His neighbor. Cute and smitten with Trick." He picked up a piece of fallen tuna and ate it.

"Of course." Mikey wiped her mouth. "Well, Kyle's version of Shay fits, if you ask me. I talked to Shay yesterday before my enlightening conversation with Carla. Shay is, or was, fed up with Lydia, didn't like Kyle, and has lousy allergies. Doesn't think too highly of her brother or mother, either. She did confirm Lydia was seeing someone, but didn't know it was Chad. She got pissed when she realized I was fishing around for clues about her family and Lydia's death, and she hung up on me. I think she was drinking too, unless she has an affinity for cough syrup."

"That whole family is a shit show." Mason licked mayonnaise off his finger. "What about Cissy? How'd that go?"

Mikey dabbed at a stain on her shirt with her napkin. "Okay, I suppose. Trick called her last night after you threw him out, and he broke up with her, then asked for Chad's boots."

"Huh? His boots?"

"Trick gave him a pair of brown and white Justins a while back. Cissy was looking for them but couldn't find them."

"Justin makes a good boot," said Mason. "I could use a new pair myself."

"Christmas is just around the corner."

Mason squinted. "Justins, not the local discount, big box store."

"Shut up, Mason."

He chuckled. "Trick didn't go see her then?"

"No, thank God. She was upset, though. Felt horrible about the whole thing. I told her to tell her attorney about Trick before the attorney gets blindsided, because it's bound to come out at this point."

"She doesn't know where Trick went?"

"No."

Mason put his sandwich down and sat back. "What's your read on her? Is she a murderer?" He paused. "Did Trick help her kill Chad?"

Mikey finished her bite and swallowed. "My take? She's stupid, and so's Trick, but they're not killers."

"Yeah, I think the same." He put his elbow on the back of the couch. "But if they aren't, then who is?"

"It comes down to Lydia. It's the only thing that makes sense. Somebody killed her, and then went after Chad."

Mason rubbed his jaw. "But why? Did they intend to frame Cissy?"

"Think about it," said Mikey. "Lydia loses it with Kyle and accuses him of abusing her. What if she did the same to Chad? She goes off the meds, then goes off the rails and accuses Chad of mistreating her. Maybe they had a big fight." She tapped her chin. "My money's on Bradley. Could Chad have killed Lydia and then Bradley kills Chad?"

"Either that or Bradley killed them both. Bradley was the executor of her will. If Lydia left him money, that's motive. Maybe Chad suspected, and Bradley did him in because he had to."

"You think it's Bradley too?"

Mason sat up. "Maybe."

"Personally," said Mikey, I'm not buying the 'Chad's a killer' theory. Whether he argued with Lydia or not, he doesn't strike me as the type."

"I tend to agree."

"But how do we prove it?"

Mason reached for his sandwich. "I think it's time to put a little pressure on Bradley Stanford. We've been too nice. If he's hiding a secret, it's time to discover it."

"His prior crimes don't indicate violence, unless you consider the bar fight, but hell, you've had a few of those," said Mikey.

"Not one of my better memories. Some jealous boyfriend slugged Trick, and I jumped in."

"You realize Trick is always the instigator in these stories?"

"You'd think I would have learned by now." Mason shook his head. "I can't plead innocence, though. I've had a few regrettable moments. I've just kept those stories to myself."

Mikey raised an eyebrow. "Trick and I need to talk."

Mason offered her a sideways glance. "Don't believe a word he says."

Mikey smiled. "Back to Bradley. I think he seems a little wimpy, if you ask me."

"If there's one thing I know about criminals, Mikey, is that when it comes to money, anything can change. I say we squeeze a little and see what pops out."

"Eww."

Mason took another bite of his sandwich.

Chapter Twenty

TRICK WALKED TO A table, pulled out a chair, and sat. He tossed his hat onto the tabletop beside him. Resting an ankle on his knee, he pointed at Valerie, who narrowed her eyes at him. "You've been following me."

Her back straight, she crossed her arms, and Trick wondered what she was thinking.

"I'm guessing it's not because of my good looks." He offered her a charming grin. "But if it is, I'll happily give you my number."

Her eyes narrowed further, and he sensed her irritation. He decided to keep pushing.

"Vain?" He tipped his head. "That name's familiar. How do I know it?" He pushed up in his seat. "You wouldn't be related to Alfred Vain, would you?"

Her eyes flared, and she walked closer. "He's my brother."

Trick nodded, beginning to understand. "My condolences."

"He's not dead, you idiot, but not from your lack of trying."

"I know he's not dead, but I still think you deserve some measure of empathy."

"You shot him."

"He pulled his weapon."

"Freddy suffers from mental illness. He's OCD, depressed, and has PTSD."

"His gun didn't have a mental illness."

Her gaze hardened. "If you weren't so damn trigger happy, you could have avoided that confrontation. But you were probably drunk and figured let's just shoot and ask questions later."

Trick recalled his confrontation with Alfred Vain when Trick was still in uniform. Vain had robbed several grocery stores and was cornered in a parking lot, threatening to shoot himself or anyone who came near him. Trick had talked to him for a good thirty minutes, until a loud backfire from a car in the lot had freaked Alfred out, and he'd panicked and raised his weapon. Trick had fired, and Alfred had been hit in the stomach. He'd survived, although whether he'd walk again remained in question. That was the last Trick had heard of him. "You two must be close. Not many people chase down a Texas Ranger to get revenge for a sibling, and then try to prove that Ranger guilty of murder. That's dedication."

"Former Texas Ranger...and if the shoe fits."

He patted his knee. "You obviously know a lot about me. How about you tell me a little about yourself?"

"I don't have to tell you shit about me."

Trick shrugged. "Suit yourself, but you've been chasing me around town. Now you've got me right in front of you. You want to talk, then let's talk." He leaned his chair onto its two back feet and balanced there. "You won't get this opportunity again."

"You want me to sit with you so you can lie to me? Why would I waste my time?"

He set his chair back down. "What are you hoping for? You're obviously smart enough to know about my involvement with Cissy Howard, and you were smart enough to go talk to Mason, knowing he'd be furious and confront me, thus sending me out to hopefully hang my head on Cissy's shoulder, and then you'd get the money shot, right? Of me with Cissy? And once you had that, Bevins and Winkler would have a pretty new photo to add to their collection, and bye-bye Trick." He leaned over. "Am I close?"

If a look could blast lasers, then Valerie's would have cut Trick's heart out. "Well," he said, "I'm still walking around, and you standing there wishing I was dead is pointless. The money shot is history, Val, so what are you going to do? Glare and hope a bolt of lightning strikes me?"

"I can dream, can't I?"

He chuckled. "If I had a dollar for everyone who wanted me dead, well..." he thought about it. "I'd probably have a crisp twenty, maybe thirty dollars, in my wallet. It's not much, but it's more impressive than most."

"You think you're so damn charming, don't you?"

The kitchen door opened, and the woman with the hairnet-covered bun walked out, carrying a slice of pie and a cup of coffee. She set them in front of Trick. "Here you are, sugar. You want anything else?"

"Charlotte, you are a lifesaver. What would I do without you?"

Charlotte blushed. "Oh, honey. You make me feel like a schoolgirl on prom night. What would I do without *you*?"

"I bet you made your handsome date very happy that night."

Charlotte fanned herself. "Honey, you have no idea." She eyed Valerie. "Can I get you somethin', sweetie?"

"Noo"

"She'll take some pie too," said Trick. "She needs it." He added a little cream to his coffee and stirred it. "And throw in some coffee. It's on me."

"Sure thing, sugar." She looked back at Val. "Our Key Lime is the best."

"Damn straight," said Trick, taking a bite.

"Be right back." Charlotte headed toward the kitchen.

"Take your time, Miss Charlotte," said Trick, through a mouthful. "We're not going anywhere." He closed his eyes and sighed. "Man, that's good." He cracked an eye open at Valerie. "Yeah, I admit. I'm a little charming." He winked at her. "But it's in my blood. I once convinced a lovely lady to let me take her husband's seat on an airline when her husband was late. Then I had to charm the flight attendant to let me keep the seat when she realized it wasn't my ticket. It's one of my better stories."

"Not that hard to do when you can flash a badge in their face."

"No badge to speak of. I was at a bachelor party and somehow ended up in the wrong city." Trick sipped his coffee. "Had to find my way back."

She jabbed a hand on her hip, her expression just as fierce as when she'd entered the room.

"How long have you been a P.I., Valerie Vain?" he asked. He perked up an eyebrow. "Assuming you are one, and you didn't lie to my partner." He took another bite of pie and sighed. Watching her, he half expected to see smoke trail from her ears. "C'mon. You know about me. Tell me about you, aside from that brother of yours. I should know something about the woman trying to throw me in prison."

Indecision flickered across her features. She seemed determined not to give in to his magnetism, and he admired her will. Trick pushed out the chair beside him with his foot. "Have a seat. Get comfortable."

She didn't move for a few seconds, but then finally walked up, pulled the chair out and sat, but leaned back and crossed her arms.

"Thank you," he said. "Well?" he asked when she didn't speak. "Don't leave me hanging." He sipped his coffee and took another bite of pie. "Tell me all your secrets."

"You want to know about me?"

"Sure. Why not? Is there something else you'd rather do because I could think of a few things." He grinned, and she smirked.

"Fine." A cleft between her eyebrows deepened. "Freddie and I were raised by our grandmother in Texas. We were taken from our mother after she beat the shit out of Freddie numerous times. Said he reminded her of Dad. My brother grew up in constant counseling, battled with addiction, and has worked very hard to get his life together."

Trick swallowed a bite of pie. "It seems he backtracked."

She glowered. "When I got old enough, I enlisted in the army. I was gone for four years, and when I came back, Alfred was running with the wrong crowd. Causing problems for our grandmother. I got my P.I. license because an army buddy of mine encouraged me to do it. We planned to open up a business together, and to be honest, I saw how cops treated my brother. In their eyes, he was guilty before proven innocent."

"If the shoe fits."

She leaned in and banged on the table. "He was trying to figure it out. The day you shot him is the day our grandmother died. And if you'd bothered to talk him down, you might have learned that." She shoved on his coffee and liquid sloshed over the edge. "And you sit there all smug as shit, trying to evade your own demons, while he sits in a wheelchair, trying to learn how to walk again."

Trick calmly put his fork down. "Forgive me, Valerie, but I've dealt with death and grief myself, and I don't recall robbing any establishments afterward. Maybe Alfred should have bought a bottle of bourbon and joined the rest of us at the bottom of it."

"He's a recovering addict."

"And that justifies him pulling a weapon on an officer?" Trick used his napkin to wipe up the spilled coffee. "Alfred could have killed me or anyone else in that lot. And then what happens to those families? To my family? Should they go rob a bank in their grief?"

"You don't have a family."

Her words struck him. "Careful, Valerie."

They held a sharp gaze until the kitchen door opened again.

"Here you go," said Charlotte, "and some fresh coffee." She held a cup, along with the piece of pie, and a full pot of coffee as only a waitress could. Charlotte placed the pie and cup in front of Valerie and pulled a fork from her pocket and set it on the table, then filled the cup with coffee. "How is it?" she asked Trick, as she added more coffee to his cup.

Trick shook off his annoyance. "You have to ask? My compliments to the chef. It's almost as good as you are sweet, Miss Charlotte." He picked up his fork and stabbed another piece of pie.

Charlotte giggled. "You are a bad boy, Mr. Trick."

He eyed Valerie. "I am at that."

"You two enjoy. Call me if you need anything."

"Will do," said Trick. "Thank you."

Charlotte disappeared behind the door, holding the coffeepot.

Valerie stared at the pie.

"Don't let your anger with me prevent you from eating," said Trick. "You've been sitting in that car all night. I know how stakeouts go. You must be starving." He ate another bite of pie from his fork. "Eat up."

Valerie set her jaw but looked at the pie. Trick kept eating and waited to see what she would do. Several seconds passed, and she finally relented, picking up the fork. "I've never been a fan of Key Lime."

"You will now."

She hesitated, but then took a bite, and then sipped her coffee. He smiled when she took another bite. "How long you been a P.I., Valerie Vain?"

"Three years."

"You like it?"

"It has its moments."

"This one included?"

She chewed. "Don't think just because I'm eating this food and talking to you that you have somehow swayed me to believe you're innocent. My determination to reveal your stripes and prove you guilty of Chad Howard's murder has not waned."

"I would hope not. That would be a lot for one piece of pie to accomplish, even if it is Charlotte's recipe."

She added some sugar to her coffee and stirred. "How long have you known Charlotte? You plan on calling her as a character witness in your defense?"

He almost chuckled. "I've known her..." he checked his watch, "almost two hours."

Valerie coughed and grabbed a napkin. "Two hours?"

"Told you charming is in my blood."

Her eyes wide, she put her napkin down.

Trick grinned. "If you really plan on taking me down with a murder rap, Miss Vain, then you're going to have to work a lot harder." He picked up a piece of fallen crust from his plate and ate it. "Especially when I'm innocent."

"Sure you are," she said with a snort. "And so's Cissy Howard." She laid her fork down. "And her husband just happens to die while you two are having an affair. And now you're trying to point the blame at Chad's lover and her family." She sat back. "You know how it looks, Mr. Monroe."

"Please. Call me Trick. We should at least be on a first name basis, considering."

Valerie barely broke stride. "And you know Bevins and Winkler are going to hear about you and Cissy eventually, so now you're covering your ass. I did my homework. I have a few contacts back home, and I know what happened in Texas. You screwed up, just like you screwed up here." She gripped the corner of the table. "You can play all sweet and nice and try to charm me like you did with Charlotte, but I don't melt like butter, *Trick*. So aim those pretty eyes of yours somewhere else, because I will prove my case, one way or another."

Trick swiped at some crumbs on the table. "You think I have pretty eyes?"

She rolled hers. "Your partner's are prettier, plus he's not so damn smug."

Trick did laugh then. "Mason? Do you like Mason? Well, I'll be sure and tell him. He'll be pleased to know."

"I doubt he'll be talking to you anytime soon."

Trick pushed his plate back. "Don't you worry about us, Valerie. Mason and I have been through more than your poor grandmother. We're partners. We bend, but we don't break."

"We'll see about that."

Trick tipped his head. "What exactly did you learn about me other than I punched a superior and had a few bad days at work?

"A few bad days?" She snorted. "Try a few bad weeks. Not everybody loves you as much as you think. I found someone willing to talk."

Trick could only imagine. "By all means, fill me in."

"You slept with a colleague's wife☐"

"Not really my fault," said Trick with a shrug. "I didn't know who she was, and she came on to me."

"You showed up to work late and drunk."

Trick cringed. "Admittedly, poor judgement on my part."

"You screwed up an investigation, got rough with a suspect, and got him set free."

Trick scratched at the table. "I remember it somewhat differently. The man was a child molester. I may have had a slight hangover that morning, and after he told me what he'd do to my child if I had one, I let him know what I thought. It may have resulted in a broken nose and a couple of cracked ribs."

Valerie went quiet.

"On the plus side, his release may have been somewhat intentional. He was followed and within two days, the cocky son-of-a-bitch had led us to a distributor of online child pornography, so all-in-all, a win-win."

Valerie pursed her lips but didn't give up. "Don't tell me. You punched your superior because he stole some kid's lunch money?"

"Close. I'm not totally faultless. He was an ass, and I was drunk, and he brought Mason into it. Called him a kook, a fraud, and an embarrassment to the Rangers. I let him know otherwise."

Valerie huffed. "Well, aren't you all unicorns and fairies?"

"I'm no angel. I know that. But what's important in any investigation is context. If I can offer you one tidbit of advice, it would be that. Sometimes, sources have their own agendas."

"Let's see if a jury agrees."

He chuckled and couldn't help but think of himself when he was new to law enforcement. "You got yourself a partner, Valerie Vain? Someone you can rely on when the chips are down? Someone you can commiserate with once I find Chad's killer and return to Texas?" He set his elbow on the table. "And please tell me it's not Alfred."

Her confidence slipped a little, and she picked up her fork. "That's none of your business."

"I'll take that as a no."

She poked at the remains of her pie.

"Let me make you a deal, Miss Vain. And if you're smart, you'll take it."

"I can't wait to hear this."

He paused, thinking. "You help me find Chad's killer."

She snickered.

"Once we do, you take your info on me and Cissy and dump it. It's not pertinent, anyway."

Valerie ate more pie. "I didn't realize you were a comedian, too."

"But here's the flip side. We don't find the killer, and you still think I'm guilty, I'll personally go with you to visit Bevins and Winkler and confess my sins." He hooked an arm over the back of his chair. "What do you say?" He waited while she chewed her bite, drank some coffee, and offered him a sideways glance. "It beats the hell out of you sitting in your car, watching me from a distance. More comfortable, too."

She set her coffee down. "You want to work with me?"

"I've always said two heads are better than one. Ask Mason."

"I don't trust you."

Trick scratched his jaw. "Listen, Miss Vain. I don't trust you either. You could just as easily turn on me. Trust is earned, but it can't grow if you don't plant it somewhere." He sat up. "You and me, we want the same thing. To find Chad's killer, right?" He paused. "Or is this just about vengeance for you, and truth be damned?"

She straightened and fidgeted in her seat. "I want the truth."

"Even if it means I didn't do it?"

"And what if you did, and you're just trying to throw me off the scent? And then you disappear, leaving me to look like a fool?"

Trick nodded. "I suppose that's a risk, just like you pulling the plug on me with Bevins and Winkler, but this is where the rubber hits the road, Miss Vain. If you're going to play this game, then you have to know when to trust your gut. No self-respecting pursuer of justice can rely solely on logic. If you do, then get in your car, drive down the road, and go team up with Bev and Wink. But, if you are who I think you are, and you really want to make a name for yourself in this world, then take two, relax, eat more pie, and consider my offer." He relaxed back against his seat. "Life is too short for vengeance, Valerie. You'll just end up with gray hair, a fat belly, and no friends. Ask my Uncle Rufus." He picked up his coffee and took a gulp. "I'm going to get a reheat from Charlotte. If you're here when I get back, I'll know your answer." He winked at her, stood with his cup, and walked into the kitchen.

Chapter
Twenty-One

MASON PULLED UP TO the small, dingy RV at the end of the trailer park and stopped his car. "Is this it?"

"According to the info Rem gave me, it is. This is Bradley's lovely abode." Mikey closed the map on her phone and put it away. "I think he's due for some renovations."

"I'll talk to him about calling his decorator." Mason unbuckled. "You stay here."

Mikey dropped her jaw. "Hell, no. I'm going with you."

"Mikey..."

"Mason, stop being so protective. This guy is more likely to collapse in tears than get in your face. Besides, I've taken a self-defense course."

Mason narrowed his eyes. "You've taken one class."

"And I kicked the shit out of marshmallow man. I told you."

"I don't think you can compare that to Bradley Stanford."

"Yes, I can. Otherwise, what's the point of taking the class?"

Mason gripped the steering wheel. "Mikey, please..."

"Is it because I'm a woman? Do we really need to get into a discussion about sexism in confrontational situations?"

"That's exactly what I'm talking about. If this gets confrontational, I don't want you around."

"So you are sexist?"

"I'm your brother."

"Good for you. Can we go now?" She popped the door open.

Mason grabbed her wrist. "What are you going to do if he gets violent?"

"Would you stop worrying? He's not going to get violent. He's probably drunk, anyway."

"Which makes it worse." He tried to think of how to dissuade her. "You know Remalla would agree with me."

"What does he have to do with this? Just because he may agree doesn't make it right. That Valerie Vain person approached you in the bar. She's a P.I. If she were here, would you be telling her to back off?"

"She's trained to deal with this."

"How do you know? She could turn tail and run at the slightest noise."

"I doubt it." He thought back to Valerie in the bar. "She didn't strike me as the type."

"And I do?"

A flare of pain behind his right eye made him grimace, and he gave in with a sigh. "If he gives the slightest indication that he's dangerous, you get the hell out of there. You understand? I don't care what's happening to me. You got it?"

"If he's hurting you□"

"Mikey, if you don't agree right now, then we're leaving." He put his hand on the keys. "We'll go to the movies instead and watch someone in a cape with superpowers save the world."

She huffed. "Fine. I'll head for the hills at the first sign of trouble."

"Thank you." He pulled the keys from the ignition and opened his door.

Walking to the entry, Mason remained aware. The neighboring RVs were quiet, and he heard the faint sounds of a TV beyond Bradley's door. He knocked. "Stay behind me," he said to Mikey.

"What for?"

Mason heard footsteps, and the door opened. A tall, heavyset man with bags under his eyes, messy black hair, and several days' worth of stubble stood in a worn brown bathrobe. "Can I help you?"

"Bradley Stanford?" asked Mason.

"Who's asking?"

Mason held out his P.I. badge. "I'm Mason Redstone, and this is my associate, Mikey. We're investigating the deaths of Chad Howard and your sister Lydia. Can we ask you a few questions?"

Bradly didn't move for a second, and his face dropped, but he showed no outward signs of distress. He stepped aside. "Come on in."

"Thanks," said Mikey.

They walked into the small RV, seeing the dirty floor, mangled blinds, dishes piled in the sink, and three beer bottles on a table beside a lumpy old couch. The TV was on, and a black and white western was playing. The RV smelled like cigarettes and sweaty shoes. "We appreciate your time," said Mason, putting his ID away. He half expected dead Lydia to make an appearance, but so far, it was just Bradley in the room.

"I talked to you on the phone, didn't I?" Bradley pointed at Mikey.

"You did," said Mikey. "We just had a few other questions to ask."

"You talked to Shay too?" he asked.

Mikey nodded.

"You got her all upset," said Bradley. "She said you're trying to pin this mess on us. Is that true?"

Mason instinctively stepped closer to Mikey. "We're not trying to pin this on anyone. We're just trying to get as much information as we can to find out what happened to Lydia and Chad."

"But they arrested his wife. She's the one you should be talking to."

"And we have," said Mason. "Believe me."

"If she did it," said Mikey. "We'll happily prove it, but if she didn't..."

"Then it has to be one of us, is that right?" His robe slightly parted and his chest hair stuck out.

"If you had nothing to do with it, then there's nothing for you or your family to worry about," said Mason. He debated how much to push. Bradley's size and likely inebriation could make him a potential threat, and Mason wished he'd stuck to his guns and made Mikey wait in the car. But that bus had left the station, and they needed more information.

Bradley yanked on the tie on his robe. "My family ain't nothing to write home about. We have our problems, but we sure as hell didn't kill Lydia." He stomped to the couch and picked up one of the beer bottles from the table.

"You've had your issues with the law, Mr. Stanford?" asked Mikey. "Have you ever been angry enough to hurt someone?"

Mason shot a glare at her, but Mikey ignored him.

"What are you saying?" asked Bradley. "You think I killed her? My sister?"

Mason opened his mouth, but Mikey spoke first. "Lydia was a successful woman. She had a good employer, a decent home, and was seeing somebody. You, on the other hand, can't hold on to a job, or money, for that matter. Were you jealous of your sister?"

Bradley's knuckles turned white from the grip around his bottle. "Jealous? Of Lydia? You think just because she had a job and a man, she was successful? She was just as screwed up as me. Took more pills than me, that's for damn sure. And her men? Kyle was a loser, and then she shacks up with some married guy." He pointed a shaky finger. And that wife of his threatened Lydia. Don't forget that."

"Lydia made you the executor of her will. Why is that? Did she leave you money? Did she have any insurance you benefited from?" Mikey kept firing questions.

Mason stood transfixed, not sure whether to clamp a hand over Mikey's mouth or stand back and admire her. He watched as Bradley's face fell, and he sputtered, trying to find the right words. Mason surveyed the room while Bradley struggled and caught sight of a jacket on a hook beside the door.

"That's a nice jacket, Bradley." He reached over and touched it. "Is that leather?"

"Must be expensive," said Mikey. "Is it new?"

Bradley turned red. "What I buy is none of your damn business. And it isn't mine. It's...a friend's jacket. He let me borrow it."

"Nice friend," said Mason. "What's his name?"

Bradley glared. "Is that what you two came here for? To accuse me of murder?" He chuckled. "You think that jacket is the smoking gun? Well, good luck proving it. I was nowhere near Lydia's the night of her death. She's the one that called me slurring and depressed, telling me her life was worthless, and I called the cops to check on her. I was here the whole time. Shay even stopped by. She can vouch for me. The only time I left was to go to Lydia's place to ID the body." He took another drink. "Which gives us both alibis, you assholes."

Mason considered that. "That's pretty convenient, using your sister as an alibi."

"Call her dammit. She'll tell you," shouted Bradley.

"I will," said Mikey. "She didn't mention anything about it before, though." She pulled out a notebook and pencil and wrote something.

"I can't help that," said Bradley. "But that don't mean shit. She'll tell you."

"You didn't answer us about the money," said Mason. "Did Lydia leave you any?"

He put his beer bottle down and pulled a new one from a mini fridge on the floor. "Hell. She left me some, but not enough to kill her over." He unscrewed the bottle and tossed the lid on the floor. "I'll show you the will if you want."

Mason studied Bradley, noting his posture and body language. "No need."

"What about your mother?" asked Mikey. "None of you seem to get along with her. Could she have done something stupid that got Lydia killed?"

Bradley laughed. "That woman can barely walk straight. If she needs anything, she'll just sleep with someone to get it. She wouldn't bother killing Lydia and risk prison just because they had a fight. Shit. If that were true, Lydia would have been dead a long time ago. Shay and me too." He drank from his fresh beer.

Mason nodded. "That leaves one other person to consider, and that's Shay."

Bradley choked on his drink, and beer ran down his face.

"But if that's true," said Mikey, "then Bradley's alibi goes right out the window. Huh." She held her jaw. "That could be a problem."

Bradley swiped at his wet robe and dabbed his face with his sleeve. "Shay didn't kill anyone. She and Lydia were close. Hell, Shay rarely leaves the damn house. Lives out in the country and even I rarely see her."

"They were close? Not according to your mother," said Mikey. She swiped at the pages in her notebook. "According to her, Shay and Lydia fought a lot. Shay likes to drink, and Lydia pops pills. Sounds like a dangerous combination."

He shot out a hand. "Is that all you got? If that warrants murder, then a lot of siblings wouldn't make it past their high school graduation." Grinning, he raised his beer. "Better have more than that if you plan to go to the cops." He sneered. "I don't deny I'm stupid, but the cops ruled Lydia's death accidental. If you plan to stir that pot, you'll just be pointing the finger at that Chad person's wife. If anyone killed Lydia, it's her."

Mason couldn't argue with that, but something about Bradley made his gut twitch. "You have a point." He walked to a window and looked out, seeing a lonely tire laying in the grass. "Maybe Lydia was an accident, but Chad wasn't. Somebody shot him." He looked back. "Do you know how to use a gun, Bradley?"

Bradley's forehead furrowed. "Now you think I killed Chad? Why would I do that?"

"He was married. Slept with your sister. Maybe lied to her. What if Lydia committed suicide over the loss? Or what if her death wasn't accidental and Chad's wife did kill her in a fit of rage? What if you knew that, and went to Chad's to confront him or his wife, and you ended up shooting him instead?" He knew the theory was farfetched, but he wouldn't put anything past this family. "Then you stood back and let his wife take the fall."

"Interesting theory," said Mikey.

Bradley hooted. "You two should be writers, because you can sure tell a helluva story."

Mason eyed the jacket, the beers, and the robe, and stepped closer. "I can tell you're amused, Bradley, and that's fine..." Bradley lowered his beer, and Mason met his gaze. "But despite the lovely aroma of this fine establishment, something doesn't smell right about you." He raised a brow. "And I intend to find out why."

"Me too," said Mikey.

Bradley held his gaze. "I think it's time you left, Mr. Redstone." He pointed. "And take your annoying associate with you."

Mikey closed her notebook and put it and the pencil away. "Just because we leave doesn't mean we're done."

Bradley stepped back from Mason. "You two are chasing windmills," said Bradley. "You go right ahead and waste your time, but you keep harassing me and my family, and I'll happily call the cops and complain." He sat on the couch. "Now, if you don't mind, *Bonanza*'s coming on, and I'd like to watch."

He stared, waiting, and Mason returned to the door. "We'll be in touch, Bradley."

Bradley drank some more beer. "I'll call the party planners. Get some balloons for your next visit."

Mason opened the door. "C'mon, Mikey." She walked out, and he followed.

Chapter Twenty-Two

VALERIE SAT IN HER car, parked along a curb down from the small house encircled by a white porch. A wooden swing hanging outside the front picture window gently rocked in the breeze. "You think Lydia's mother knows something?"

Trick held Valerie's binoculars and looked toward the house. "Despite your belief to the contrary, Cissy and I did not kill Chad. Which leads us to Lydia, Chad's mistress, who drowned in a pool two weeks before Chad."

"And you're convinced her death is connected to Chad's?"

"I am."

"And Cissy didn't do it?"

"No."

Valerie chuckled. "You really are something, aren't you? The lengths you'll go to convince me you and Cissy are innocent. Let me ask you something. How long do we play this game before I take you in?"

He put the binoculars down. "We play it until we know."

"But I do know."

He resumed watching. "You have much to learn, Miss Vain. Anger and revenge have no business in a murder investigation. You want to find a killer? Keep your emotions out of it."

"You're a regular Ranger Yoda, aren't you?" She eyed the house. "You're trying to tell me you're keeping your emotions out of this?"

The side of his mouth quirked up. "Touché, Miss Vain. But if I thought Cissy had killed someone, I'd reluctantly bring her in and fight like hell to defend her." He lowered the binoculars. "Like you with your brother."

Valerie frowned.

"You and I have more in common than you think," said Trick. He grinned. "Doesn't that just piss you off?"

"I want to shoot you just thinking about it."

"Get in line, Miss Vain. Get in line." He returned to watching the house.

"Why are we surveilling the home? Why don't we just go talk to her?"

"Patience, Valerie. Sometimes it doesn't hurt to get the lay of the land before we approach."

She ran her thumb over the steering wheel. "What makes you so convinced she knows something? What if Lydia really did get drunk, hit her head, and fall in the pool? It sounds like she was messed up enough."

"If Lydia died in an accident," he thought of Detective Bevins, "I'll eat my hat."

"Remind me to buy you some Pepto Bismol."

"Give it to Detective Bevins. He's going to need it." He continued watching the house. "But I do like your spirit, Valerie. Keeps me on my toes." He pointed. "There's a car in the driveway."

"Wow. You are good at this. Let's call Bevins and Winkler and let them know."

"It's not her car, or her husband's."

"How do you know?"

"Because Mason's not the only one with connections. I still have a few friends on the force. Much to your dismay."

She scoffed. "That car could belong to a friend, or a repairman, or her damned psychic."

"Or...perhaps someone else."

Valerie squinted to see movement on the porch. A woman stood at the front door with a man. Based on their nearness, and their body language, he was more than a friend. "Let me see."

Trick handed her the binoculars, and she eyed the couple standing outside the door. "That's not her husband?"

The woman smiled, and the man pulled her close.

"No. It is not."

Valerie saw the woman's hand on the man's butt, and the couple kissed.

"I think Lydia's mom has a secret," said Trick.

"What secret? She's basically kissing this guy in her front yard."

Trick shrugged. "If she's been drinking, I suspect she doesn't care. And the neighbors may be used to it. Question is, is the husband?"

Valerie lowered the binoculars. "How in the world does this help us...I mean, help you? Who cares if she's cheating on her husband?"

"All information has value. She has some, and now so do we."

"What information does she have?"

"Family, Miss Vain. If anyone knows their kids, it's a mom." He pointed. "And if her kids are somehow involved in Lydia or Chad's death, then she knows something. Maybe not everything, but something."

Valerie handed him the binoculars. "I take it back. You're not Ranger Yoda. More like Ranger Scooby-Doo."

His grin flashed again. "Learn from me, Miss Vain. You might be surprised what you find out." He took the binoculars.

"Just don't give me anything I need to take a pill for."

"That, my dear, is entirely up to you."

The man left the porch, went to his car, and drove off as the woman watched and then returned inside.

Trick gestured toward the house. "How about we go pay a visit to the lovely Mrs. Stanford, or whatever her name is now?"

Valerie debated, her mind warring with her, but she started the car, and drove down the street.

Mason sat at the small table and handed Mikey her cone with a scoop of chocolate chip. He set his cup down and grabbed a napkin.

"Don't tell me," said Mikey, eyeing his ice cream. "Vanilla. You really should branch out more."

"I like vanilla. It was mom's favorite, too."

"True, but she lathered hot fudge all over it, added whipped cream and a cherry. It's called a sundae."

Thinking back, he laughed. "I remember when she bought a shake and spilled it down the console of Max's new car. She and I furiously tried to clean it up, and she swore me to secrecy for life."

Mikey laughed too. "Max knew. He found the cherry under the front seat."

Mason smiled and took a bite. "I miss her."

"Me too," said Mikey, licking her ice cream. "She'd have been all over this case. She liked Trick, and he was smitten with her."

"I know. He took it hard when we lost her."

"He did," said Mikey. "I remember seeing him at the funeral. He looked as lost as you did."

Mason scooped up some ice cream and recalled the heaviness of that day. "I should have been a better friend."

Mikey lowered her cone. "What are you talking about? You were always good to Trick. And you were a grieving son. Cut yourself some slack."

"It's not just the funeral. He was my partner. And when the time came, I sided with Victor." He sighed. "And we both know how that turned out."

Mikey grimaced. "Don't remind me."

Mason thought back. "Maybe I should have stayed in Texas. It would have saved us both a lot of trouble."

"Mason, you did what you felt was right at the time. You can't second guess yourself now, nor blame yourself for Victor's actions and what stemmed from them. And as much as we may both hate to admit it, it's because of him you're following your gut and doing what you love. But that comes with a price. As much as you may want to, you can't make everyone happy. You were given a gift, and you had to follow where it led. Trick's a big boy. His happiness can't be based on your choices. Besides, he found his way here, so it seems life managed to get you two back together."

"Couldn't it have found a less challenging path?" He licked his spoon. "Maybe a football game or a party?"

"You hate those things." Mikey licked a drip of ice cream that was about to fall from the cone. "And when it comes to you and Trick, nothing less than a murder case will do."

"I'm guessing you don't mind it either."

Mikey dabbed her mouth with a napkin and leaned in. "Can I admit something?"

"Since when have I stopped you from doing anything?"

She grinned. "That interview with Bradley was the most exhilarating thing I've ever done." She curled her fingers into a fist. "I wanted to get in there, break down his will, and get him to confess." Her eyes widened. "I was stoked."

Mason raised his hand. "Okay, there, policewoman. Hold your horses. I'll admit. You did a great job, but let's not go too crazy. These things take time and patience."

"Are you kidding? I'm ready to speak to Shay, and then that mother of theirs. I bet I could get her to talk in no time." She slurped at a chocolate chip.

Mason scraped some ice cream from the side of his cup. "How about we talk about Bradley first? What'd you think of his answers?"

Her eyes narrowed. "Oh, please. He knows something. He got all touchy when we asked about money. And that jacket? It was his."

"No question. If Lydia did leave him some money, then that would explain the fancy jacket. But considering his living arrangements, he hasn't made major changes to his lifestyle. What did you think about his alibi?"

"Lying."

"I got that impression, too."

"Now we talk to Shay?"

He sat back. "Probably, but the likelihood that she backs up her brother is high, and then where does that leave us?"

"She might hang him out to dry. They don't seem too close."

"You never know with something like this. I've seen families that hate each other close ranks, and defend their loved ones to the death. They can kill one another, but God help anyone else who tries to."

"What then?"

Mason thought about it and wondered what Trick would do. "I say we go to the source. Let's talk to the mother."

"Michelle? You think she'd speak to us?"

"Depends. But there's only one way to find out." He scooped out some more ice cream.

"If you think so." Mikey took a bite of her cone with a crunch, and Mason's cell phone rang.

He eyed the display. "Oh, boy. It's Serita Avery."

Mikey leaned to look. "Your client? I talked to her. I scheduled you for next week."

Mason sighed and debated whether to answer, but realized he also had a duty to his paranormal work and clients that couldn't be ignored. "I should talk to her."

"You want me to answer?" asked Mikey.

Mason shook his head and answered. "Serita?"

Several minutes later, and the remains of his ice cream melted, Mason hung up. "I need to go over there. She's in crisis. Keeps thinking she's seeing a dead man staring at her in the mirror."

"But I thought you talked to her about it, and she'd made peace with it. At least that's what she'd told me."

"Well, apparently, whoever's haunting her in the mirror hasn't found the same peace. I told her I'd swing by and take a look."

Mikey finished her cone and sipped from a water glass. "But what about Michelle? Aren't we going to talk to her?"

Mason nodded. "If there's time when I get back, then we'll go. Hopefully, Miss Avery won't take too long. You go back to the office and wait for my call." He paused. "And do not, under any circumstances, go out on your own. You got that?"

Mikey's shoulders fell. "You are no fun."

"Promise me."

Mikey hesitated. "Fine. I promise."

"Okay." He sat back and rubbed his chin, thinking.

"What's that look? Something bugging you?"

Mason recalled the previous night. "Listen. I need you to do me a favor while I'm gone."

"What's that?"

Mason searched his gut for an answer, and his gut confirmed it. "Call Trick for me."

"Call Trick?" Mikey tossed her napkin and Mason's cup in a trashcan beside the table. "After last night? Don't you want to call him?"

"I would, but I don't need to get in an inane argument right before I see a client. I need to keep a clear head to deal with Serita's mirror man. Just tell him to stop by this evening, and we'll go from there. We need to talk."

"If that's what you want."

"Thanks. I appreciate it." He stood. "You want me to drop you off at the office?"

Mikey relaxed back in her chair and pulled out her phone. "No. I'll find my way back. You head out to Serita's. I'll call Trick and maybe get another ice cream cone."

"Another?"

"What? I'm hungry."

Mason shrugged. "Suit yourself. I'll call you when I'm done."

Mikey held up her cell. "What if I call Shay? See if I can get her to fold like a napkin?"

Mason pointed. "Mikey□"

"Okay. Okay. Just thought I'd ask."

"You behave, and maybe when I get back, I'll let you kick down Michelle's door."

Mikey sat up. "Seriously?"

"Of course not."

Mikey made a face at him, and Mason headed out.

Chapter
Twenty-Three

REM SAT AT HIS desk with a pencil in his mouth and typed. Across from him, Daniels shuffled through some papers and cursed.

Rem removed the pencil. "What are you looking for?"

"That receipt for our lunch the other day when we interviewed that guy who thought he saw a body in the river."

"Oh, yeah. That place served a good hot dog." He stopped typing. "Did you take it out of your wallet?"

"Yes. It was right here. I just had it." He checked the papers again.

"You sure? Maybe it's still in your wallet."

Daniels slumped. "I think I'd know if I took it out of my wallet or not."

"Maybe. Maybe not. Did you check your desk drawer?"

Daniels offered him an exasperated look. "Yes."

"The floor? Did it fall off?"

Daniels leaned over and looked. "It's not there." He sat up. "Did you take it?"

"Yes," said Rem. "I'm hiding it. I secretly hide receipts to drive you nuts. Having fun yet?"

Daniels did another check of the pile. "Maybe you're embarrassed because you ate three hot dogs that day, and they'll probably only approve two."

"I was starving. Besides, that guy wouldn't stop talking. I needed a distraction."

"No. You just wanted me to talk to him. Not you."

"You take better notes than me."

"What notes? His floating woman was a mannequin that had fallen into the water after some photo shoot up river."

"Good thing we saw the photographer desperately trying to save it. He almost fell in himself." He patted his stomach. "Those three hot dogs helped save a life."

Daniels rolled his eyes. "You pulled a plastic woman out of the water, lectured the photographer on not polluting, and then told him where he could get a new pair of shoes on sale since the ones he wore were drenched."

"That new discount store has some great deals. You should check it out."

"Yeah, well. When I'm looking for fake designer shoes, it'll be my first stop."

Rem threw out a leg. "Check it out. I got these last month for thirty bucks." He bounced a sneakered foot.

"There's already a hole in the toe."

"That's why I bought three pairs."

Daniels narrowed his eyes and stared at Rem.

The squad door opened, and Rem looked to see Bevins and Winkler walk in. He put his foot down and returned to typing. "I think we have some company."

Daniels swiveled as Bevins and Winkler approached their desks.

"Remalla. Daniels," said Winkler.

"Winkler," said Daniels. "Bevins. How are you two today?"

"Going through receipts?" asked Bevins, eyeing Daniels' desk. "Pain in the ass, isn't it?"

"You should take a picture, then toss the receipt," said Winkler. "Works better than the paper system."

Daniels straightened a pile. "Thanks for the tip. I'll keep it in mind."

Rem paused his typing. "You guys need something, or is this a social visit?"

Winkler made eye contact with Bevins. "We're looking for Mason Redstone and his partner, Trick Monroe. You two know where we might find them?" asked Winkler.

Rem poked at his watch. "I suppose I could check my Redstone locater. I told him to wear it at all times."

"He did take it off that one time, though," said Daniels, leaning back.

"Darn it, that's right," said Rem. He shrugged. "You may be out of luck."

Bevins raised the side of his lip. "Funny."

"Have you tried calling?" asked Daniels.

"We'd rather talk in person," said Winkler.

Rem didn't like the looks on their faces. "Any reason why?"

Winkler looked between Rem and Daniels. "We just came from talking to a co-worker of Cissy Howard's. Claims she saw Trick Monroe and Cissy making out after Chad's funeral."

Bevins hitched up his pants. "Doesn't sound like a grieving widow to me." He smiled. "Nor a grieving friend."

Daniels sat forward and eyed Rem across the desk.

"We'd love to hear Mr. Monroe's explanation for this little tryst, but we need to find him," said Winkler. "We went to Redstone's place of business and his home, but no luck."

"You talk to Cissy yet?" asked Daniels.

"We're going to this afternoon," said Bevins. "I can't wait to hear what she has to say." He chuckled. "That hole we're digging for her just got a little deeper. But now, maybe she won't be in it alone."

"We have a patrol watching Cissy's place in case Trick shows." Winkler leaned over and rested a hand on the edge of Daniels' desk. "Something tells me Monroe will find a way to weasel out of this, so the sooner we can find him, the better. You two know Redstone, and Redstone can lead us to Monroe, so if you know something, say something."

Rem recalled their dinner at Mason's. "I have no idea where either of them is."

"Me either," said Daniels. "We haven't talked to them today, but if we hear from them, we'll contact you."

Winkler nodded her head. "Good. Thanks." She straightened. "Maybe you could arrange a meeting with Redstone and Monroe, and we can join you. It can be a pleasant surprise."

"I love surprises," said Bevins.

Rem took a breath. "We'll see what we can do."

"While you're at it," said Winkler. "Think about who may have been impersonating me."

"Impersonating you?" asked Daniels, raising a brow.

"Carla," said Winkler, "Cissy's co-worker, said she'd already talked to me yesterday, and that I'd agreed to take care of an unpaid parking ticket."

Bevins cleared his throat. "Our impersonator is petite, with light brown hair and pink highlights, wearing all black, and has a nose piercing. She should be easy to find." He paused. "Ring any bells?"

Rem slapped a flat look on his face. "No clue."

Daniels scratched his jaw. "A piercing, huh?"

"Can you believe that?" asked Bevins. "Carla told this imposter the same info about Monroe and Cissy. Since Redstone's investigating Chad's murder, we think this woman must work for Redstone. Which means we need to find Monroe fast, before he disappears on us."

"And we don't need to tell you that if Redstone is helping his friend evade a murder, then that makes him an accessory," said Winkler.

"Let's not jump the gun," said Rem. "Maybe you should talk first and assume later. Making out with someone, even though the timing's lousy, doesn't make them a killer."

Winkler frowned, and Bevins smirked. "You're friends with Redstone," said Bevins. "You trying to protect him and his cocky partner?"

Rem sat up. "Cocky or not, he and Redstone still deserve a fair shake." He paused. "And not a rush to judgement."

"Our judgement is based on the facts, and they're adding up fast," said Bevins. "And if you weren't friends with this guy, you'd be all over his ass for this."

"Maybe, but I'd be checking all the facts, not just the ones I like," said Rem.

Bevins curled his lip. "Sounds like you're a friend first and a detective second. Maybe you need to question your own judgement before they embarrass you when we arrest them."

Winkler took Bevins' arm. "Take it easy, Bevins."

Rem held Bevins' look. "The only judgement I'm questioning is yours. Just because somebody says 'boo' doesn't make them a ghost."

"Ghost, huh?" asked Bevins. "Sounds fitting, coming from you. Redstone's a kook. Maybe you are too?" He grinned. "'Cause I've heard a few things."

Daniels stood. "I think you've said enough, Bevins." He faced Winkler, his face stony. "You need anything else? Because if not, I think we're done here."

Winkler tugged on Bevins. "Come on, partner," she said. "Relax. We're all on the same side, right?"

Bevins and Rem glared until Bevins finally looked away. "Yeah," said Bevins. "Sure we are."

"You two have a nice day," said Daniels, his expression unchanged.

"You let us know if you hear from Redstone," said Winkler, guiding Bevins out of the squad room.

"You'll be the first," said Rem, holding his stare.

Bevins glanced back before he and Winkler walked out.

Daniels sat. "Anybody ever tell you that you have a horrible bedside manner?"

"Lots of people," said Rem, picking up his phone.

Daniels nodded. "Makes sense."

Rem pulled up Mikey's number. "I don't like that guy."

"Really? I thought you two were hitting it off," said Daniels. He sighed. "Let me guess. You calling Mikey, our imposter?"

"Damn straight. I'm going to kill her." He punched the button and listened. "Do me a favor. Pull out a five."

"A five? What for?"

"Humor me."

Daniels hesitated, then shrugged, and pulled out his wallet. He shuffled through some bills. "Don't tell me. You want a milkshake from the□" His face dropped, and he pulled out a small piece of white paper. "It's the receipt."

"Told you," said Rem.

Trick surveyed the house as Valerie pulled up into the driveway. He opened the door, but stopped when his cell rang. Grabbing it, he hesitated when he saw it was Mikey. "I need to take this."

Valerie waited while he walked to the end of the driveway and answered. "Mikey?"

"Hey, Trick."

"Don't tell me. Mason is pissed I haven't picked up my stuff."

"On the contrary. He wants to talk to you."

Trick watched Valerie as she stood with her arms crossed and leaned against the car. "Then why didn't he call me instead of you?"

"Because he's on his way to Serita Avery's."

"Serita who?"

"A client with a ghost in her house. He asked me to call and see if you can come by tonight to talk."

Trick rubbed his forehead. "Uh, yeah. Of course." He paused. "Is he still pissed? Is he going to have the authorities waiting for me when I get there?"

"Guess you're going to have swing by to find out."

"Lucky me."

"Would you rather face them, or Mason's wrath?"

"I'll have to think about that one." Valerie pointed at her watch. "Listen. I'm about to talk to Lydia's mom. I'll call when I'm on my way to Mason's."

"Michelle? We're planning on talking to her when Mason gets back."

"Well, hold off for now."

"We spoke with Bradley this afternoon. He definitely has a vibe we don't like."

"Then I'll hold off on him. We'll compare notes this evening unless I'm hauled off in handcuffs."

"We won't call the cops until we talk about the case. Then they can haul you off."

"I'd appreciate that."

"See you later."

"See you." He hung up and put his cell in his pocket. "You ready?" he asked Valerie, and started walking up the driveway.

She followed. "You're the one taking calls and making me wait."

"Sorry about that. Some calls need to be answered."

They stepped up to the porch, and Trick knocked on Michelle's door.

Mikey hung up with Trick and walked to the counter. She ordered a scoop of chocolate in a cup, and went back to the table and sat, still thinking about the case. Mason would be gone for at least an hour, and she debated what she could do during that time, but Mason had basically forbidden her from completing anything useful. Since Trick was talking to Michelle, that was no longer on the table, so she and Mason would have to discuss what to do next, which would likely be talking to Shay. Mikey hoped Trick could get some solid information from Michelle and looked forward to their evening when maybe, between the three of them, they might discover some plot within the Stanford family.

She took a bite of her ice cream and almost called Rem. They were supposed to go to the movies that weekend, but she figured he'd be busy, and didn't want to bug him at work. He wouldn't be pleased when he learned about her helping Mason interrogate Bradley. Sighing, she took another bite, thinking she might keep that to herself, but then changed her mind, relishing again in the memory of Bradley's questioning. These protective men in her life would just have to get over it. Her next self-defense class was in two days, and she looked forward to confronting the marshmallow man again.

Her cell rang and, seeing Rem's number, she chuckled and answered. "Hey. What's up?"

"You want to tell me why you're pretending to be Detective Winkler?"

Mikey froze and thought of Carla. "Umm, well...I um..." She tried to think.

"Please tell me you aren't going to respond to Winkler like that."

"I can explain."

"What the hell were you thinking? Did you agree to take care of a parking ticket?"

Mikey closed her eyes. "It's not as bad as it sounds. Carla assumed I was Detective Winkler□"

"Did you clarify you weren't? You realize impersonating a police officer could land you in jail for a year, plus a generous fine to go with it. Winkler asked us about it."

"She did? Winkler talked to Carla? Did Carla tell her about Cissy and Trick?"

"She did. They're looking for Mason and Trick as we speak. It's not good. And if they see you, they're going to know you're the one who pretended to be Winkler. The piercing and pink highlights are hard to miss."

Mikey groaned. "Hell."

"Hell is right. Do you know where Mason and Trick are? Because Trick's about to face his demons, and if he's not careful, he could take Mason down with him, and you'll be right behind them."

"They're both busy, but I can contact them."

"Good. They need to be prepared."

Mikey's cell rang again, and she checked her phone. Recognizing the number, her heart raced. It was Shay. She spoke to Rem. "I'll tell them. Listen, I have to go. I've got a call I have to take."

"Mikey, we need to talk about Winkler□"

"We will. Soon. I'll call you back later." She hung up on him, quickly pulled out her notebook and pencil, and with a shaky finger, answered Shay's call. "Hello?"

"What did you say to Bradley?" Shay's snuffy voice crackled over the line. "He is upset. Said you came to his place and accused him of killing Lydia? Is that true?"

Trying to shift from Rem's call, Mikey nibbled her lip and wondered what Mason would say in this situation. "We just asked him a few questions."

"Questions? You did a lot more than that. He's trying to get his shit together, and the last thing he needs is for you two assholes making him think he's going to prison. He's had enough jail time as it is."

Mikey didn't think for a second that Bradley was trying to get his shit together, but was rather trying to keep his shit secret. "Shay, listen. There is more to this story about Lydia and her death. I think you know that, and I think you know Bradley has some culpability. It's not adding up."

Shay sneezed loudly into the phone, and Mikey held the phone out. "Sorry." Shay sniffed. "I think you guys are grasping at straws. Bradley has his moments, but he's a good guy at heart."

"Did you know you're his alibi for the time of Lydia's death? He said you stopped by his place the night she died." Mikey hoped she wasn't revealing too much, but she wanted to note Shay's reaction. There was a brief silence. "Is that true?"

Shay sniffed again. "I think this whole damn thing is a mess. Lydia was an accident. Why can't you people leave it alone?"

Mikey leaned over the table, trying to think. "But what if it wasn't, Shay? What if it comes out that Lydia didn't accidentally fall into the pool? If you don't come clean, then someone will take the fall, and we want to be sure it's the right person."

"Nobody's taking any falls. If anyone killed Lydia, it would be Chad's wife. She's the most likely suspect. Stop trying to make our family look guilty. We didn't do anything. If you keep harassing us, we'll be forced to call the police."

Mikey squeezed her temples. Shay was right. No matter what they did, they still didn't have anything directly tying the family to Lydia's death, and Cissy would remain the main suspect. She took a breath, deciding to take the risk, and pushed a little harder. "Cissy might be the main suspect, but the cops will do some digging. They'll have to. Any good defense attorney is going to look for other possible suspects. Your family has issues, and I suspect Lydia may have done a few things to make you all angry. We talked to Kyle. According to him, Lydia went off the deep end, and accused him of crazy things he never did. Did she ever do the same to you, or Bradley? Could she have done anything that might give you or Bradley a motive? Because if she did, it could put you both in a difficult position, and with Bradley using you as an alibi, it makes it look like you're both working together."

"That's ridiculous." Shay said, but without the fervor she had at the beginning of the call. "This whole thing is stupid." She sighed deeply and blew her nose. "Bradley and I...I mean...we just..."

Mikey held her breath. "Just what?"

"I...I'm so confused. I don't know what to do."

"Shay, is there something you're worried about?"

Shay hesitated. "There was this one thing, but it was so long ago..."

Mikey swallowed. "What was it?"

There was a pause. "Nothing. It was nothing." Shay almost whispered.

"Obviously it was something." Mikey gripped her pencil, and prayed Shay would answer.

"It's very personal." Shay groaned softly. "I'm not comfortable talking about it over the phone."

Mikey straightened. "It's okay. I can meet you."

"No. Never mind. It's not important. Forget I said anything. I should go."

Mikey scrambled not to lose her. "Tell me where you'd feel comfortable. I can come now. I promise if you want to get something off your chest, now's the time to do it. Carrying something like this around takes its toll. Believe me, I know." Mikey waited for what seemed like hours for Shay to answer.

"Okay," said Shay, sighing softly. "Let me give you an address."

Chapter
Twenty-Four

TRICK KNOCKED AGAIN.

"What if she doesn't answer?" asked Valerie.

"She'll answer."

Valerie smirked. "How can you be so sure?"

"Because right now, she's looking through the peephole and seeing my handsome face. She'll be too curious to stop herself."

"You really are a piece of□"

The door opened, and Trick smiled at the woman who stood there, wearing the robe he'd seen her in earlier. She smiled back, and her eyes traveled over him, then her smile faded when she spotted Valerie. "How can I help you?"

"Michelle Stanford?" asked Valerie.

"Who's asking?"

Valerie held out her identification. "I'm private investigator Valerie Vain, and this attractive fellow is my..." she cleared her throat, "...assistant, Trick Monroe." Trick raised a brow at her, but Valerie barely offered him a glance. "You mind if we ask you a few questions about your daughter, Lydia?"

"Lydia?" asked Michelle. "She died."

"Yes, we know," said Trick. "Our condolences."

Her gaze met his. "Thank you."

"But we have some questions about her death," said Trick. "We also understand she may have had a relationship with a man named Chad Howard, who was murdered."

Michelle held her chest. "I was about to get in the shower."

"I promise, ma'am." He took off his hat and aimed a tender look at her. "We won't take much of your time."

"I already talked to someone on the phone about this. Was it you?" She looked at Valerie.

"No, ma'am. It wasn't me. But we do have additional questions, if that's okay?" asked Valerie.

"Well, all right. I guess so. Come in." She stood back and opened the door wider.

Trick stepped inside, and Valerie followed. "We appreciate it, ma'am," said Trick.

"Call me Michelle." She shut the door behind them.

Trick surveyed the austere room with muted colors. A blue sofa sat against a paneled wall with a glass coffee table in front of it and a piled gray carpet beneath it. The linoleum floor kitchen with yellow cabinets and a small four-person breakfast table was to his right, and a small bar with two shelves of liquor and a few highball glasses stood against the wall in front of him. Trick spotted a glass half-filled with amber liquid on an end table beside the couch. He put his hat on the coffee table and ruffled his hair. "And you can call me Trick."

Michelle straightened her robe and ran a hand through her own brown hair, which was pulled back, but slightly out of place, as if she'd hastily thrown it into a ponytail.

Valerie stood off to the side and surveyed the room, her gaze settling on the glass on the end table.

"What can I do for you, Trick?" asked Michelle. She ignored Valerie.

"I'll get straight to the point, ma'am...I mean Michelle. We're wondering if Lydia's death wasn't an accident, and that whoever may have killed her, killed Chad too."

She stared for a second, but then sighed. "That wouldn't surprise me in the least." She walked into the kitchen. "You want some coffee?"

Trick and Valerie made eye contact. "Love some," said Trick.

"Why do you say that wouldn't surprise you?" asked Valerie.

Michelle grabbed a coffee pot and glanced at Valerie. "My daughter didn't always make smart decisions, and she wasn't good at social graces, either. She didn't make friends easily and chose her lovers poorly. On top of that, let's just say she had a wealth of experience with medication that would impress a pharmacist. In my mind, it was just a matter of time before her behavior caught up with her. I'm just surprised the police haven't figured it out." She added water to the pot and poured it into the coffeemaker.

"Can you get into more specifics about her behavior?" asked Trick.

"You mean like erratic outbursts, dramatic highs and lows, sleeping too much or too little, and strange phobias and OCD issues, like having to put her food in specific places on her plate, and some nonsense about not wanting her picture taken." She pulled a bag of coffee grounds from a cabinet and pointed at a picture on the wall. "I think that's the only one I have of her, and that's from her college graduation. I had to blackmail her to get it." After opening the bag, she scooped out some grounds and added them to a filter in the machine. "That girl even refused to get a driver's license because it required a photo. Said she didn't particularly like driving anyway, so it didn't matter. I could never convince her otherwise."

Trick wandered over and looked at the picture on the wall. Two women and a man stood on the steps in front of an impressive building; one woman wore a cap and gown, her bangs barely showing from beneath the cap, and looked annoyed. He guessed it was Lydia. The other woman, with her dark hair blowing in the wind and smiling, had to be Shay. Bradley, with broad shoulders and a stocky build, stood between them, his dark eyes narrowed at the camera and his arms around both women. "Nice photo."

"Oh, please," said Michelle, flipping on the machine. "It's terrible. But it's one of the few times I could get all three of them together without Lydia snarling, Shay arguing, or Bradley incoherent."

"It sounds like all the siblings have their issues," said Valerie. "How'd they get along?"

"Get along?" Michelle snorted, closing the bag of grounds. "None of us get along." She put the bag away. "Like I told that other woman I spoke with, we've had our share of ups and downs. I've been married a few times, which is where Lydia probably inherited her luck with men." As the coffee percolated, she launched into her history, starting with Lydia and Bradley's dad and ending with the dissolution of her marriage to Shay's father, and her current marriage, which, according to her, was going smoothly. Trick let her talk, remembering how Mikey had told them that Michelle liked to make herself the center of attention, and he wanted her to get comfortable. His hope was she'd stay that way once the questions got harder.

The coffee drips slowing, she pulled down a couple of mugs.

"None for me. I'm not much of a coffee drinker," said Valerie.

"More for me then," said Trick. "I didn't sleep much last night."

"It must be catching," said Michelle, pouring coffee into two mugs and handing one to Trick.

"Thanks," said Trick. "After all you've mentioned, I can see why there must be friction in the family."

She added some sugar and stirred her coffee. "I can't remember the last time we were all together where we didn't argue. It seems my children don't like me very much. But that's the way it is, I suppose. I'm the mother, so I get all the blame."

"What would they blame you for?" asked Trick. "Did they do something wrong?"

Michelle smiled. "Do they do anything right?" She put down her spoon and cup and wrung her hands.

Trick blew on his coffee and took a drink. "Surely there's something you can brag about, Michelle. I mean, Lydia graduated college. She held down a job. Supported herself."

Michelle rubbed her temple as if she had a headache. "I suppose. Except for the men she dated and the pills. And Shay completed beauty school, and at least managed to marry, although she ended it after nine months." She walked to the end table and picked up the glass with amber liquid. "I only gave it six. I think she stuck it out to nine just to spite me." She swirled the amber liquid, returned to the kitchen, and added it to her coffee.

"And Bradley?" asked Valerie.

"He got through high school, but only because his teachers passed him. They didn't want him back, not that I can blame them. He was a bully. Tormented the other kids. You wouldn't believe the number of parents that complained." She shrugged. "I told them to toughen up, along with their kids. Everyone's such a pansy nowadays. I learned that life is tough when I was a kid, and so can they. The sooner, the better." She took a healthy sip from her doctored coffee.

Trick and Valerie shared a glance. "You said Lydia took pills," said Trick. "What kind?"

"Anti-depressants, mostly, but I know there were more. I went in her bathroom once. I saw Valium, painkillers, and a few other things I didn't recognize. God knows where she was getting it all."

"What about alcohol?" asked Valerie, eyeing Michelle's drink.

"She drank," said Michelle, "but strangely, not to excess. Shay takes the prize for that. Girl has a drink in her hand wherever she goes." She raised her mug. "Lydia got my taste in men, and Shay my taste for liquor. Lucky girls."

Trick nodded, holding his coffee. "And what about Bradley? We know he's done some time, but mostly for petty stuff. Did he ever get violent?"

Her face fell. "Bradley's...well...he's a schemer. He doesn't use fists because he knows how to land on his feet. Although if he's backed into a corner, he might come out swinging."

"Has he come out swinging before?" asked Trick.

Her expression fell. "You're asking a lot of questions about my children, but you said you wanted to talk about Lydia and this man Chad's death. What does that have to do with Shay and Bradley?"

"Well, ma'am...Michelle," said Trick, wandering around the room and stopping at the fireplace mantel. "We have to consider the possibility that one of them may have killed Lydia, and even Chad."

Valerie shot him a hard glance and Michelle glared. "Excuse me?" asked Michelle.

"I think my assistant here may be taking his own medication," said Valerie. "What he meant to say was□"

"I didn't misspeak, Valerie." Trick eyed another picture on the wall of Bradley and Michelle together wearing party hats. "I think either Shay or Bradley killed their sister."

Michelle lowered her coffee. "That is insane. Are you crazy?"

"I don't think so," said Trick. "Although I know some will disagree." He gestured at Valerie, who was aiming those laser eyes at him again. "But I don't see the point of beating around the bush."

Michelle walked to the bar and added more amber liquid to her cup. "I think we're done talking. You should leave. Now."

"Actually, Michelle, I think we're just getting started," said Trick.

"We should go," said Valerie, heading to the door.

"Let's begin with Bradley," said Trick. He took a sip of his coffee. "Why would he want to kill Lydia? Is it money? She made him executor of her will, but why? He doesn't seem like a logical first choice. And did he know he was executor? And if he did, and there was money involved, did that make him think twice? Could he be more violent than you realize, and it just stayed beneath the radar until something set him off? Maybe he never liked Lydia. She's his older sister. She's got the smarts, the education. Did she hold it over his head? Make him look like a fool?"

Michelle whirled. "Bradley would never do that. He and Lydia were close. She helped him when he needed it. She only made him executor because..." Her drink shook from her hold on it.

"Because why?" asked Trick, sensing he was near to something important.

Michelle turned away.

Trick continued to press. "Because she didn't trust you, her own mother, to take care of things in the event of her death? And why is Lydia even thinking about death? Hell, most people never think about a will or what happens when they die until they're near death themselves." He stepped closer. "Was Lydia near death?" A thought occurred to him. "Or did she think she was?" Michelle stiffened. "Is that it?" asked Trick.

"You've said enough," said Michelle.

"She's right," said Val. "We should leave."

Trick's mind raced. "She didn't choose you, though, to handle her affairs. Is it because you couldn't be trusted? Is it because if you're cheating on your husband, you might cheat her too?"

Michelle dropped her jaw. "How dare you."

"How dare me?" Trick pointed. "How dare you, I think is the correct question. Why didn't Lydia want you involved? Are you the one that caused her to name Bradley, a man who can't rub two pennies together, as the person to handle her affairs?" He narrowed his gaze. "Were you two so at odds with each other that you considered killing her?"

Michelle sputtered. "I would never□"

"No, I agree," said Trick. "It doesn't make sense, because as much as you may be willing to let your family collapse around you, you don't strike me as the murdering type." He swiped his hand. "You've got pictures of your kids, and diplomas." He eyed one on the wall. "So if you're telling me Bradley didn't do it, and neither did you, that leaves Shay. Did she have a reason to hurt her sister?"

"You don't know what you're talking about," said Michelle. "None of us hurt Lydia. We argued, but we loved her."

Trick sat his coffee on the end table. "No. You didn't. You sat back and watched her fall apart. According to Kyle, Lydia was doing okay, but then she introduced him to the family, and between Shay and Bradley's interference, Lydia went off the wagon and their relationship ended soon after." He crossed his arms. "You say Shay's the drinker, but what else is she?"

"I don't want to talk about this," said Michelle.

"And I don't want to have to tell your husband that the man who just left here wasn't him." Trick leaned a shoulder against the wall by the sofa.

Michelle tensed, and her face fell. "What are you saying?"

Trick pulled out his cell. "I'm saying I want to know about Shay, and you don't want me to make this phone call to your husband."

"Are you blackmailing me?" Michelle asked.

"Blackmail seems harsh. Let's consider it a challenging moment. We all have to face them. Like you said. Life is hard," said Trick.

Michelle slammed her drink on the bar. "You want to play this game? You want to threaten me? That's child's play. My husband isn't stupid. Call him for all I care."

Trick raised the phone. "What's his number?" Michelle leveled an evil look at him that rivaled Valerie's, but Trick didn't budge. "If you don't give it to me, I'll get it some other way. You know I will."

"You son-of-a-bitch," said Michelle.

"I've been called worse," said Trick. "I take after my momma." He held the phone in front of him. "What's it gonna be, Michelle? Tell me about Shay or I make my call."

Michelle began to pace. "Fine."

Valerie eyed daggers at him, but he ignored her. "Fine, what? Did Shay have a reason to hurt Lydia?" he asked.

"Shay...Shay...," Michelle ran a hand through her messy hair. "Shay never liked Lydia, no matter what she may have told anyone. Shay loved to lord everything over Lydia. Her father was alive, and Lydia's wasn't. Shay was pretty and Lydia was ugly. She never stopped comparing herself to her sister out of some desperate attempt to prove she was better. Lydia and Bradley were close, and Shay hated it. Lydia did well for herself, and Shay hated that, too. She'd undermine Lydia any chance she could. That's why Kyle and Lydia broke up, because Shay kept telling Lydia that Lydia would never be able to hold on to him. He'd leave eventually." Michelle paused, took a healthy swig of her coffee, and put it on the counter. She hugged herself, her body taut. "For a while, Lydia broke off ties to Shay. They were estranged for several months, and then somehow, Shay wiggled her way back in and changed tactics. Now it was all about Kyle. He was no good and didn't care about Lydia, only about himself. Lydia had been stable on the pills for a while, sticking to her prescribed doses, but I think the stress of Shay's interference made her start to abuse again. Lydia seemed to be only half aware of what Shay was doing and began to believe her. The damn drugs messed with her head, which was already messed up enough. Shay destroyed the relationship, and Kyle disappeared. And then Chad came into the picture, and Lydia went berserk." She held her head, then found her drink.

"Berserk? What happened?" asked Valerie.

Trick stepped closer.

Her fingers shaky, Michelle took another healthy gulp of her coffee. "I don't know. Lydia barely spoke to me at that point, and neither did Shay, but I heard things through Bradley. There was some sort of argument between them. Shay was jealous and Lydia was livid, or vice versa. If I were to guess, Lydia liked Chad. Shay found out and pursued him because of it. They were hell bent on killing each other, and when Lydia died and Shay didn't show up for the funeral, I thought..."

Trick waited to hear her finish the sentence. "You thought what?" he asked. Noting the diploma on the wall, he saw the picture of Shay and the name of the beauty school.

"I thought...I...I...couldn't help but wonder if Shay could have...have..." Michelle put a palm over her eyes. "Oh, God. I can't even say it."

"Killed her?" asked Valerie.

Something on the diploma caught Trick's eye, and he looked more closely. A chill ran up his spine, and his skin prickled. "Michelle," he said softly. "What is Shay's name?"

Michelle dropped her hand, and Valerie frowned. "What are you talking about?" asked Valerie.

"Her...her name? Why?" asked Michelle.

Trick pointed toward the diploma, his heart thumping. "What is her given name?"

"It...It..." Michelle foundered at the change in subject. "Her given name is Serita. Serita Alvarez. But we've called her Shay since she was a child."

Trick set his jaw. "That man she married. What was his last name?"

Valerie came over and eyed the diploma.

Michelle shook her head. "What on earth...?"

"What was his name?" asked Trick, sharpening his tone.

"Uh...Umm...let me think." Michelle's brows knitted. "Shaun. It was Shaun. Shaun Avery."

Trick cursed. Shay's actual name was Serita Avery.

Chapter Twenty-Five

MASON SAT IN SERITA Avery's bedroom, much as he had a few days earlier, and stared into her mirror. When he'd arrived, Serita had flung open the door, thanking him for arriving so quickly, looking disheveled with her hair in disarray and sputtering about how the man in the mirror wouldn't let her be. The man continued to appear and accuse her, and she didn't know what to do. And then that morning, in the bathroom, she'd seen a woman with him, and they'd both pointed at her. She'd run out, terrified and confused, convinced she was hallucinating, and if Mason couldn't do something, she'd have to see a doctor. Either that or move.

Mason tried to reassure her, went back into the bedroom, and studied the mirror. The room's window shades remained closed, the only illumination coming in from the light shining from around the edges. The bed was unmade, and the room untidy. Suitcases sat along the wall, and the closet was open. Half of it was empty, but the man's clothes he'd seen before still hung in the same place.

Mason had to consider the possibility that whatever tragedy had befallen this woman was causing her visions. Guilt could create a number of symptoms, and he worried that he might have to ask Serita to call that doctor, or at least suggest counseling, but he'd have to see first if the man in the mirror had indeed returned, and if he was truly the source of the problem.

After sitting for several minutes, he'd had no success in his attempts at contact. Deciding to try the other mirror, he stood and entered the attached bathroom, and stared into it. It was slightly smeared, and he grabbed the hand towel to wipe it. The mirror popped and Mason realized it was a medicine cabinet. He opened it. Several pill bottles were lined up on the shelves, along with over-the-counter allergy medication. Eyeing the bottles, something pricked at him, as if he'd seen something out of the corner of his eye but couldn't make it out. Deciding not to pry further, he closed the mirror and went back to staring and waiting. Nothing happened, and he returned to the bedroom, where he tried again with the larger mirror. Sitting silently, he was about to leave when familiar tingles traveled up his arms. Opening up, he listened.

Like before, a male presence emanated, and a voice echoed in Mason's mind. *Help her. It's not her fault.* The voice had said the same on his previous visit. "How can I help?" Mason asked aloud. The mirror turned a misty gray, as if it was fogging up. "What is your message?" he asked.

Help her. She needs help.

"Who needs help?" asked Mason. "Serita?"

The mirror clouded more, and Mason watched it swirl, and then slowly, the fog began to take shape. "Who are you?" asked Mason.

The tingles grew, his skin chilled, and the room turned frigid. Mason rubbed his shoulders. "What do you want me to know?"

The fog turned dense. Mason's reflection twisted and contorted. A man appeared in the mirror, his face pale, and with a garish wound in his head.

Mason froze, not sure he was seeing properly. The man staring back at him was Chad Howard.

Trick raced to Michelle and took her arm. "Where does Shay live?"

"What?" Michelle tried to pull away. "What for?"

Valerie stepped closer. "What's going on, Trick?"

"I need her address. Right now." Trick squeezed harder. "Because if you don't give it to me, you're looking at accessory to murder, Michelle."

"Wh...What?" asked Michelle.

"Trick, what is wrong?" asked Valerie.

Trick pulled Michelle close. "My partner is on his way to Serita Avery's house, not knowing what he's about to walk into. Give it to me. Now."

Michelle stammered. "Shay would never□"

"Now," yelled Trick. He mentally calculated in his mind how long it had been since he'd talked to Mikey and, in his gut, he realized it was too long. Mason didn't have much time left, if any.

"It's in my phone," Michelle yelled back. "I'll get it." Trick let her go. She pulled her cell out of her robe pocket and accessed the address with trembling fingers. "Here."

Trick memorized it, and Valerie looked over his shoulder. "Find out where we're going, Valerie. I have a call to make." He grabbed his own phone and punched the button for Mason.

Mikey double-checked the address and pulled into a vacant lot. Large trees with heavy branches and thick leaves encircled about an acre of land and the driveway was almost completely overgrown with grass growing through cracks in the cement.

For the millionth time, she second-guessed herself, knowing she was breaking her promise to Mason, but didn't want to lose this opportunity to talk to Shay. She pulled in and parked under a canopy of tree branches, and wondered why Shay chose to meet here, but assumed she wanted privacy. Her anxiety over the phone had been acute, and Mikey hoped Shay wouldn't change her mind and not show. Mikey had promised she'd head straight there. Holding her phone, Mikey surveyed the area. It was quiet, and the lot was big enough so that the nearest neighbor would likely not even know a car was there unless they drove by and looked.

Feeling antsy, but keeping an eye out for Shay, she texted Mason, telling him where she was and giving him the address. Maybe if he was finishing with Serita, he could join her here. Based on her rough recollection of Serita's address, she didn't live too far away.

After sending the text, she tapped on the steering wheel, checked the time, and almost jumped in her seat when her phone rang. Not recognizing the number, she realized it was a business call which had been forwarded to her cell since she and Mason were out of the office. Mikey answered. "You've reached SCOPE. How can I help you?"

A woman replied. "Hello. I'm looking for Mason Redstone. This is Daphne Stewart."

Mikey recalled Daphne as being Chad's assistant and the woman Trick and Mason had spoken to at Chad's office. "He's actually in a meeting, but I'm his assistant, Mikey. Is there something I can help you with?"

"Well, I suppose," said Daphne. "He asked me to call if I remembered anything that I thought might help with the case. I debated calling those two detectives, but...well..." her voice lowered. "...I really don't like them very much."

Mikey pulled out her notebook and pencil. "I can help with that. What did you remember, and I'll let Mason know."

"It's not really what I remember, it's what I found."

"What was that?"

"I was going through some of Chad's things, and getting rid of some paperwork..." Her voice caught. "...I'm sorry. It brings back memories."

"It's okay. Take your time."

She sniffed. "Thank you." Hearing the sniff, Mikey thought of Shay. "Anyway, I was going through some stuff, and it triggered a memory of us in Chad's office."

"Us?"

"Me, Chad, and Lydia. We were working on a large project. Tony came in to surprise Chad for achieving some sort of benchmark, brought a cake and congratulated him. Tony asked me to take a picture of them to include in the newsletter."

Mikey had no idea where this was going. "Okay."

"Lydia didn't like her picture being taken, and she tried to avoid the photo, but I half caught her in one before she disappeared with some excuse that she had to be somewhere. I just checked my phone and I still have the picture. Since Mr. Redstone seemed interested, I thought I'd send it to him."

"That's a great idea. Let me give you my number and you can send it to me. I'll make sure he gets it."

"Okay. That's fine."

Mikey gave Daphne her cell number and her phone pinged when the message came through. "Let me check to see if I got it. Hold on." Mikey put Daphne on speaker and opened the photo. Mikey recognized Chad Howard, looking fresh-faced and smiling, standing next to a tall man with thick dark hair, holding a balloon. A woman sat just at the edge of the shot, barely in the photo, and looking like she wanted to be anywhere but there. She wore a blue business suit, and her features were average, although she had pretty brown hair and bangs framed her eyes. Her face was sullen, and she held something white in her hand.

"That's the closest you'll come to a picture of Lydia," said Daphne. "Sorry."

Mikey studied it, noting Lydia's eyes. They looked tired and a little puffy and the item in her hand appeared to be a tissue. "She looks like she's been crying. Is she that upset about the picture?"

"Crying?" asked Daphne. She paused. "Oh, no. I think Lydia was always a bit of a hypochondriac. She always had a tissue in her hand. Maybe she had a cold."

Mikey went still. "Lydia had a cold?" A lump formed in her stomach.

"Yes. Or thought she did. You could never tell with Lydia."

Shay's sneezes echoed in Mikey's mind. "Thank you, Daphne. This is helpful."

"You're wel□"

Mikey hung up before Daphne could finish. Something stirred in her gut and Mikey didn't like it. She studied the photo of Lydia and thought of Shay. Lydia's face stared back, her eyes sad and weary. Chad's face beamed, his excitement for whatever reward he'd received evident. Mikey flicked her gaze back to Lydia. Did she look like someone who was in love with the man beside her, or annoyed with him?

"Shit," Mikey said aloud. Fumbling with the phone, she shifted screens to call Mason.

The sound of a car approached, and Mikey looked through her rearview mirror. A vehicle drove up and parked behind her. A man jumped out, and realizing she had nowhere to go, Mikey's stomach flipped. Just as the man approached the driver's side, her phone rang, and Trick's name popped up on the display. The man aimed a gun at her, and Mikey froze. It was Bradley Stanford.

"Get out of the car," he growled. "Now."

Mason took an unsettled breath at dead Chad's appearance. It wasn't uncommon that cases could overlap. Ghosts weren't restrained by location or timing. Was Chad trying to tell him something about his own case? Mason blinked, checking to be sure he wasn't hallucinating himself, but dead Chad remained. "What do you want?" he asked.

Help her. She's confused. The voice echoed in his head.

"Who's confused? Why are you here?" asked Mason.

She needs help.

"Serita needs help? You want me to help her?" He had another thought. "Or is it Cissy?"

Help them all.

Mason groaned. Now he was more uncertain. Why couldn't Chad's spirit be clearer? He considered maybe he was asking the wrong questions. He figured if dead Chad was choosing to communicate, maybe he should ask the obvious. "Who killed you, Chad?"

Dead Chad stared back, and the mirror swirled again, the mist shifted, and a woman's face took shape and came into focus. It was the same woman from the interview with Cissy. Her wet hair plastered against her face and her blue lips twitching, she laughed, and her voice bellowed in his head.

She did, Lydia said. *She did*. Then she opened her mouth and cackled, just as she had done before. Mason shivered and broke out in goosebumps as dead Lydia kept up her mantra. *She did. She did. She did. She did. She did.*

A cold, clammy sweat broke out on his skin, and his heart thumped. Everything swirled much like the mirror, and he stood, wondering what to do. Chad and Lydia had both appeared in the mirror at Serita's, but why? Trying to think, he recalled his conversations with Cissy Howard and Trick, and tried to put the pieces together. Why were Chad and Lydia haunting Serita Avery?

A thought flickered, and he returned to the bathroom, opened the medicine cabinet again, and grabbed one of the pill bottles. It was Valium, recently prescribed to Serita. He took another one, which was a painkiller, also prescribed to Serita. He dug through a few more until he found one that made him stop cold. It was another painkiller, but this one was prescribed to Lydia Stanford, as was the bottle beside it. The blood rushed in his ears and his heart thumped. What was going on? He returned to the mirror and saw Chad and the cackling woman together, swirling but starting to fade, and fought to put the pieces together, when Chad pointed to a spot behind Mason. Mason turned, seeing the half-filled closet.

He whirled toward it, seeing the men's clothes hanging from the rod. Telling himself to stay calm, he walked over, slid the door back, and flipped through the shirts and pants. There weren't many and there was no way to know whom they'd belonged to. Seeing a shoe poking out from below, he shoved the pants out of the way, and froze when he saw a pair of worn, scuffed brown and white boots in the back. He reached for them, pulled them out and almost dropped them when he turned them over and saw the familiar *Justin* logo stamped on the bottom of the boot. *Chad's boots,* he thought. *The ones Trick asked Cissy to find.*

"Oh, shit. Oh, shit. Oh, shit," he mumbled to himself. Putting the boots down, he grabbed for his phone, seeing the missed phone and text messages from Trick and Mikey. His habit was to silence his phone when meeting with a client, and he'd missed them. His fingers racing to call back, he reached for the gun in his ankle holster when a woman's voice stopped him cold.

"Put the phone down, Mason."

He stopped and saw Serita standing outside the door, aiming a gun at him. He slowly let go of his weapon, which was still in the holster, dropped the phone onto the bed, and raised his hands. "Hi, Serita." He paused. "Or do you prefer Shay?"

Serita encroached, and he stepped back into the room, forcing himself to take slow breaths. She grinned. "How did you know?"

He swallowed. "Chad's the one in the mirror, and you have his boots. Are those his clothes?" Her grip tightened on the gun, and Mason kept his arms up. "I saw Lydia in the mirror." He thought about that. "You must have known that I would see them. And that would give you away."

"I figured, but it didn't matter. I needed you here. You saw Bradley today, and you and that damn sister of yours won't stop snooping around."

His adrenaline racing, Mason tried to think. "Why did you invite me here the first time?"

Her face flickered with uncertainty. "That was legit. Chad was haunting me. I knew it was him, but I couldn't get rid of him. Bradley and I were planning to leave town, but I don't want Chad following. I called you on a whim, hoping you could take care of it, but imagine my surprise when your sister called the next day, wanting to talk about Lydia and Chad. I realized you were investigating Chad's death and were suspicious of Lydia's. If you'd have left it alone after I talked to your sister, it wouldn't have mattered, but you didn't."

"You and Bradley killed Lydia. Why?"

Her eyes narrowed. "I did it. Bradley just helped. He covered for me."

"You killed Chad too?"

Her eyes blinked, and her head twitched, and he didn't like the look on her face. "He deserved it." The gun shook in her hand. "He knew...he knew...and he was going to talk."

"He knew you'd killed Lydia? How did he know?"

She blinked again. "I don't want to talk about this." She waved the gun. "I'm just waiting for Bradley. He'll be here soon. Then he'll finish it, and we're out of here."

Mason kept his eye on her weapon, wondering if he could take it from her. "What's Bradley's going to finish?"

"You. My guess is he'll shoot you, but that's up to him. I'd do it, but I don't want you and Chad both haunting me. You and your sister can pester Bradley."

Mason stopped breathing, and he clutched his hands into fists. "My sister? What are you doing with Mikey?"

"I called her not long after I talked to you. She couldn't wait to meet with me, only Bradley's waiting for her instead."

A cold well of hatred bubbled up in Mason's stomach. "You touch her□"

"Too late," said Shay. "She's probably already dead."

Mason's vision went white, and he launched himself at Shay just as she fired the gun.

Chapter Twenty-Six

VALERIE FLEW THROUGH A light as a car horn blared. "Are you sure about this?"

Holding the phone to his ear, Trick cursed when Mikey's phone rang and went to voicemail again. He'd tried both her and Mason several times with no luck. "I'm sure." Lowering the phone, he disconnected. "It's got to be Shay and Bradley. Mason and Mikey got too close, and Shay and Bradley are scared. They're getting rid of the threat, and then they'll disappear."

Valerie slowed her speed and turned down a tree-lined street. "Where?"

Trick checked the map. "Keep going. We're close."

"We need to call this in. The cops need to know."

Trick shook his head. "Not yet. We have to see what we're dealing with."

"Trick☐"

"Turn here," said Trick.

Valerie hit the brake and turned.

"Go slow. It's just down the road." He pointed as a driveway came into view. "Stop."

"Here?"

"Here."

Valerie slowed and pulled over. Trick saw a small one-story house on a multi-acre wooded lot. The trees provided ample privacy, and if he hadn't seen the dirt and gravel driveway with a mailbox out front, they might have driven past it. Valerie had stopped just short of the entrance to the driveway, but Trick could still see the small house through the trees. He grabbed Valerie's binoculars and peered through them. The house backed up to more woods with a rutted, narrow road behind it, leading deeper into what looked like a forest. Not far from the house stood a smaller structure, wooden and dilapidated, and Trick guessed it had once been a barn. The door to it stood slightly open.

"If they're in trouble, why don't we call the cops?" asked Valerie.

Trick spotted a four-door red sedan parked off to the side of the house, but saw no movement. "Shay and Bradley are unstable at best. You call the cavalry, and they come in guns blazing. They'll likely get Mikey and Mason killed."

"You want to do this alone? Is that what you're saying? Are you crazy? We'll end up dead, along with Mason and Mikey."

"Chin up, Miss Vain. We have surprise on our side. Are you armed?"

She reached over and popped open the glove compartment. "I am." She pulled out a small revolver. "Are you?"

"Unfortunately, no."

"Then what the hell do you plan to use? Being a smart-ass will only get you so far."

He lowered the binoculars. "On the contrary, I find my wit frequently works better than a weapon."

"Not with my brother, it didn't."

He raised a brow at her and went back to looking.

"I still think calling for help is our best shot at this."

"Hold on," he said, seeing movement through the binoculars. The front door opened, and a man walked out. He was burly and broad-shouldered. "It's Bradley."

Bradley stomped down the front steps and over to the car. After reaching the driver's side door, he stopped. Trick saw a woman leave the house and stop at the edge of the porch. She yelled something at Bradley, who yelled back. The two were definitely on edge. The woman pointed toward the old barn and threw out a hand. She wore jeans and a large t-shirt, her disheveled hair blew in the wind, and her long bangs hung in her face. Studying the woman and recalling the photos on Michelle's wall, Trick sucked in a breath. "I'll be damned."

"What?" asked Valerie, leaning up. "What is it?"

Trick watched her a second longer, confirming his suspicions. "That's not Shay."

"What do you mean it's not Shay? Who is it?"

"It's Lydia. She's alive." He watched Lydia return to the house and Bradley got in the car, started it, and backed up. Trick started to tell Valerie to get down, but instead of heading toward the driveway, Bradley drove the car behind the house and down the narrow trail into the woods.

Mikey moaned, and her head flared. Hearing muffled sounds and jostled by the bumpy movements beneath her, she slowly became aware of her surroundings. Opening her eyes, she blinked, trying to clear her vision, but it was dark and difficult to see. Lying in a small, enclosed space, she shifted. Her side hurt and her mouth was so dry she could barely swallow. Her mind sharpening, she raised her arm, touched the back of her head, and felt the wet warmth of blood. A memory flashed in her brain.

Bradley had pulled a gun on her. He'd yelled at her to get out of her car, and she had, asking him to relax and not hurt her, and trying to get him to tell her what he was doing. He wouldn't talk though and told her to get in his car. Mikey had no intention of getting in his vehicle, though, and had tried to think of how to escape.

He'd yelled at her again, and she'd turned, ready to make a run for it, when something hard had hit the back of her head, and she'd crumpled.

Moaning again, she tried to get her bearings. Touching hard surfaces above and around her, she determined she was in the trunk of a car. The noises and the bumpy movement were coming from the crunch of tires rolling over dirt and gravel. Her side ached and feeling around, she touched a small tire, probably the spare, beneath her. Exhaust fumes made her cough, and she prayed she wouldn't die from carbon monoxide poisoning.

Trying not to panic, she told herself to think. It was the only way out of this. She searched the rest of the trunk, hoping to find a tire iron or something that could be used as a weapon, but had no luck. Coughing again, she wiped her burning eyes and thought of Mason. Was he okay? Instinctively, she knew he wasn't. If they'd come after her, they'd have come after him too.

The car slowed and came to a stop. The fear welled up, and Mikey stifled a sob, sending out a silent prayer for help.

Trick put the binoculars in the seat. "You ready?"

"Ready? What are we going to do? You have a plan?"

"I do." He closed his eyes and envisioned in his mind their next steps. A series of actions played out, and he opened his eyes.

"Trick. I really think we need help."

"You're right." He grabbed his phone, searched for a number, and dialed.

"What are you doing?"

"Calling for help."

She grunted and put her head back. "You're going to be the one to kill me before anyone in that house does."

"Have faith, Miss Vain." Trick listened to the ringing until someone picked up. "Yes," he said. "I need to speak to either Detective Daniels or Remalla. It's urgent. Tell them Trick Monroe is calling. I'll hold, but the longer I wait, the sooner someone will die."

He heard a gruff "hold on" and seconds later, Detective Daniels answered. "Trick? What's wrong?" Trick gave him the fastest possible answer and explained the situation, telling them he was with Valerie Vain and not to shoot her, and then gave him the address.

"We're on our way," said Daniels. "You two should wait for us."

"My partner's in there, and probably Mikey, too, Detective. Time is short if not already up."

There was a pause. "Be careful."

"I will." He hung up. "Cavalry's coming." He popped the door open. "Let's go, Miss Vain."

Chapter
Twenty-Seven

VALERIE CLOSED HER CAR door quietly, and holding her weapon, jogged around the front of the vehicle to meet Trick. They ran into the trees, just off the side of the driveway. Getting closer to the house, Trick squatted, and Valerie did the same beside him. "How do you want to do this?" she whispered.

Trick studied the property for a second. "You take the barn. I'll take the house."

Valerie surveyed the area. "Barn? You mean that shack over there? Why don't we both go to the house?"

"Because Lydia pointed toward it. If Mason drove here, then I suspect they put his car inside the barn to hide it, which likely means he may be in there. It needs to be checked and cleared. If you get there and find nothing, head to the house."

"What are you going to do?"

"I'm going to find Lydia and hope I can either subdue her or get her to see reason before Bradley returns. Once we take care of Lydia, then we'll go after Bradley."

"What about Mikey? Where is she?"

Trick sighed. "I'm not sure. Which is why we need to move fast." He rose and leaned over to stay hidden. "You ready?"

Valerie nodded. "I'll see you at the house. You be careful."

"You too."

Valerie took off through the brush toward the barn, and Trick headed in the opposite direction. Moving quickly and dodging roots and branches, she came up beside the barn and squatted again, waiting and listening. Nothing moved, and she jumped up and ran toward the side wall and plastered herself against it. Advancing cautiously, she peered around it and could see the front of the house, but there was no sign of Trick or Lydia. Everything was quiet.

Sliding around the corner, her gun aimed down, she stuck close to the wooden slats and approached the barn's entry. She reached out and grasped the rusty handle, and pulled. It opened enough for her to glance inside, and she saw tufts of hay, stacks of bags that looked like dirt or maybe fertilizer, a few stalls, and Mason's car parked carefully between them. Taking a last look at the house, she pulled the door wider and slipped inside the barn.

Careful to stay low and not be seen, Trick crept as far back into the trees as he could while making his way toward the rear of the house. Once there, he saw a vegetable garden, an old tire swing hanging from a branch, and a small back porch leading to a ripped screen door. Taking a second to double-check the area, he stepped out and sprinted into the vegetable garden, landing on his knees, and ducking down.

Peering up, he checked the back windows of the house, but seeing no movement, he dashed up to the wall, pressing his back against it. He slowly moved up to a window, ducked below it, and glanced quickly inside, but all he could see was furniture and bookshelves. Staying down, he darted to the other side of the window, straightened, and, sliding sideways, neared the screen door. He hooked a finger into the latch and slowly pulled. It squeaked, and he stopped, listening, and then pulled again. It squeaked again, and he held back. Continuing the delicate balance of trying to open it without alerting Lydia, he finally had it wide enough that he could fit through and try the knob.

This is where he would be the most vulnerable. If Lydia was waiting for him, he had no escape plan. He'd have to hope she'd hold fire long enough for him to start talking. He had no doubt she'd be armed.

On high alert, he turned the knob, and the door opened. Gently, he pushed it wider and swiveled, looking around the frame. Relief bloomed when he didn't see anyone, and pushing the door farther, he stepped inside.

Valerie held her weapon low and away and approached the back of the car, hearing only the crunch of the dirt beneath her heels and her heavy breathing. Stopping at the trunk, she peered into the back seat, but it was empty. Coming around to the side, she kept an eye on the stalls. The barn smelled of hay, rotting wood, and the lingering scent of manure. She tried the driver's side door, and it popped open. Leaning down, she checked inside, but saw nothing out of place. It was clean and tidy.

Retreating, she straightened and moved to a stall, checked it, and moved on to the next. The barn was unoccupied, and after checking the last stall, she began to head toward the door when she heard a thump.

Swiveling fast, she aimed her weapon, her heart thudding, and her breathing escalating. The thump came again, and she squinted. Taking a couple of steps, she cursed herself for her stupidity. The trunk. Someone was in Mason's trunk.

The thump banged harder, and she walked up to the rear of the car, holding her gun, and backed up to the driver's door. Taking a shaky breath, and keeping her gun leveled at the trunk, she pulled the door wide, leaned over and popped the trunk. It lifted and moving fast, she came around and aimed her weapon toward the inside. "Don't move," she yelled, then stopped cold when she saw Mason Redstone lying inside, his face pale, and his shirt covered in blood.

Trick stepped softly into the kitchen, every nerve ending on alert to the sound of anyone's approach. The house remained eerily quiet, and he slowly pushed the door closed. Staying close to the wall, he surveyed the kitchen, seeing dishes, two mugs in the sink, and crumbs on the breakfast table. Trying to stay relaxed, but failing, he took a few steps and peered into an empty laundry room, then quickly passed it and stopped just outside the entry to the main room. If he was to guess, Lydia would be frantically packing, preparing to leave, and he hoped he could surprise and restrain her before she could fight back. He spied a block of knives and debated taking one, but it would be useless in a gunfight, and he had no desire to stab Lydia. If he could get close enough to injure her, then he'd be close enough to take her gun and restrain her.

Sliding to the edge of the wall, he looked around it and saw the quiet living area. The front door stood open about an inch, with two suitcases to the side of it. A worn couch sat against the back wall and a small TV with rabbit ears was perched on a square table across from the couch. A pair of slouching bookshelves stood on either side of the TV. Glancing out the front window, Trick didn't see Lydia, and he moved into the room, taking quick steps, and heading toward the hallway which led to the bedrooms. He stopped just outside of it when he heard a noise. Turning, he saw Lydia, her eyes wide, standing near the front door, aiming a gun at him.

He stopped cold and raised his arms.

"Well, well, well," she said. "Who the hell are you?"

Running up to the trunk, Valerie lowered her gun and stuck it into the back of her jeans. "Mason?" She grabbed his arm, and his eyes fluttered. "Are you okay?"

He groaned.

"Mason?" She gently shook him.

He blinked and became more alert. His gaze met hers and he grimaced. "Valerie?" he whispered. "Where am I?" He gripped his bloody arm and chest with red fingers.

"You're in the trunk of your car. Can you get out?"

Trying to move, he sucked in a pained breath. "She shot me."

Valerie tried to assess his injuries. Blood soaked his shirt, but he was lying sideways, so it was hard to determine where it originated. "You're bleeding. A lot. Maybe you should stay still."

He grunted and shifted, gritting his teeth. "Help me up."

"Are you sure?"

He raised a bloody hand, and she took it. "Yes," he said.

Pulling, she helped to lift his upper body. "Where are you hit?"

Once sitting up, he took hold of the edge and strained to ease himself out. "Shoulder," he said with a groan. "I think."

"Be careful." Worried it might be worse than a shoulder wound, she tried to stabilize him as he rolled out, threw a leg over, and almost fell into the dirt. Grabbing him, she held on until he could get his feet under him, and he sat on the bumper. Sweat poured down his face, and his knuckles were white as he held his arm. "You need an ambulance."

"You alone?" he asked, panting. "How'd you find me?"

"Trick," she said. "He's going after Lydia."

"Lydia? You mean Shay."

"No. I mean Lydia. We saw a picture of her at her mother's. It's Lydia who's alive."

"But Serita Avery is Shay."

"True. But Serita Avery is dead. Lydia killed Shay with Bradley's help."

At the mention of Bradley's name, Mason paled more than Valerie thought possible. "Bradley. Where's Bradley?" He pushed up from the car and tried to stand.

Valerie held him up. "What are you doing?"

"I have to find Bradley. He has Mikey."

Valerie supported him until he stood on his own and walked to the door. "He drove into the woods. There's a path, but we didn't see anyone with him."

Mason made it to the door and pushed it open. "What path?"

"There." Valerie pointed.

Mason followed her finger and nodded. "I see it." Holding his shoulder, he took a deep breath, and straightened.

"What are you doing?"

Mason eyed the house. "Is Trick armed?"

"No."

"Hell," said Mason. "Check my ankle holster." He grabbed at a pant leg.

Valerie leaned over and pulled on his jeans. "It's empty."

He sucked in a shuddered breath. "Valerie," he said softly. "Go help Trick. Lydia is armed. She'll shoot him. I'm going after Bradley."

"You can barely move."

"Trust me. I'll be moving in no time. Bradley's going to kill Mikey if she's not dead already." His stricken face turned stony. "And if she is, then I'm going to kill Bradley."

"Mason□"

"Go now. Trick will need your help." And he darted out of the barn with way more vigor than Valerie expected and disappeared into the woods.

Trick didn't move an inch. "Hi, Lydia."

Lydia's wide eyes narrowed.

"There's no point in denying it. I talked to your mother. Nice lady, if not a bit high-strung. I saw your picture on the wall."

Lydia straightened her aim. "You talked to my mother?" She paused. "Who are you?"

Trick spoke gently, in hopes of keeping her at ease. "I'm Trick Monroe. Chad Howard's stepbrother. I came to investigate his death." At the mention of Chad, Lydia's face furrowed. "I understand you used to work with Chad. Were you two close?"

Lydia scoffed. "He was an idiot. Like all of them."

"I do admit. Men can make some stupid mistakes. I've made a few myself." He forced in a slow breath. "What mistake did Chad make with you?"

She hesitated. "I don't want to talk about him."

Trick projected as much calm as he could muster. "Yes, you do. I bet you're dying to talk about it. My guess is that Bradley's not a good audience. How did you manage to sway him to help you kill Shay and Chad? He doesn't strike me as the brains of your partnership."

"He only helped..." She tipped her head. "I see what you're trying to do. Get me to confess."

Trick chuckled. "We've gone way past confession time, Lydia. You're holding a gun on me. Mason came here believing you were Shay, and he and Mikey are missing. All roads lead to you and Bradley. I'd say the jig is up."

"Cissy did it. Cissy killed Chad and Lydia, or so everyone thinks." She smiled, and the gun shook in her grasp.

Trick shook his head. "Since we've got a few minutes, or at least I hope we do, let me take a guess at what really happened." He paused and when Lydia didn't shoot, he continued. "You and Chad were co-workers. You liked him, and maybe he liked you. An affair ensued. I'm just not sure if Chad slept with you or Shay, but there was funny business going on. You and Shay, however, weren't too happy with each other. One was jealous of the other. You like your pills, and she liked her booze. It's a tricky combo, and once the fuse was lit, well, it led to murder." He lowered his voice. "Am I on the right track?"

She just offered him a dull stare.

"It appears I am. Let's keep going. You and Shay have an altercation by your pool. Maybe she meets you or you meet her, who knows? But you fight. You hit Shay in the head with something hard, and she falls into the pool. But she's drunk, you make no effort to save her, and she drowns. You panic. You've just killed your sister. What do you do?" He paused, but Lydia didn't react.

Trick took a small step toward her. "You called the only person you could. Bradley. He's the only one you trust. You tell him what happened while Shay's floating in your pool. Strangely enough, Bradley gets a bright idea. He tells you to leave and come here, to Shay's, and he'll take care of it. He contacts the authorities. Tells them you called, upset and unstable. He was worried, suggested you were suicidal and requested someone check in on you. The police arrive and find you dead, or at least they think it's you. They can't find a photo ID because you don't like your picture taken, which is a form of Scopophobia, in case you didn't know, but Bradley arrives at the scene and happily offers to identify the body. Tells them it's you, not Shay. They zip Shay up, take her off, nobody questions it, Bradley authorizes cremation because you'd made him executor, there's a memorial which unfortunately Shay refuses to attend due to the contentious issues with her sister, and everyone thinks Lydia's dead." He tipped his head. "How am I doin' so far?"

She set her jaw.

"My big question is why, though? Why pretend to be Shay? But then your mother told us Shay got a nice payday when her dad died, so you and Bradley slowly withdraw her funds and wait for the dust to settle. Only Chad interrupts the closing credits." He took another step closer. "That one I am a bit confused about. Why kill Chad?" He thought about it. "Did your interest in him precede your logic? Did you go see him or call him, hoping he might run off with you into the sunset? Is that why he stayed home that day? Because it freaked him out that a dead woman had contacted him or because you'd threatened him when he didn't return your devotion? Did you watch from the vacant apartment, smoke a few cigarettes, and when Cissy disappeared, knocked on his door, tried one more time to sway him, and when he said no, or worse, threatened to call the police, you shot him?"

Lydia cocked her head. "You all finished with your lovely story?"

"Not quite." Trick glared. "Where's Mason? Where's Mikey?"

She sneered. "You're the one who knows everything. Take a guess."

Trick kept an eye on the gun. If he could get a little closer, he might be able to grab it before she could fire. "My guess is Bradley's earning his keep."

"You got that right. And once he's done, we're out of here, and you and the rest will be nothing but an afterthought."

"I'm not too sure of that, Lydia."

"I'm pretty sure of it, Trick."

Trick raised his hands higher. "Put the gun down. There's been enough tragedy. We don't need more. Let me help you."

"Your death will not be a tragedy. More like overdue."

Trick relaxed his posture. "Lydia. It isn't worth it. None of this is. You can't kill all of us and expect to escape. They'll know it was you. And what happens when Bradley gambles away all the money you've taken from Shay? Then where do you go?" He took another step. "If you turn yourself in, you can get the help you need."

Her posture turned rigid. "I don't need your help," she yelled. "I don't need anyone's help. Maybe if my mother had done her job and not looked the other way when..." she faltered, but just as quickly recovered. "...the only thing I need is time and you're taking way too much of it."

"I'm not alone, Lydia. Others are on their way. Your precious time is up."

"Then I guess I better hurry."

Trick took a step closer and eyed the gun. "Lydia□"

"Get back," she spat, and Trick stopped.

Lydia's sanity was unraveling, and Trick was quickly running out of options. "This is your last warning." He paused. "I'll give you to the count of three."

She snickered. "Count us down then, and we'll see who's left standing."

"Please, Lydia..." Trick mumbled a curse when she straightened her aim. "Remember. This was your choice." He braced himself. "One..." He paused. "...two..." Lydia's finger tightened on the trigger. "...three." Trick dove to the side and hit the floor, just as Valerie flew in from the open door, her gun raised and in firing position. "Freeze," she yelled. "Put down your□"

Lydia swiveled, turning the gun on Valerie, and Valerie fired.

Chapter
Twenty-Eight

MIKEY WAITED. THE CAR had stopped, and she heard faint footsteps, then the trunk popped, and bright light made her squint. Bradley stood above her, holding his gun. "Get out."

Mikey pushed up. Her eyes adjusting to the light, she held the edge of the trunk. "Please. Let me go."

"I said get out," said Bradley. His expression left little room for argument.

Shaking, Mikey slid out of the back of the car, got her feet on the ground, and stood. "Don't shoot me." She raised her hands. "Please."

"We're going to take a little walk in the woods. Let's go." He waved the gun.

Her stomach knotted in terror. Mikey knew if she walked away with him, she would never return. "Bradley, don't do this." Her fingers trembled.

"You've left us no choice. You and your brother should have stayed out of it."

Her mind raced with thoughts of how to escape. "Just leave. Right now. I'll keep my mouth shut, and by the time I find my way back, you and..." She paused, wondering if her theory was correct. "...is it Lydia? Is Lydia the one who's alive, and Shay's dead?" Maybe if she could distract him, she'd get an opportunity to run.

He scowled at her.

"Chad slept with Shay, didn't he? Not Lydia. They argued over him. And you helped Lydia kill Shay?" Her heart knocked against her ribs, and she prayed she could delay him long enough for Mason to... She fought back panic. Where was Mason?

He grinned. "You're pretty smart, but that's why you're in this mess, isn't it? Except you missed that Serita was Shay."

"She disguised her voice, didn't she? Acted sick?"

"It worked."

"Was that your idea? It was a good one." Maybe she could appeal to his ego. "Did you help Lydia drown Shay? Did you plan all of this?"

He straightened as if proud. "I didn't help Lydia with anything. She made this mess all by herself by stupidly falling for Chad."

"What happened between them?" asked Mikey, desperate to delay Bradley.

He kept talking. "Shay showed up at Lydia's while Chad was there working, and it didn't take Shay long to realize that Lydia liked him, and she set out to pursue him. He was dumb enough to fall for it. They'd meet up out here, and when Lydia found out, she was livid. My two sisters hated each other. Shay threatened Lydia. Lydia threatened Shay. Chad finally realized the mess he was in and got out, but Shay didn't like to be told no. She went to his office, confronted him, and he told her to leave."

Mikey eyed her surroundings while he spoke, trying to determine where she could run. The woods were thick, and if she could reach them, she could disappear before he could shoot. Her thoughts returned to Mason, and she prayed with everything she had that he wasn't dead. The fear bubbled up, and she fought back tears.

Bradley's face hardened. "I'd hoped that would be the end of it, but Lydia taunted Shay when she learned it was over, and Shay lost it. Lydia came home late one night to find Shay waiting for her by the pool. Shay was drunk and told Lydia that she'd thwart Lydia till the day she died. Said she'd turned Kyle against her, and she'd do it again with the next man. Lydia grabbed a loose brick and slugged Shay. Shay went in the water and never came out." He cocked his head. "Just like you will never leave the woods."

Mikey bit her lip, telling herself she had to survive this. "You're the one who made it look like Lydia died instead of Shay."

"Everybody thinks I'm so stupid. But I've always got a few cards up my sleeve. It wasn't hard. I told Lydia to take Shay's purse. I identified the body as Lydia. The authorities were satisfied, and Lydia and I laid low at Shay's, biding our time. It was easy because Shay kept to herself, and no one came looking. We siphoned Shay's money and were planning to leave. It was all good, but then you called." He raised the gun and took a step.

"Bradley, this is wrong." Mikey moved back and away from the car. "Where is Mason? Is he okay?" She braced for the answer. If Mason was dead, she might as well let Bradley shoot her.

He smiled. "I stuffed him in the trunk of his car. Lydia shot him, and hopefully, he's bled out by now, but if he hasn't, I'll take care of it when I get back."

Mikey's stomach twisted, and she bit back her anguish. This was her fault. If she'd figured out the clues sooner, maybe she could have saved Mason. Despair overwhelmed her, but anger fueled her. "You won't get away with any of it. They'll find you and Lydia. Mason and I aren't the only ones looking." She thought of Rem and Daniels and hoped they'd piece together the answers if she wound up dead.

"Let 'em look. By the time they find you and Mason rotting in the weeds, Lydia and I will be someplace with warm sand and strong drinks." He aimed the gun. "Now move."

A kernel of courage sparked in her gut. She needed a distraction because there was no way she could let Bradley lead her away. Desperate, she remembered a prank she'd pulled on her older sister Margaret when they were kids and fighting over a toy. Mikey had pointed, Margaret had turned, and Mikey had grabbed the toy.

Praying her idea would work, Mikey widened her gaze, stared off at a distant point, and yelled. "Oh, thank God."

Bradley turned to look, and Mikey sprinted across the path and darted into the trees just as Bradley fired. A bullet slammed into a tree in front of her and the bark exploded, sending shards of wood flying and hitting Mikey in the cheek. She yelped but didn't break stride and kept running.

Trick jumped up as Valerie ran over to Lydia, who'd collapsed to the floor, blood pooling beneath her as it gushed from her abdomen. He grabbed a blanket from the couch and raced to Lydia's side.

Valerie stared in shock. "I shot her." Her breathing came in rapid gusts. "God. I shot her."

"Calm, controlled breaths, Miss Vain." He pressed the blanket over Lydia's injury and knocked Lydia's gun away. "Here." He grabbed Valerie's wrist, which shook. "Hold down with pressure. We need to slow the bleeding." Valerie followed his instructions. She put her gun down and leaned over Lydia, pressing against the wound.

"Is she going to be okay?" asked Valerie.

"Only time will tell," said Trick. "Where's Mason? Was he in the barn?"

Shaky, Valerie nodded. "Yes. He's been shot. He's bleeding badly."

Trick looked out the window. "Where'd he go?"

"Into the woods down the trail. He's after Bradley. Says he has Mikey."

"Damn it. Is the fool armed?"

"No."

Trick made some quick deductions in his head. "You stay with Lydia. The cavalry should be here any minute. You tell them where we went."

"We? Where are you going?"

"After Mason. He won't survive long, injured and pissed. Especially if Bradley has a gun."

Blood soaked the blanket, and Valerie pressed harder. "I should go with you."

"No. You stay with her. You're the one keeping her alive right now. I'll find Mason and Mikey." He stood, wiping his bloody hands on his jeans.

"Wait."

He stopped.

Valerie grabbed her gun and handed it to him. "You'll need this."

He took it. "Thank you, Valerie." He watched Lydia, who moaned softly. "I owe you my life."

"You just make sure I can collect on the debt. Now go get Bradley."

He checked the gun. "With pleasure, Valerie. With pleasure." And he raced out of the house.

Mason ran, staying in the cover of the trees and following the narrow dirt road with the rutted tire marks. Hoping Bradley wasn't too far ahead, he sent out a silent plea that he would get to Mikey in time. His shirt soaked, he held his shoulder, trying to staunch the flow of blood. His adrenaline kept him moving, though, and he pushed harder, moving faster. His vision swam, and he had to stop and hold on to a tree until the dizziness faded. Once he found his balance, he took off again. Gulping in air, he kept looking for the car or anything that would indicate Mikey's location. Seeing a divergent path, he wondered if Bradley had stayed on the original trail. Had he driven deeper into the woods or veered off? Mason prayed he was on the right road.

Stumbling, he went to his knees and almost collapsed. His injury throbbed, his head pounded, and he struggled to catch his breath, but wouldn't give up. Holding a fallen tree for support, he pushed up and forced himself to focus when a shot rang out. The sound fueled him, and he ran out onto the road, knowing he wasn't far.

Cresting a hill, he spotted the car and ran faster. Nearing it, he saw the open trunk, but there was no sign of Mikey or Bradley.

Mason surveyed the area, looking for any sign of where they went, when another shot rang out to his left, and he heard a scream. He turned and sprinted into the woods.

Mikey moved as fast as she could, going deeper and deeper into the foliage, hoping to find a house or someone who could help her. Bradley fired again, and she screeched when the bullet smacked the tree beside her, spraying more shards of bark. She diverted then, trying to put some distance between them, and get out of sight of Bradley. Her side ached, and she gasped for air, but kept running. She prayed Bradley would slow eventually when his physical conditioning caught up to him, and Mikey trusted her recent jogs with Rem would keep her moving long enough to outlast Bradley and evade his bullets.

Dodging roots and branches, she ran until she was forced to slow. Her heart was beating so fast, she worried Bradley could hear it, and he'd find her. Seeing an area with thick cover, she squatted beneath it, trying to catch her breath. Bradley had stopped firing, and she didn't hear him behind her. Had she lost him? She couldn't be sure.

Waiting and listening, she debated what to do and where to go. She had no idea where she was or even what direction she'd come from. She'd darted around so much that she was lost. Mikey figured that was the least of her problems though, and her heart rate slowing, she took a shaky breath, ready to keep moving. After another look, she stepped out, ready to run, when a force hit her and knocked her to the ground. The breath left her, and she tried to scream, but hands locked around her throat, cutting off her air, and she saw Bradley on top of her, his face a menacing sneer.

"If I can't shoot you, then I'll strangle you." And he squeezed.

Mikey saw stars when her oxygen flow stopped, and she grabbed at his hands, scratching at his skin, and kicked out with her feet, but Bradley was like dead weight on top of her. Panicking, and her throat burning, she flailed, fighting to breathe, and she thought of marshmallow man, and how her instructor had told her to never give up. Use everything you have to get free. Mikey grabbed at Bradley's fingers, grabbed one, and pulled on it, yanking hard. Mikey heard a snap and Bradley cursed, pulling back. His weight on her shifted, allowing her to get her arm under her and twist, knocking him off balance. Shoving herself upward, she bucked and kicked, fighting to get away from him. Recovering fast, he fought to drag her back and grab her throat again. Mikey dug her fingers into the ground, looking for anything to use as a weapon. Just as his fingers closed over her neck, she grabbed onto something solid and swung it. It was a dead branch, and she slammed it into the side of his head. The blow knocked him back, and he let go of her. Coughing and sputtering, she tried to scream, but nothing emerged except a whisper.

Blood spurted from Bradley's temple. Mikey scrambled out from under him, kicking harder with her feet. Making solid contact with his legs and stomach, she prevented him from grabbing her again. He grunted when she drove a heel into his thigh, and she rolled, digging her toes into the dirt, trying to find traction, and almost standing, she lunged forward. A hand yanked on her ankle though, and she went down again, and he pulled her toward him. She managed to scream, but her bruised throat muted the sound. Fighting and determined not to let him win, she thrashed and flailed, and he grunted and cursed, but his size and strength gave him the edge. He grabbed her arm, reared back a hand, and slapped her, and she went face down in the dirt, her head spinning, and her hands grasping at the leaves and roots. Pulling on her, he turned her back over, and his hands found her throat again, and she knew then that he'd won. She was going to die, but with one more surge of strength, she scratched at his hands and fingers, then clawed at his face. The lack of air, though, made her vision blur, her ears ring, and her strength ebb. Pure terror flooded her body, and she said a prayer for forgiveness that she couldn't fight harder.

A thunderous bellow shattered the roar in her ears and something white and red shot out of the woods and tackled Bradley. The weight suddenly off of her, Mikey held her throat as the air whooshed back into her lungs. She coughed and gagged. Getting to her knees, she heard and saw the scuffle. A man was on top of Bradley, and he was slugging him in the face, over and over.

Mikey blinked, trying to get her bearings and catch her breath, and she recognized the wild man as Mason. The red and white she'd noticed was his blood-soaked white shirt. Her momentary relief that her brother was alive turned to terror again when she realized the seriousness of Mason's injury. Mikey struggled to stand, wanting to help, but not knowing how. Mason continued to beat Bradley, but Bradley fought back and got his own punches in. Mason flinched, and Bradley took advantage. He attacked Mason's wounds, and Mason, weak and at a disadvantage, fell back.

Bradley scrambled to get away, but Mason came again, punching and fighting. Bruised, his head and nose bleeding, Bradley grabbed at Mason's shoulder and squeezed. Mason cried out and toppled.

"Mason," yelled Mikey, with a croak.

Bradley scurried away, and Mason tried again, but Bradley was faster, and he kicked at Mason, knocking him back. Wounded and gasping, Bradley stood, his shirt ripped and his hair askew. He reached around his back and patted for something. Not finding it, he searched the ground, leaned over, and picked up his gun that had fallen in the dirt.

Barely able to move, Mason managed to get to his feet with Mikey's help. He was covered in dirt and leaves, and blood ran from his sodden shirt and onto his pants. Wobbling and breathing rapidly, he pushed Mikey. "Get behind me," he said.

"Mason, no," said Mikey, holding his arm to support him.

"Run," he said, trying to get her to move. "Into the trees."

"No. I'm not leaving you."

Bradley held the gun. "Isn't that sweet? Somehow, I don't think Lydia would do the same for me." He wiped the sweat from a swelling eye.

"Bradley," said Mason, "Shoot me. Let Mikey go."

"Can't do that," Bradley sneered. "But you've done me a big favor. Now I don't have to drag your ass out here. I can bury you both right where you stand."

"Are you prepared for both of us to haunt you? The way Chad haunts Lydia?" asked Mason.

Bradley chuckled. "Haunt me all you want. But you'll still be dead, and Lydia and I will be laughing all the way to the bank. I can handle a ghost or two for that."

"It doesn't matter where you go," said Mason. "Your problems will follow." He sucked in a breath and grabbed his shoulder.

Mikey put her arm around him and wondered how he was still standing. "I love you, Mason," she whispered.

"I love you, too," he whispered back.

Bradley aimed the gun. "Time to say goodbye."

Mikey braced and gripped Mason, who tried again to shove her back and stand between her and Bradley. Mikey clutched at him, anticipating the shots. Time seemed to stand still when three rapid fire booms shattered the quiet of the woods. Mason jumped and Mikey screamed and closed her eyes, expecting Mason to fall., When he remained upright, she opened them. Bradley stood, his gun arm drooping, with three spots of blood dotting his shirt. The blood stains grew and began to streak down Bradley's chest. He stood for a second, but his arm fell along with the gun, his knees buckled, and he collapsed into the dirt.

Stunned, Mikey didn't move, and Mason looked back. Mikey followed his gaze and saw Trick standing behind them beside a tree, his arm up and holding a weapon.

Relief flooded through her, but shock prevented her from moving or even speaking. Trick ran up, passed them, and stood over Bradley. He squatted, took Bradley's gun, and checked for a pulse. "Bye, bye Bradley." He straightened and came over, putting both guns in his waistband. "You two okay?"

Mason, still breathing hard and looking ashen, wobbled again. "Where the hell have you been?"

Trick looked Mason over. "Thought I'd take a hike first. Pretty country. Did you catch the wildflowers on the trail?"

Mason grunted and turned toward Mikey, who fell into his arms and hugged him. The relief of seeing him alive and surviving her own encounter with Bradley rushed over her, and she couldn't hold back her tears.

He hugged her back. "Are you all right?" he whispered.

She nodded into his neck.

He held her for a second, but she felt the warmth of his blood seep through her clothes and pulled away. "You're hurt." Her gruff voice caught, and she wiped away her tears.

"You need a hospital," said Trick, taking Mason's arm.

"I'm okay," he said. "Just a scratch."

"You're bleeding like a water bucket full of holes," said Trick. "Hold on to me." He grabbed Mason's arm and slung it over his shoulder.

Mason tried to walk, but stumbled. Mikey tried to support him from the other side. "I suppose you think this means that I owe you twice," said Mason, his voice weak.

"I'll make you a deal," said Trick. "You don't die, and we'll call it even."

"I'm fine. Check on Mikey," said Mason.

"I'm okay," Mikey's voice cracked. Her body ached, her throat throbbed, and her cheek burned, but she tried her best to hold up Mason, who was getting heavier as his pace slowed. If he collapsed, it could take hours to get him help.

"C'mon, partner," said Trick. "It's called one foot in front of the other. Don't pass out on me."

Mason grimaced and almost stumbled again. "I'm trying." He took a slow step. "Where's Shay...or is it Serita?"

"You mean Lydia. Valerie shot her."

"Valerie's here?" asked Mason. "She shot Lydia?"

"I'll explain later. Valerie found you in the barn, remember?" said Trick. "I think she likes you."

Mason attempted a smile. "Of course she does."

"There's no accounting for taste, but if you want to pursue the lovely Miss Vain, we've got to get your ass back and patched up. So keep moving." Trick shifted and adjusted his grip, and Mikey did the same.

"I'm tired," said Mason.

"You have to keep going," said Mikey, feeling her own exhaustion sap her strength.

"Hang in there, Red. Don't give up on me," said Trick.

Mason slowed further, his head bobbed, and Mikey began to shake from exertion and worry, when she heard her name called from a distance.

"Mikey? Mason?" Men's voices reverberated through the woods.

Trick stopped and yelled back. "Here. We're over here."

Mikey almost dropped to her knees when she saw movement, and Rem and Daniels, along with two uniformed police officers, darted out of the trees.

Rem heard the yell and spotted the threesome. "There," he said.

"I see 'em," said Daniels.

They sprinted forward, the officers behind them.

Approaching the trio, Rem saw Trick supporting an injured and bloody Mason and Mikey, her clothes ripped and dirty, looking like she might drop where she stood. Getting closer, he saw the marks on her throat, and her red and swollen cheek. Despite her injuries, though, she was alive, and relief coursed through him.

After arriving at the secluded house and finding Valerie Vain with a bleeding Lydia, they'd called EMTs, and jumped into a car with two other officers. They'd followed the rutted road to Bradley's vehicle and, heading into the woods, Rem had braced for the worst. He'd already been dragged through the hell of grief after losing someone close to him, and he didn't want to go through it again. They'd struggled to follow the tracks when three gunshots rang out and they'd raced toward the noise.

"Mikey," said Rem, running up with Daniels. Mason stumbled and Trick struggled to keep Mason on his feet. Mikey tried to offer support but was about to collapse herself.

"Rem," she said, her voice rough.

"Bradley's dead. I have his weapon," said Trick. "I need help with Mason."

Daniels directed the uniformed men to take care of Bradley and ran up to Mason, taking Mikey's place and helping Trick. "I got him," said Daniels, adjusting his hold. "Let's go." Daniels and Trick hauled Mason back toward the trail.

Rem took Mikey's arm and could feel her trembling. He caught her before she fell, and she latched onto him. "Are you okay?" he asked. His arms went around her, and he kept her upright.

Her arms encircled him, and her head fell into the nape of his neck, and she nodded against him. Seeing the blood on her shirt, he worried. "Are you hurt? Are you bleeding?"

"No," she whispered. "It's Mason's blood."

"You're shaking like a leaf," he said. "Hold on." He scooped her up and carried her.

"I'm...okay. I...I can walk," she sputtered, her voice barely audible.

"Would you shut up?" he said. "Stop trying to be so damn strong. I got you. You helped me when I was a mess. Let me help you this time. Okay?"

Her fingers dug into his shirt, and she curled into him. Whatever dam she'd erected began to break, and he heard a sob. Thinking of what she must have endured, he half considered returning to Bradley and shooting him again just to ensure he was dead. He rested his chin on her head and offered soothing words. "You're safe now. You're okay."

The last bit of the dam crumbled and, her shoulders shaking, she cried into the hollow of his neck as he walked with her back to the trail.

Chapter
Twenty-Nine

TRICK WALKED OUT ONTO the back porch with a pitcher of margaritas. "Let the party commence." He poured some into Valerie's glass as she sat in a patio chair beside Daniels and his wife, Marjorie.

Sitting at the table, Mason held up his hand. "I'll stick to beer. Thanks." He held his bottle and rubbed his achy shoulder. His arm hung in a sling, and he tried to adjust it.

"Don't forget me," said Rem, standing and holding out a glass. He'd been sitting with Daniels' and Marjorie's one-year-old son, J.P., in the grass and playing with him and his toys.

Trick leaned over and filled it. "Enchiladas will be ready soon."

Rem grinned, and Mason half expected him to drool. "I can't wait," said Rem.

Daniels laughed. "I may have lost a partner." He grabbed a chip from the bowl on the table. "Think you can put up with him, Trick?"

"I've already got my hands full with this guy, who's taking loads of my time." Trick nodded at Mason.

Rem pointed at Daniels. "You start cooking enchiladas, and I'm not going anywhere."

"I thought I had you with my Chicken Marsala," said Marjorie.

Rem's shoulders fell. "That's true. Sorry, Trick. You're stuck with Mason."

"Lucky me," said Mason.

Trick put the pitcher on the table. "Remember now, you owe me twice." He held up two fingers at Mason.

"I thought we called it even," said Mason.

"I lied," said Trick. He held up his glass. "A toast."

"Wait. Where's Mikey?" asked Rem.

The back door opened, and Mikey came out with a bowl and her own glass of margarita. "Here's the queso." She set it on the table with the chips.

"This just keeps getting better and better," said Rem.

"We're toasting, Mikey," said Trick. He raised his glass.

Mikey held her margarita as everyone lifted their drink. Mason watched her, though, seeing the dullness behind her eyes. Her cheek had healed, but splotchy, yellow bruises still marked her throat. A week had passed since Bradley's death and Lydia's hospitalization. Lydia had survived but remained in the hospital. Mikey still seemed haunted, though, and he sensed it was about more than just Bradley's assault.

"To good friends, good food, and good women." He winked at Valerie, and Mason rolled his eyes. "All of whom at this gathering have saved our asses."

"I'll drink to that," said Daniels, lifting his drink and holding Marjorie's hand.

"For sure," said Rem, looking at Mikey.

Mason raised his bottle to Valerie, and she clinked her glass to his. "To good women," he said.

"And good men," she said, holding his gaze.

Trick held up his glass again. "And to Bevins and Winkler. May Bevins enjoy eating the hat I sent him. Hopefully, the Pepto Bismol I included will help with the digestion."

"You didn't?" asked Mason.

"Oh, I did," said Trick with a grin.

"I hope he poops felt for days," said Rem. "Maybe Winkler will request a new partner."

"Don't get your hopes up," said Daniels.

"I'll check the enchiladas," said Mikey, and she disappeared into the house.

"So, what happens next, Trick?" asked Daniels, leaning up to check on J.P., who chased a ball into the yard. "You going back to Texas?"

Trick drank his margarita and settled into a chair. "For a while, at least. I have a few fences to mend."

"What about Cissy?" asked Rem. "Any future there?"

Trick shook his head. "No. The water has washed way under that bridge. I think that was more about grief and loneliness than anything, for both of us. She's another good woman who deserves better than me. She's moving back to Texas. May already be there."

"What happens after you mend those fences?" asked Valerie. "You plan on returning to the Rangers?"

Trick grinned, and Mason sighed. "You want to answer that?" asked Trick.

Mason gritted his teeth when he moved his shoulder. "I may have temporarily been affected by my injury and offered to share my office space with Trick, provided he plays by the rules."

Daniels' eyes widened, and Rem dropped his jaw. "Are you serious?" asked Rem.

"Are you going to do paranormal work, too?" Marjorie asked Trick.

"Ah, no," said Trick. "I'll be sticking to the strictly normal side of things. I'll handle the straight up stuff and Mason can handle the woo-woo side. We figured it might serve us well to broaden the business." He sunk down in his seat. "Although, I think we're going to have to change the name."

"SCOPE stays," said Mason. "You want to create your own agency and get your own name, that's fine with me. But SCOPE is the sign on the wall. I get plenty of stuff that turns out to be just nosy neighbors or pesky lovers. You can handle all that."

"Gee. I can hardly wait." Trick pursed his lips. "Maybe I should consider creating my own name."

"What about MNPI?" asked Valerie. "Monroe's Non-Paranormal Investigations."

"Or MINT," said Marjorie. "Monroe's Investigations of Nutty Terrestrials."

"That one has potential," said Rem with a smile, and he walked to the brick planter with his drink and leaned against it. He kept an eye on J.P. in the yard, who squealed as he pulled on a handful of grass.

"What about you Valerie?" asked Daniels. "You going back to Texas?"

Valerie dunked a chip in queso. "I'll visit my brother, but I actually live here. I moved after I left the military."

"Isn't that nice, Red?" asked Trick. "Maybe we'll have the opportunity to work with the lovely Miss Vain again." He smiled and reached for a chip. "I know how much she enjoys my company." He bit into the chip.

"I think I've had as much of your company as I can handle," said Valerie. "But I believe Mason, here, still owes me a drink."

"I do," said Mason. "Plus a lot more." He gestured at Trick. "Our butts might still be in the woods if it wasn't for you."

"Nah," said Rem. "We'd have found you by now. You just wouldn't be looking as pretty."

"I'll collect on that debt," said Valerie. She sipped her margarita and eyed Mason. "Eventually."

"Somehow, I don't think she's referring to me," said Trick. "What a shame."

Daniels chuckled. "You have your own agency, Valerie?"

Valerie picked up the conversation with Daniels while Mason stood and joined Rem beside the planter.

"How's the shoulder?" asked Rem.

"Better," said Mason. "I can move it now without crying."

"That's always a bonus," said Rem.

After Valerie answered Daniels, she sat up and took another chip. "I know Mason's background with the paranormal, but have you two ever had a paranormal encounter?" She looked at Rem and Daniels. "With your history, surely you've experienced a few strange things."

"Other than Rem's taste in clothing and bad jokes?" asked Daniels, trying the queso.

Rem's face fell. "Go ahead, smart guy," he said to Daniels. "Tell her about your grandad's house and the lovely town of Dumont. Maybe she'll want to visit."

"The Lady of Black River," said Marjorie, shaking her head. "Wait till you hear this, Valerie."

Daniels took a sip of his margarita and launched into the story.

Mason listened for a bit, but his thoughts returned to Mikey. "You mind if I ask you something?" he asked Rem.

"No. What is it?" asked Rem.

"It's about Mikey," said Mason, noting she hadn't returned. "You notice she's a little quiet since what happened with Bradley? Hasn't been herself?"

Rem nodded. "Yeah. I noticed. But that asshole almost strangled her to death. It's not easy dealing with that kind of trauma. Especially when she was just getting past Victor and what he did."

Mason was familiar with Rem's own troubles after dealing with Victor and his followers, and how Mikey had helped him cope. "Hell." He held his head. "I should have considered that. She survives one madman and then has to face another." He sighed. "You think I should leave it and let her work through it? I'm not asking you to betray any confidences, but I know she talks to you, and she hasn't said much to me."

Rem studied his margarita. "My advice? Don't let her wallow. I tried to hide from the world, and she got in my face and wouldn't let me. Maybe she needs the same treatment. But not from me. From you."

Mason sighed. "Is she mad at me? Does she blame me?"

Rem glanced over. "She's mad at herself, Mason. Thinks she almost got you killed. She's laying a guilt trip on herself so heavy it would weigh down an elephant. Granted, it's only been a week, but it only took her a week to get onto me. That, and the nightmares, lack of sleep and flashbacks, don't help, so I'd say the sooner you can talk to her, the better."

Mason made up his mind. "That's all I needed to hear." He put down his beer. "Thank you, Detective."

"Anytime," said Rem.

Mason left the backyard, while Daniels continued his story and Rem joined in. He entered the house and saw Mikey in the kitchen, pulling the enchiladas from the oven. "They're ready," she said.

Mason approached her. "We need to talk."

Mikey put the oven mitts away. "What? Are you guys already out of queso? Jeez. I'll get some more."

"Never mind the queso, Mikey. And screw the enchiladas. What's going on with you?"

She frowned. "Nothing's going on. I'm fine."

"No, you're not. You and I have barely spoken since everything happened."

"You've been in the hospital, Mason and I've had a bit of a sore throat□" She touched her neck.

"Don't make light of it. You almost died."

She stopped in mid-search of the utensil drawer. "So did you."

"And that's not your fault."

Mikey straightened. "I don't want to talk about this right now. Can we just eat?"

"Too bad if you don't want to talk. Remalla said to get in your face, so I'm getting in your face. You're carrying way too much baggage over this."

She eyed herself. "I don't see any suitcases..."

"Mikey, don't□"

She slammed the drawer and threw out her hands. "What do you want me to say, Mason? That I'm sick to my stomach and have been all week? That I close my eyes and see that animal, Bradley, hovering over me? That I still feel his hands on my throat?" Crossing her arms, she leaned against the countertop. "Or that I still remember the terror I felt when he said you were dead, and how he was going to take me into the woods and kill me? Or how stupid I was when I spoke to Shay and Serita, and couldn't tell I that was talking to the same woman?" She dug her fingers into her arms. "My stupid gut couldn't even detect that Bradley was violent, and I was dumb enough to ignore you and go meet Shay by myself." She kicked out an open cabinet, and it banged shut. "The list of my mistakes is long and embarrassing. I should have known better. And now I have to live with the fact that it almost got us both killed." She turned away from him.

"None of that is your fault," said Mason.

"Then whose fault is it?"

"Who exactly do you think you are? Superwoman?" He stepped closer. "Hindsight is always twenty-twenty, Mikey, and you can use that to blame yourself all day, but it's a lousy barometer for success. We did our best. Hell, I was with the woman, and I didn't know something was up. And I'm supposed to be the one who sees things and knows things. If anyone is to blame, it's me. I almost got *you* killed, and I will never forgive myself for that."

Mikey dropped her head. "That's not what I want, and certainly not what I meant."

"Then what should we do? Sit in sadness and regret? God knows I've blamed myself for Mom enough, and I don't want you to do the same. Not for me, or anyone. It's not worth it."

She hesitated and stared off. "I think..." Her bottom lip quivered. "...I think it's going to take some time."

Mason walked over and took her arm. "Just so long as you talk to me. I can't do this job without you. But I need to know that you're okay. You went through hell with Victor and now this. It's a lot to handle, and I know how you are. You'll act as if you're strong enough to manage it. But if you need help, I want you to ask for it."

Going quiet, she nibbled her lip, and her eyes welled with tears. "Rem told you to get in my face?"

"He did."

Mikey sniffed. "Asshole."

"Sucks when your own tactics get used against you."

She swiped at a tear. "It does, and I'm going to let him know about it."

"I'm sure you will." He walked closer. "Do you hear me, though? Will you let me help?"

After a few seconds, she nodded at him.

"Good," he said, and took her hand. "Now, can I get a hug? I could really use it."

Mikey smiled, walked into his arms, and squeezed him. "I love you, big brother," she whispered in his ear.

"Love you right back," he said, trying not to groan when his sore arm pulled.

The back door opened, and Mason heard Rem's voice. "Umm, sorry to interrupt, but the natives are getting restless for some enchiladas."

"You mean you are," said Mikey, pulling back and wiping away a tear.

Mason turned to respond when a loud slam reverberated through the house. Mikey jumped, Rem squealed, and Mason winced when Mikey jostled his shoulder.

"What was that?" asked Mikey.

Rem pointed toward the hall, his eyes wide. "That...that bathroom door. It slammed shut."

Mason walked into the living room. "It's been doing that."

"What?" asked Rem. "That's not the first time? Is it a draft?"

Mikey came around and tried the door. It opened, and she looked inside. "Nothing."

"No. It's not a draft," said Mason. "It's a spirit trying to communicate."

Rem paled. "Then I'll be using the outside facilities, because I'm not going in there."

"What outside facilities?" Mikey swung the door back and forth.

"Take a wild guess," said Rem.

"Sorry I asked." She left the bathroom door open. "They slammed it hard, like they're trying to get our attention," said Mikey to Mason. "You have any idea who it could be?"

"Whoever it is, they're not talking," said Mason. "Just slamming."

Rem raised his hand. "I'll just wait outside. You two have fun with that. Just bring the enchiladas when you get a chance." He backed out and closed the door.

Mikey stood for a second and pointed. "You realize Mom used to do that? Slam the door?"

Mason stilled, and a memory flashed of him and his siblings, fighting over something miniscule, their loud shouting bouncing off the walls and reverberating through the house. Mom had had enough, and she'd walked to a door and slammed it hard, the loud noise stopping everyone in their tracks. "I'll be damned. Do you think...?" He approached the door.

"Maybe she's talking to you," said Mikey. "And maybe you should listen before she starts aiming for your fingers."

Mason stood slack-jawed, wondering if it was true, when Trick came into the house.

"I hear your ghost is back," he said. "But I'll be damned if it's stopping us from eating. I'm getting the food." He headed into the kitchen.

"I'll help you," said Mikey.

"You better figure it out, Mason," said Trick from the kitchen, "cause if that keeps up, you're going to have to put in some outdoor plumbing."

Mason shook off his surprise and headed for the kitchen. "Has Remalla peed in the bushes?" He grabbed some plates.

"Not yet," said Trick.

"It's just a matter of time though," said Mikey. "So be prepared to either share your bathroom or get complaints from the neighbors." She smiled, and it was the first genuine smile he'd seen from her in a week. Mason smiled back and grabbed some silverware. "I'll keep that in mind."

The enchiladas served, Mason excused himself. "Be right back," he said. "I'll get more chips."

"And grab the other pitcher of margaritas," said Trick.

"I've got one arm, remember?" asked Mason.

"You want me to help?" Valerie started to sit up.

Mason waved her off. "No. Enjoy your food. I'll manage."

"Keep an eye on that bathroom," said Rem. He shifted in his seat. "I may have to use yours in a minute, unless you'd rather I use the lawn."

"I'd let him, Mason," said Daniels. "He'd likely kill the grass."

Rem smirked and Mason chuckled and went into the house. Before going into the kitchen, he detoured into his bathroom, closed the door, and stared for a moment in the mirror. Smoothing his mustache, he noted the slight shake in his fingers. Gripping his injured shoulder, he let go a long breath, groaning through the discomfort. He opened the medicine cabinet and eyed the bottles of pills on the shelf. One had been prescribed by his doctor for pain. Ignoring that one, he pulled out the other two and read the labels. They were prescriptions for two other painkillers □ one for Serita Avery and the other for Lydia Stanford.

He stared at them, thinking back. Closing his eyes, he recalled standing in Serita's bathroom. After Chad had pointed toward the closet, Mason had made a hasty decision and tucked the pill bottles into his inside jacket pocket. After Lydia had shot him and he'd been thrown into the trunk, he'd slid the jacket off to staunch the flow of blood. The jacket had remained in the trunk and was still there when Mason's car had been returned, the jacket untouched.

Looking at the pills, Mason questioned his sanity. He'd risked his career and reputation by taking them, but now that he had them, he told himself that keeping them wasn't that big of a deal anymore. They were just pills. He figured somebody should have them.

Still staring at the bottles, he thought of his mother slamming the bathroom door. Was this why? Was she trying to chastise him? Get him to stop? Probably, he thought. She'd be furious, but even though Mason hated the thought of disappointing his mother, he didn't see the point of stopping. It wasn't like he couldn't end it when he wanted to. He'd done it before, and he could do it again.

He opened a bottle, shook out a pill, and swallowed it dry, then opened the cabinet beneath his sink and hid both bottles in a box with his razors. If his guests were going to use his bathroom, he needed to keep them out of sight.

The bottles secured, he closed the cabinets, checked his reflection in the mirror, tweaked his mustache once more, and left to rejoin the party.

What Happens Next?

Get ready for *Lost Dreams*. Tricks joins SCOPE, and his first case is to help a wealthy woman locate her missing brother. His investigation becomes complicated, though, when Mason's brother is accused of murder and an entity whose presence reveals more than Mason and Trick are prepared for harasses Mason. When the two cases collide, it could lead to yet another murder—one of their own.

Enjoy an excerpt below.

Want more from J. T. Bishop?

Sign up for her newsletter at jtbishopauthor.com to get the Daniels and Remalla prequel novella, *The Girl and the Gunshot*, plus future books, short stories, missing scenes and excerpts for **free**.

Reading Detectives Daniels and Remalla?

If you are, then you know *The Redstone Chronicles* is a spinoff of the detective series. Mason and Mikey were introduced in book two, *Of Breath and Blood*. If you're reading in order, then enjoy *Of Body and Bone*, book three in Detectives Daniels and Remalla, which follows the events of *Lost Souls*. A list of books in chronological order follows below.

If you're new to Daniels and Remalla, then meet the two charismatic detectives who battle psychopaths, unexplained evil and unsolved cases. In *Haunted River*, book one in the series, the ghost of a woman haunts a small town where she lived and died. When a second woman's body turns up twenty-five years later, Daniels and Remalla become suspects, and the next targets.

Or start with *Murder Unveiled*, the prequel novel to *Haunted River*. A prominent art dealer is found murdered after the unveiling of a famous, but cursed, painting. When Daniels and Rem are assigned to investigate, they'll learn that a curse may prove more deadly than a killer and they could be the next targets.

Or pick up the omnibus *Shadows and Secrets*, which includes *Haunted River*, *Of Breath and Blood*, and *Of Body and Bone* (books one through three) of the paranormal mystery thriller series.

Discover the series that introduces Daniels and Remalla.

The Family or Foe Saga introduces the bantering and affable detective duo. This set of four books follows the trail of a murderer determined to exact revenge on the family he believes wronged him. But there's more to the story when his secrets reveal unexpected connections, and shocking revelations come to light.

Do you like light sci-fi with urban fantasy and a delicious romance thrown in?

Discover Bishop's first series, *The Red-Line Trilogy*. One woman holds the key to unlocking a secret that will ensure the existence of a secret community. One man, assigned to protect her, will risk everything to keep her alive, but when he falls for her, will their destiny be enough to save them both?

And the Red-Line series continues with the sister series to the trilogy, *The Fletcher Family Saga*. A distant but deadly threat risks the lives of three unique siblings, but life can't stop because of who they are. They'll endure love, loss and a dangerous enemy determined to destroy them.

Either Red-Line series can be read first. Take your pick. Boxed sets are available, too!

A Note From J.T.

I love to hear from my readers about their experiences with my books, and I'd love to know what you thought about *Lost Souls*. This book was a little challenging at first because I had to shift out of the Detectives Daniels and Remalla mode, which came first and I love to write and focus on a new series. Once I got into the story, though, Mason, Mikey and Trick blossomed into full-fledged characters, and I was hooked. I've embraced the Redstones. They're going to provide fun storylines to explore, plus offer opportunities for a lot of crossover between the *Redstone Chronicles* and the *Daniels and Remalla* series. While Daniels and Remalla must cope with the paranormal events they witness, Mason is accustomed to it and expects it. It's an intriguing viewpoint to work from and allows me new creative opportunities. Plus, there's the thrilling possibility of romance. (We'll see what happens between Remalla and Mikey.) The romance angle will definitely be covered in the Daniels and Remalla series, so make sure to keep up with that one.

And what happens with Mason and his addiction? That was a last-minute addition, since I decided Mason needed a flaw or two. It makes him much more interesting as a character and it's going to provide some great insight into our other characters. There's lots of good stuff to come, so get ready.

Reviews are a huge plus and big help for an author and potential readers. I would love it if you could please take a couple of minutes to leave a quick review for *Lost Souls* . And if you'd like, please leave a few comments, too.

As always, thank you for your time and readership. It is deeply valued and appreciated.

Now, on to the next book!

Books in Chronological Order

Although recommended but not required, in case you prefer to read in order...

Red-Line: Prelude to the Shift, a short story (subscribers only)
Red-Line: The Shift
Red-Line: Mirrors
Red-Line: Trust Destiny
Curse Breaker
High Child
Spark
Forged Lines

———ele———

The Girl and the Gunshot, a novella (subscribers only)
A Hamburger Christmas, a novella
The Magic of Murder, a novella (subscribers only)
First Cut
Second Slice
Third Blow
Fourth Strike
Murder Unveiled

Haunted River
Of Breath and Blood
Lost Souls
Of Body and Bone
Lost Dreams
Of Mind and Madness
Lost Chances
Of Power and Pain
Lost Hope
Of Love and Loss
Lost Lives
Dominion
Lost Time
Illusions
Lost Love
Vendetta
Black Bird

Acknowledgements

ANOTHER BOOK IS COMPLETE, and again, I have many to thank. This doesn't happen alone, and I am indebted to family and friends for their help, support, and encouragement. It is truly appreciated.

I love writing about the bonds between loving family, deep friendships and the ties that hold them together. Plus, my fascination with the unknown thrown into the mix makes for a satisfying story and hopefully, adds a little more thrill for my readers.

I especially want to thank my fans. Hearing from you and knowing that you're enjoying my books makes all the hard work worthwhile. None of this would matter without your tremendous support. If I can help you escape from this crazy world for a short period each day, then I've done my job.

Here's to more stories, more fun, and more time for yourself. If you can have a little of that each day, you're on the right track.

Enjoy an excerpt from Lost Dreams, Book Two in The Redstone Chronicles.

MASON REDSTONE WALKED THROUGH the old farmhouse that had recently been renovated into a beautiful two-story ranch-style home. High ceilings and big windows gave the house a light and airy feel and the gorgeous view of the rolling hills reminded Mason of his grandparent's home in the hill country of Texas.

The owners had contacted his agency, SCOPE, the previous week and had asked Mason to investigate their property. They'd bought the farmhouse a year earlier and had envisioned it as the place where they would enjoy their eventual retirement. But once construction had begun, they'd had nothing but issues. Workmen came and went, never staying longer than a couple of weeks. They'd say the place had a vibe, or that they'd seen or heard something they couldn't explain. Renovations had come to a halt more than once until new workers could be employed. Eventually, the home had been completed, although eight months behind schedule, and the owners, an older couple in their mid-sixties, had moved in a month later. Having had no experiences themselves during the renovation, they were unconcerned about the activity, believing it to be the result of overactive imaginations and superstitious beliefs.

They'd made it three months before calling SCOPE.

SCOPE stood for the Study of Cryptids or Paranormal Entities, and Mason had thought it was the perfect name, although his sister Mikey had disagreed.

After a two-year stint as a Texas Ranger, several talks with his brother Max who lived in San Diego, and listening to the advice of his best friend Victor, Mason had taken the leap and left the Rangers, moved to California, and had become a private investigator in hopes of using his gifts to help others. Mikey had followed soon after.

It had been a rocky start, especially after his estrangement from Trick, his partner on the Rangers, his falling out with Victor, the murder of his cousin, and the gut-wrenching loss of his mother. But life was improving and business was picking up. The acceptance of the paranormal as more mainstream had kept Mason on his toes, and he was happy now that Trick had joined SCOPE.

Mason had been reluctant at first, especially after working a recent risky case with Trick, in which he and Mikey had almost lost their lives. But that case had resulted in repairing their fractured friendship, and now that Trick was here, Mason could see the benefit of a second investigator. One who could handle the non-paranormal cases, which also seemed to be on the rise despite the agency's name. Trick had completed the requirements for a P.I. license and had started work that week. He already had a client coming in later that day, and Mason was anxious to hear about it once he returned to the office, but right now, he had some spirits to clear from the old farmhouse.

The minute he'd walked into the home, he had sensed the presence of two souls who still wandered the property. One was an older man and the other a young child, a girl, maybe ten years of age. Odd noises and spectral voices, footsteps on the stairs and in the hallways, and objects falling from the shelves had thwarted the owners. They'd installed cameras and had caught an apparition moving past a door frame and the wife had called Mason the next day, telling him they needed help and threatening to sell the property if the activity continued.

Mason had arrived two days later, and had walked through the house, sensing the two presences who Mason felt sure had lived here before. After spending some time on the property and reaching out to the entities, he'd learned it had been a father and daughter. The daughter had died in the home after a long illness, and the father had grieved for her and had died himself years later from a heart attack, likely brought on from the long period of grief.

The strange part of the visit, though, was why they chose to remain. The renovations had disturbed them, and although they weren't dangerous spirits, they believed they still owned the property and didn't care for the changes.

Mason had discussed the problem with the homeowners and they'd asked him to encourage the spirits to move on, and let them live in their house in peace. He'd agreed, believing he could do some research on the property, prepare, and would return to move the father and daughter on and into the light.

Now, a week later, as he walked through the main hallway, he opened himself up to the energy of the space, sensing the presence of the spirits. He'd communicated to them, telling them the situation, and letting them know it was time to leave. Honesty was the best policy with both the living and the dead, and Mason trusted that once the father and daughter understood their situation, they would happily move on. But as Mason continued to walk down the hallway, he sensed another presence, one he hadn't felt on his earlier visit, and he realized that the father and daughter remained not only because they felt a connection but also because they were being prevented from leaving. The additional presence was stopping them.

Mason paused at the entry to a guest bedroom and eyed the closet. In his research, he'd found little to justify any lingering evil spirits, but he could never rule out the land itself. He could only go so far back in his search. Most history was lost to time, and would never be known. Mason sensed that there was more to this property that had nothing to do with the home itself.

Stepping into the small room, he eyed the bed, a sitting table with an attached mirror, and a bureau with a chest of drawers. Nothing seemed out of place, and Mason studied his reflection in the mirror. He wore his boots, jeans and a pressed long-sleeved forest green shirt. His groomed handlebar mustache dusted his cheeks, and not having shaved that morning, he sported a slight five o'clock shadow on his jawline. He'd left his cowboy hat in the front room and he noted again when he saw his longish hair reaching his ears that it was time for a cut.

But now was not the time to worry about his appearance, because in the reflection, he saw and heard the closet door creak open behind him.

Mason turned, his heart beginning to thump, and allowed himself to open up to the presence. Curious, but also careful, he approached the closet door, and nearing it, he reached out and touched it. He pulled on the knob, opening the door more, and peered inside. The closet contained little other than a few items of clothing hanging from the bars and a couple of boxes on the floor.

Taking a steady breath, he moved closer, mentally asking who was present, but got no response. Reminding himself that fear never solved any problems, he took slow steps and entered the closet, asking again for the presence to make itself known. He sensed that whatever had beckoned him held the answers as to why the father and daughter remained. Mason wanted those answers, and he asked again.

A cold breeze became a sudden drop in temperature, and a chill ran up Mason's spine. His body tingled, and Mason had the sudden understanding that perhaps he'd made a mistake. That what had lured him into the closet had not done so in kindness, but in malevolence. Realizing his mistake, he turned to leave, when he heard a low growl, the light went out, and the closet door slammed shut.

www.ingramcontent.com/pod-product-compliance
Lightning Source LLC
Chambersburg PA
CBHW060902250626
47159CB00008B/2836